orders from the

DESERT FOX

The bombing continued all night. The men and vehicles were dispersed, but the screams never stopped. At dawn, Rommel drove up in his mammoth English truck. Shells were still flying.

"Who's in charge here?"

Peter sat up and put his shirt on.

"I guess I am, General."

"You guess? Don't you know? Who are you, a Limey cook?"

"Oelrich. Lieutenant, 7th E.B."

"Oelrich, eh? Know anything about 88's?"

"Yes, sir, a little."

"A mile west of here you'll find three Flak 88's disabled. Flying shale. Get over there and fix them."

"Yes, sir."

Peter took two men and drove off in the mobile machine shop. He was glad to get away. Generals seemed to draw fire.

No sooner had he repaired the 88 than Major Dreieck drove up.

"Oelrich, load up and head west."

"West? What about Cairo?"

"Forget about getting to Egypt. Load up."

Peter looked at his bloody hands and greasy fingers, and wondered what he was doing in the desert.

SWASTIKA

Robert Kail

BELMONT TOWER BOOKS
NEW YORK CITY

A BELMONT TOWER BOOK

Published by

Tower Publications, Inc.
Two Park Avenue
New York, NY 10016

1

"Schatz, mein Schatz,
Reise nicht so weit von mir..."

Vreneli was stroking his cropped dark-blonde hair and humming a folksong about a soldier going to war. Peter rested on her breast and felt the humming coming from deep inside her.

"You were sleeping..."

"Mmm..."

"Oh, Peter! Come home with me for Christmas. The family would love to have you. My little sister thinks you're the best thing that ever happened since William Tell invented marchpane."

"I'll try—but I can't leave father all alone. Besides, we'll see each other for the whole two weeks in St. Moritz."

"And then you'll go to Basel and leave me all alone."

"In the bosom of your family," he murmured low, pushing her breast against his cheek. He kissed her. "You're wonderful. I don't think we'll get in much skiing in St. Mortiz."

"Yes, we will! We'll be out on the slopes every day at eight with the rest of the kids. That's what those trips are for!"

"Oh, no. If there's a cloud in the sky we'll spend the whole day together under a goose-down comforter and the whole night learning to jitterbug."

"You're terrible!" She pulled the blankets from him and laughed as they fought for them. "Come on. I have to leave. Get some clothes on."

Peter grabbed a heavy dressing gown and went over to put some kindling into the porcelain stove. As Vreneli dressed, Peter lapsed into distraction staring at a projection of a huge bridge that was tacked on his drafting board in the afternoon sun. Outside, Zurich lay cold and busy as Citroens and horse-drawn carts bustled by on the wide avenue that had replaced the medieval city walls only a hundred years before.

After Vreneli pulled on her knitted wool underclothes and her tweed skirt and fixed her hair before the tiny mirror, she picked up her violin to go back to the Conservatory. Her hair, a little blonder than Peter's, made short ringlets around her rosy cheeks.

She went over and stood behind him, wanting to reach around and into his dressing gown. In her sensible English walking shoes with their low heels, she was taller than he as he stood barefoot on the parquet floor. Her lips touched his ear.

"What is it?" she asked. "*Rhine Bridge No. I: Basel-Oelrich.* That's where your father's factory is."

"This is just a school project. But someday we'll build it. Connect it with the autobahns. Eight lanes. We'll do it someday—if they ever make peace."

"Hitler's famous autobahns."

"Don't laugh. They're the way of the future. Someday every family in Switzerland will have an auto."

"And we'll all be part of the greater German Reich?"

They heard a finely-tuned car engine idling beneath the window. A huge black Mercedes with a Basel licence plate was in front of the door, and a tall blonde man in Homburg and Chesterfield was ringing the eighteenth-century house bell.

"It's my brother!" Peter scurried to pull on trousers and shoes, shirt and sweater.

"Do you want me to go?"

"No. You'll have to meet him someday. Pull the latch and let him in."

Peter was still adjusting his clothing when his brother knocked on the door to his room. He nodded to Vreneli to open the door.

6

"Hello, Peter. I was hoping you'd be in."

"Hello. This is Vreneli Schmid—my brother Hans-Jörg."

"How do you do." Peter's elder brother kissed Vreneli's hand in the German way. She found it as distasteful as the way he slapped his mocha gloves against his thigh.

"Having a little afternoon tea?" Hans-Jörg smiled wickedly.

"I was just leaving. I hope you'll excuse me. I have to get back."

"Honored to make your acquaintance, Miss Schmid."

"I'll see you at the station Saturday, Vreneli. 'Bye."

"*Ciaou*, Peter. Don't forget about Christmas."

"I'll try to make it." He waved to her as she went down the stone steps and unlatched the big wooden door. Then he turned to face his brother.

Hans-Jörg was ten years older than Peter, and unlike his younger brother, he was tall and blonde, a shining example of the Master Race. One of his greatest pleasures was to keep Peter away from the boardroom and out of the business affairs of the Oelrich Factories Corporation, the family firm. Hans-Jörg was a great believer in the Führer principle, and there could be but one leader at a time. Hans fully intended to be the unquestioned head of the family business when his father died, and he hoped to keep Peter as far back in the drafting department as possible.

"Nice little doxie. But I wish these little local girls would shave their legs."

"I like her very much. I may marry her."

"Don't be absurd. You can do better than that. I'll introduce you to a Rumanian Countess tonight. You don't know what life is all about until you've romanced some of those *haut monde* fugitives at the Baur au Lac. They're chic, svelte, and rich. Their jewels are worth more than that girl's whole family."

"I like Vreneli."

7

Hans-Jörg watched out the window as the girl bustled away on her sturdy legs.

"Built close to the ground."

"She's a good skier."

Hans-Jörg peered at the drafting table. He could just barely read engineering plans.

"What is this? Rhine bridge..."

"For school. But we'll build it someday."

"Don't be an ass. There's no money in bridges. I can make more for the company on a hundred cannon barrels than you'll ever make on a pipe-dream like this."

"If you can get the steel."

"Don't you worry about that. I'm on the way over to the German Consulate right now. Actually, that's why I came to see you. I have to go to Berlin for Christmas to negotiate some contracts. You'll have to stay with father."

Since their mother had died, Christmas was a cold and formal affair at the family house in Basel—the servants away, ever richer gifts under the huge tree, and ever fewer people to enjoy them."

"I was planning to be with Vreneli. Perhaps I'll bring her."

"Don't be absurd. She wouldn't know how to behave. You'll just embarrass her and get father angry."

"Why can't you stay? Surely it's not hard to sell cannon these days."

"What do you know about it? I'm entertaining a group of Ruhr people tonight. Champagne—dancing—some of the prettiest young war widows in Europe. And then Christmas—a ball at the Reichs Chancellery. The Führer will be there, and Schacht, and Ribbentrop."

"A champagne salesman, a renegade American, and the little corporal."

"It's the New Order, and it will last a thousand years. And *we'll* make the cannon that build the state."

Peter looked again at the huge suspension bridge. There was no steel in Europe in 1941 to build bridges.

8

"Very well. I'll be in Basel for Christmas. But you get back as soon as you can."

"Fine. I knew you'd be a good little brother. Come now, how about coming over to the Baur au Lac tonight? Black tie. The Lakeside Suite. If you don't like the Countess, I'll introduce you to two Greek girls who will make you forget all about your little Swiss Miss."

"I have a project to finish."

"The good student. All right, have it your way. I'll see you after Christmas then."

"All right. Have a good trip. And don't accept any medals."

"Shh—" Hans-Jörg smiled. "We're not supposed to talk about that." He waved and went out the door and down to his waiting car.

Peter picked up his steel dividers and adjusted a work lamp. He had another four days before turning in his bridge plans.

Peter had worked every summer in his father's factory helping design military bridges and guns for Germany. Now, with a two-front war, there was no more steel except for cannon, and it hurt his soul to design components for death.

Ever since he had graduated from High School two years before, Peter had dreamed of designing bridges and railways for the united Europe he felt was inevitable. Even before that, when he was supposed to go away to the fine boarding schools in the mountains where his brother had been educated together with sheiks and shahs, industrialists children and the nobility of Europe, Peter had preferred to go to a public school in Basel, commuting by bicycle and streetcar, for the extremely serious Swiss public schools gave far better math and science preparation for an engineer than did the private schools for the rich. When he was admitted to the Federal Institute of Technology, the school for which Einstein had once failed the entrance exams, Peter felt he was coming into his own.

9

His family had migrated from Alsace to Basel in the 1860's. Three generations of Oelrichs had made rifles, cannon and steel bridge components for the armies of Europe. They retained their German citizenship through three great wars. From their Swiss vantage point they sold to both sides in each war—the French, the English, the Germans, the Italians. Between wars they had consolidated their profits until they owned six acres of factories on the other side of the Rhine. Technically it was Swiss territory, but it had been easy to buy up since it was on the German side of the river, protected only by a wire border fence. The Swiss preferred land surrounded by mountains or protected from invasion by the Rhine.

2

Peter had enjoyed helping to design bridges for Germany in the firm's drafting offices in Basel. He felt that their company could become bridge builders for all of Europe. Then the war had erupted, and his brother, taking over more and more of the sales, had converted the factories to the production of proximity fuses for the British, and Flak 88's for the Germans.

Peter's approach to life had been very serious until he met Vreneli. After his mother died, Peter's father had withdrawn into himself and seemed to shun Peter, perhaps because he looked so much like his mother. Business kept coming to them, and old Hans Oelrich was proud of the way his eldest son was making million mark deals with the Third Reich, selling to the French, and licencing designs to England. But Peter he shunned.

So Peter had grown up with a more serious approach to life than had his brother. He liked technical work, and he would be happy someday to be the inside man at Oelrich's—in back designing while his brother was out selling and representing the firm.

Peter had been educated with the Swiss, and he spoke Swiss-German better than anyone in the family ever had. His steady and careful approach to life was more like that of the Swiss than like his volatile and avaricious German forebears.

And then he met Vreneli. She was taking a diploma in music at the Conservatory, and he met her at classes she was auditing at F.I.T., classes in literature and music history. She was from a middle-class family in Aarau, a family that had all the warmth and kindness that was missing from Peter's home.

They had gone to movies together, and then to one of those all-night balls at the University. Vreneli had also visited Peter's modest student room near the Institute. When he took her to the Baur au Lac for dinner, she was shocked.

"Are you sure you can afford it? Only princes and kings go there!"

"My name is Oelrich, Schatzi."

"What does that mean? There's a whole town named Oelrich."

"It was named after my grandfather."

"Oh, come on. What would you be doing at the F.I.T. if you were related to them? You're not even in a fencing club, and they hobnob with diplomats."

"And design bridges."

Peter and Vreneli had signed up for a pre-season ski trip to St. Moritz. They met at the railroad station in Zurich on the Saturday after school let out for Christmas vacation. It was a long trip through the alps in a third class carriage filled with noisy students who parked their skis and their canvas bags on the overhead luggage racks and clomped down the aisles in their heavy ski boots to have tea in the restaurant car.

Peter and Vreneli held hands and listened to the singing and watched the black-haired Italian Swiss kids going from one village to another on the train, and listened to them chattering away with a vivacity seldom seen in the cold north.

Most of the students were checked into the big Post Hotel by the station. Peter had arranged for two rooms at a hotel halfway up the mountain. He loaded Vreneli's bags and his in a horsedrawn sleigh and put their skis in the back. The sleigh bells tinkled in the fresh snow as they drew up to the hotel.

"Looks like fresh powder snow," Peter said.

"It'll be wonderful. Maybe we can do some cross-country."

Peter tipped the driver and they walked into the lobby with their skis and bags.

"Guten Tag, Herr Direktor Oelrich."

Just call me Mister, if you please."

"Yes sir, Mr. Oelrich. We have a nice suite for you with two bedrooms. Southern exposure."

"Very good. This is Fraülein Schmid. Shall we go up?"

The suite was spacious and glowing in the afternoon sun. A bathroom with a huge marble tub separated the bedrooms.

"Thank you." Peter gave five francs to the bellboy and closed the door after him.

"Oh, Peter. This is so luxurious. Are you sure you can afford it?"

"Yes, dear. Get used to it. I want you to have the best."

"What's this?"

"A bottle of Kirsch, compliments of the management apparently."

"And a basket of fruit!"

"I'll show you a new way to eat peaches."

She kissed him, and they began warm to each other.

"None of that," she said. "Dinner is at seven, and we have to change."

"Spoilsport!"

He took her bags into her bedroom.

"Ooh—look at that tub. I get the first bath."

"There's room enough for both of us."

"You're terrible. Is that what you learned on your Paris business trips?"

He started the steamy water flowing into the tub and threw in some bath salts from a colored bottle on the marble ledge.

By the time he got back after hanging up his clothes, Vreneli was already lying back in an ocean of steaming fragrant bubbles.

"Hey, that's not fair!"

He got into the tub with her and rinsed himself off.

"Here, let me." She made him stand up above the perfumed bubbles and rubbed him with a sponge.

"Hey, that hurts."

"You're a softie."

"Just you wait." He sat down. "Now it's your turn."

He ran the sponge up and down her firm, muscular legs and kissed her wet navel.

"Did you ever shave your legs?"

"No. Is that what the girls do in Paris?"

"Yes. Shall I shave you?"

"You'll cut me!"

"Never." With a smile he reached over to get his razor and shaving cream, spilling water all over the floor.

Sitting down in the tub, he took her legs one at a time, covered them with foam, and shaved them carefully from the ankles up.

"You'll make me look like a little baby."

"So much the better." He looked up at her, her breasts erect and shining, her sturdy body towering over him, and he dropped the razor.

"Oh, Peter!" Her legs almost gave out under her. "Kiss me again!"

3

When the local train from Aarau pulled into Basel station, Peter was waiting beside the tracks.

"Hello, darling. You look wonderful," she said. He kissed her and took her bags.

"Your sunburn is better."

"Well, it proved we got out of the hotel at least once."

"How was your Christmas?"

"Wonderful. We had the biggest goose you ever saw. And Anneli knitted a heavy ski sweater for me. It must have taken her forever."

The big Mercedes was parked in the taxi rank outside of the main station entrance. Peter handed the bags to the chauffeur and opened the door for her.

"What a monstrous big car. How do you get gas for it?"

"We have our own tanks."

They drove across the great Rhine bridge toward the high smoking chimneys of the Oelrich factories.

"Cannon for the glory of the greater German Reich!"

Vreneli took his hand.

They drove past the factories and out to a private road where a small bridge connected to a tiny island in the Rhine. The stone pile of a house brooded over the river in the dusk.

"It's huge."

"My grandfather's house."

"And just the three of you live there?"

"And the staff. The old wing is closed off. It's impossible to heat in winter. They used to bring in whole barge loads of soft coal from the Ruhr to heat it."

Vreneli's hand clutched his. They drew up to the heavy stone *porte-cochère*, and the chauffeur came around to open the car door. A maid appeared at the door to the house.

"Good evening, Klara. This is Miss Schmid."

"Good evening, Mr. Peter. Here, let me take your coat, Miss Schmid."

Peter dropped his loden coat on a chair. He was wearing a dark blue Savile Row suit and a white shirt of Egyptian cotton.

"You look so different."

"English tailoring. It's expected of me here."

They went hand in hand into the great hall. In the curve of the stairway a fifteen foot Christmas tree gleamed beneath a skylight.

"That tree is certainly big enough."

"An old family custom. There used to be a lot of us, but the older generation died off. Fewer family, fewer servants, but the old habits linger on."

He took her hand and brought her up the stairs. In her room a fire was burning in a little fireplace topped by a marble mantelpiece.

"It's so nice to have a lady guest, Miss Schmid," said the maid.

Peter smiled. "It certainly is. Come along and meet father. Klara can unpack your things."

"Let me straighten up a little first."

"I'll wait in the hall."

Peter looked down the long hall at the vacuous old Barbizon paintings, now darkened with age. The walnut gewgaws on the Biedermeyer chairs gleamed dully in the yellowish light of the old chandeliers.

Vreneli came out. "Shouldn't we wait until dinner? Then I could take a bath first."

"No. Come on. Let's beard the old lion in his den."

Peter knocked on the big walnut doubledoors of his father's upstairs study.

"Herein!"

"Father, this is Vreneli."

The old man turned from his desk. A fringe of white hair surrounded his bald head, and a well-trimmed white

16

moustache that contrasted with apoplectic red complexion made him look like Bismarck. A saber scar ran down his left cheek. He stared coldly at Vreneli from her cotton stockings up to the sunburned cheeks devoid of makeup.

"Grüezi wohl."

"Grüss Gott," the old man answered. "Won't you sit down?"

He laid aside the steel pen with which he had been checking the books, and closed his ink bottle.

"Well, young lady, I understand your father is a mathematics instructor in Aarau."

He spoke in an old-fashioned court German that reminded her of a preacher or a school professor.

"Yes."

"An old Swiss family."

"Back to the thirteenth century."

"Well, isn't that wonderful. In the thirteenth century my ancestors were serfs. But we've improved ourselves a bit since then."

"You're very fortunate."

"Fortunate? It's unremitting industry, and planning, and meeting the right people. Hitler—we were already sending him money when he was rotting in Landsberg prison. And the Quai d'Orsay? You could buy the whole Ile de France for a pittance."

"Father, let's not get started on that. I'd like you to make Vreneli feel at home here. I hope she'll be here often."

"So. Well, come along then. Let's go down into the cellar and pick out some wine for dinner. Do you like good wine?"

"Oh, a glass of Beaujolais is about my limit."

"We'll do better than that. Come."

They crowded into a little elevator that sank noiselessly into the solid bedrock of the Rhine basin. The musty cellars stretched away in the distance, lit by naked electric bulbs of ancient vintage.

"Here's a Chateau Rochefoucauld that my father laid in, in 1873. *Premier cru.*"

"That's enough, father. There are only three of us."

"Don't be a boor, Peter. We have to have a white to go with the fish course."

"We'll all catch pneumonia down here."

The old curmudgeon stalked down an aisle. "I have a nice little white wine here. Von Ribbentrop's old firm. A 1939."

"Is he always this way?" Vreneli whispered.

"No, dear," Peter kissed her cheek. "Sometimes he's worse."

"All right, all right," the old man came back with a bottle in each hand. "Let's not stand around. Come along upstairs. Come along."

The dinner table was laid in a vast shadowy room. Beside the table a mousy little man dressed in a shabby wool suit was waiting for them.

"Good evening, your Honor, Herr Peter."

"Hello, Neider," Hans Oelrich nodded, jerking his head toward the little man. "My accountant," he said.

"Herr Neider, may I present Miss Schmid?"

"How do you do."

Klara and a butler served the soup.

"Neider is here with the books," the old man explained.

"How are things going, Mr. Neider?" Peter asked.

"Oh, swimmingly, Mr. Peter. The payments from Manchester are coming in regularly through Lisbon, and we..."

"Fraülein Schmid would not be interested in that, Neider," Herr Oelrich cut him off with a contemptuous gesture.

The plates clicked as a fish course was served in silence. There were five glasses and eight pieces of cutlery at each place. The plates were cold.

"These are lovely glasses, Mr. Oelrich," Vreneli said timidly.

"A gift from Prince Napoleon when he was President," the old man answered. "A pompous ass."

Gilt forks scraping on china echoed in the vast chamber.

"And how are your studies progressing, Herr Peter?"

"Very well, thank you, Herr Neider. My professors seem satisfied."

"They'd better be," Hans Oelrich grunted.

A small Black Forest cake was served for dessert. Vreneli discovered that she had run out of forks. She smiled at Klara.

"Hänt-Sie 'n Gabeli, Fraülein Klara?" she asked in Swiss-German.

The maid blushed and bustled off to get a fork.

"We speak High German in this house!" Hans Oelrich thundered.

"Oh come on, Papa. Don't insist on being a foreigner in your own country."

"Europe is my country," answered the autocrat, and he switched the desultory conversation to French, which made Herr Neidig uncomfortable. "Do you know, those damned Bolsheviks have stolen our timer? God knows how they got one—probably from England—but they've copied it. And there's no way to stop them. No way to sue them. Lawless *communardes! Canaille.*"

"The revolting peasants are revolting."

"Is that funny? You may laugh. You've never worked all your life just to have your designs stolen."

"They'll never be able to produce them, Papa. Not without trained Swiss workmen."

The old man gave a short laugh. "Not even the Germans can do it. Slave labor—hah! They've drafted all their best workers, the fools." He stood up abruptly. "Shall we go into the library?"

Their footsteps echoed on the cold stone floors. A fire was burning in the huge library, taking the chill off the air. Hans Oelrich slumped in a leather chair, leaning forward

19

to get closer to the fire.

Vreneli admired the leather-backed volumes that gleamed with gold stampings from behind the metal grillwork that protected them from use.

"They're all in Russian!" she exclaimed.

"Basil Zaharoff! Now there was a man. I could tell you some stories about him."

Peter was contemplating the eight foot high portrait that glowed above the stone mantelpiece. It was a dark-haired woman in a satin evening gown. Vreneli followed his eyes.

"My mother," he said.

"And there was a woman," Hans Oelrich smiled. "We used to have the Crown Prince here. He'd stop off on his way to St. Moritz. She would give a dinner for fifty as easily as I add a column of figures."

"She was a lovely woman," old Neidig put in meekly.

"Neidig, you are an ass. Go up and get the ledgers. They're on my desk. And be quick about it."

"Father, we'll say good night. Vreneli is a little tired after her trip."

"Next time, send a car for her." The old man stood up. "Fraülein Schmid, it has been a pleasure to meet such a charming daughter of William Tell. I trust you enjoyed yourself."

"Thank you, Herr Oelrich. An honor, I'm sure."

"Good night." He eyed the swing of her hips as Peter escorted her to the tall double doors. Going up the stairs, Peter and Vreneli heard the old man shout.

"Neidig! Gott verdamme, mach schnell." His voice echoed in the marble hall.

Klara was waiting in a high-backed chair in the corridor outside of Vreneli's room.

"We'd better keep the door open," Peter murmured.

They sat down primly in front of the small coal fire.

"He's a terror," Peter said.

"I've never met anyone quite like him."

"And you won't. He's one of a kind. Don't let him bother you."

They sat quietly talking for a few minutes, and then stood up to say goodnight.

"He's all right. Nobody will ever change him," Peter said.

"I did so want to make a good impression."

"Well, go to bed, and don't worry about it." He kissed her primly. Klara was still waiting in the hall.

"You can turn down Miss Vreneli's bed now, Klara," he said. "Good night, darling."

"Good night, Peter."

Shortly, Vreneli lay back in the huge canopied bed and watched the shadows flickering on the panelled walls. In spite of all the things she had on her mind, she was very tired, and she fell asleep almost instantly.

4

When school started again after the Christmas vacation, Peter was so busy that he seldom got away from Zurich. He spent one weekend in Aarau with Vreneli's family, but didn't get to Basel, and didn't see Hans-Jörg. Peter wasn't even aware that the Swiss Army had been put on a red alert for mobilization.

In Hans Oelrich's office overlooking the belching chimneys of his factories, conferences were the order of the day. A representative of Albert Speer's war production procurement office had flown down from Berlin accompanied by a high-ranking officer of the Waffen S.S.

"We must have our payments in gold," Hans-Jörg insisted. "Reichsmarks do us no good. It takes forever to trade them off through the international market the way things stand, and we take a large loss."

"The Kaiser paid us in gold," Hans Oelrich interrupted. "Prince Bismarck paid us in gold."

"That can be arranged," said the German procurement agent. "But for our part we need a guarantee of continued delivery. We know you're being paid off by the British. And if things go badly for us, you can just stop delivery to us. We know how you Swiss think. You want to be with the winners."

"Mein lieber Herr," Hans-Jörg interposed. "We are German through and through. Our firm has supported the National Socialist Party since 1923. As for our Manchester factory, I cannot control those licences. Certainly we're being paid, but the funds are blocked. After the war, of course, with a little help from the conquerors, we should be able to drain that money out of England and put it to use to strengthen the continental system. But in the meanwhile..."

"Then why do you insist upon gold? Krupp von Bohlen..."

"He's buying up half of the Saar with his Reichsmarks. We cannot do that. We need a gold-backed currency to make our investments. And then, too, Krupp can pay off his workers with black bread and bean soup. We need Swiss francs."

"My dear Herr Oelrich," the S.S. representative smiled. "We don't like to quibble. Surely you are aware that one of the best armored divisions in Europe is idling its engines just ten minutes from here. And your own Army has mobilized with its little popguns."

"You wouldn't dare."

"Hitler has dared many things, and he rules Europe!"

"Nonsense and you know it," Hans Oelrich interjected. "If you come in here with your damned tanks, you'd be razing the very factories you covet."

"This little plot of land is totally indefensible, and your army knows it."

"But they would blow up everything before they retreated, and they'd take the workers with them. The explosives are already in place."

"You may have heard—we have invented something called a Blitzkrieg. It is as quick as a bolt of lightning." The officer touched the lightning bolts of the SS insignia on his collar. "And just as deadly."

"How dare you stand in my office, on my property, and threaten me?" the old man thundered.

"Be calm, father. Let me handle this." Hans-Jörg tried to quiet him.

"Gentlemen, my father is very excitable. Let us adjourn for lunch. Come back at two and I feel sure we can come to an agreement. We are not really too far apart."

"Very well, at two. But you had better be ready to make a committment."

"Of course, of course."

The Germans stalked out, and Hans Oelrich slumped

back into his chair, his face an alarming shade of red.

"My God," he said. "They're not gentlemen at all! That miserable little corporal sends me auto mechanics and pencil pushers and expects me to treat them as if they're gentlemen!"

"Calm down, father."

"Calm down?" The old man was wringing his hands. "They can roll over that border in a matter of minutes. If they start firing those 88's, there goes the factory. Everything we've worked for for three generations—a mess of rubble."

"The Swiss wouldn't dare set off those demolition charges. They're too respectful of property rights."

"Do you think they're bluffing, Hans-Jörg? You're a fool."

"Switzerland is surrounded by the Third Reich. They wouldn't dare resist the Führer. He took France in six days, and Poland in six hours. He could take this place in six minutes."

"The Swiss would blow it up and take all the workers with them. We can't produce proximity fuses with slave labor. Do you think you can train a Russian prisoner over night? They can't even handle a screwdriver."

"Father, you're getting too excited. Go home. Let me handle it. They told me that the gold was no problem. I'll find a solution."

"I don't feel well," the old man whined. "Where's Peter? Peter should be here."

"Go home. I'll take care of everyting." Hans-Jörg pressed a button under the table to summon his father's chauffeur. Between the two of them, they got the old man out.

The January sun was glinting off the river as Hans-Jörg paced in front of the grimy windows. The Germans returned promptly at two.

"Gentlemen, my father was not feeling well, and he

24

begs to be excused. I can assure you that any agreement I make with you will be binding upon the firm."

They sat down at the glass-topped conference table with its gleaming ashtrays and sharpened pencils lined up neatly next to the note pads, and there was a silence.

"The problem is ostensibly simple," Hans-Jörg said. "I want gold, and you want a delivery guarantee. It's the solution that is not so simple."

The S.S. officer smiled nervously.

"Herr Oerlikon, it is incumbent upon me to suggest a solution which may not have occured to you," he said.

"Yes?"

"You have a younger brother, I believe. A student."

"Yes."

"Our attitude is that it is the duty of every German national to serve the Fatherland, just as you and your father have done with your fine work here. Now if the younger Mr. Oelrich were to volunteer for some work in Germany..."

"A hostage then..."

"Oh, let us not say that. My leader's house has many mansions."

"Well, perhaps not a mansion. But I wouldn't want him harmed, or put in jail or anything."

"Of course not. We are very punctillious, you know that."

Hans-Jörg paused.

"To change the subject for a moment," he said, "the gold deliveries could be made by courier across the border..."

5

Late in January Peter went home to Basel for a weekend. The house was deserted—his father and brother at the factory, only the maid in the kitchen.

"Herr Peter! What a surprise!"

"Hello, Klara. Do you have enough for another plate tonight?"

"Of course. I'll have to call Mr. Hans-Jörg to tell him you're here; and I'll have to get some of your favorite bread. No one else eats it these days. Why, I remember when your mother was alive . . ."

"Oh, never mind, Klara." Peter looked into the pantry. "I'll go over to the bakery myself. I need the exercise."

Peter got out the worn bicycle he had used ever since he was old enough to straddle the seat. He couldn't use one in Zurich. It was too hilly there.

The bakery was only a few minutes away. No sooner did he cross the border into Germany, however, and go around a corner, than he was stopped by a Gestapo car.

They took him to Gestapo Headquarters in Schopfheim. He expected to pick up a telephone and be home in thirty minutes, but something went awry. The Gestapo made all the telephone calls, and then drove him in a big Mercedes to a camp deep in the Black Forest, and a detention room in another Gestapo headquarters.

"You're making a mistake." Peter was beginning to be worried. "I'm a student from Zurich. I've got my student I.D., my border pass—everything in order."

Peter knew something about Germans. He was getting nowhere trying to be humble. He had often seen his father berate foremen, shouting so loudly that his face turned an apoplectic red that made his saber scar stand out. Peter dropped his light Swiss accent and spoke in the most brutal, clipped, High-German he could muster.

"Enough! Take me to your commanding officer. Do you know who I am? I demand to speak to the highest ranking officer on the premises! Immediately!"

He kept up the shouting for five minutes, feeling more like an actor every minute. He felt very foolish and was running out of steam when a black-clad officer with silver eagles on his sleeve came in and beckoned to him.

"Follow me."

They went down a corridor and paused outside an office.

"Der Schweizer, Herr Oberstgruppenfuehrer."

"Hereintreten."

Peter stood in front of the desk. The Colonel was studying a clean, new, red-tabbed file. Even upside down, Peter could read his name on the file. The Colonel looked up.

"Are you Peter Oelrich?"

"Yes. I have all my papers here. There must be some mistake. I'm from Zurich. I'm a student at F.I.T. I ..."

"Let me see your papers."

The Colonel took Peter's identification papers and read them carefully line by line. He seemed to take forever.

"I was just going over to the Roebling Brothers bakery to get some bread. I go almost every week when I'm home. The black bread on this side of the border..."

"You are Peter Oelrich of Basel?" The Gestapo Colonel was cold as ice.

"Yes. My father is the chairman of the Oelrich Fabrik. We..."

"Herr Oelrich, I am now going to enlist you in the Army of the Third Reich. You are going to have an opportunity to serve your fatherland."

"Fatherland? I'm Swiss for two generations. You can't draft me."

"What does this say?" The Colonel pointed at Peter's

27

border pass. In a space inscribed 'Citizen of' was a 'D'. "What does that stand for?"

"*Deutschland.*, but we've been in Switzerland since 1870. My father and I were born there. And my brother..."

"Peter Oelrich, you will take one pace forward and become a private soldier in the Army of the Third Reich."

"I..."

Peter felt a blow in the middle of his back, and stumbled forward.

"But I..."

"Wegfuehren. Heil Hitler."

Old Hans Oelrich was not aware that Peter had disappeared. It was not unusual for him to stay away from Basel for many weeks. From time to time the old man, more irritable than ever, would complain.

"Where is Peter? He should be familiar with these specifications. He understands these things."

"Oh, he's probably off in Aarau with that sweet little thing he's shacking up with," Hans-Jörg answered. "You didn't much care for her, I take it?"

"Totally unsuitable. As a petite amie perhaps. That I could understand. He could keep her out of sight. But as a wife! *Unwahrscheinlich.* No culture, no beauty, no background. A nothing."

"Ah well. He's very young and naive. Those trips to Paris did him no good. All he wanted to do was walk around and look at the buildings."

"*Komm doch.* How about that steel?"

"We can save enough from the breech block mechanisms to turn out as many timers as we wish."

"And how will you get them to England?"

"By air, if necessary. They're small, and light."

"And irreplaceable."

"Precisely."

Peter was put into a basic training company of sixteen-year-olds. They were all former Pioneers and Hitler Youths, who had been inured to the entire drill and manual of arms since early childhood. All were fanatically nationalistic, if little else. Peter soon learned not to ask questions. Every time he went to visit his company commander's office he got three hours of punishment drill in the cobblestoned barracks square with full field pack and helmet. Although he wrote letters home, he got no answer.

He learned to adjust to the military. Rifle drill and close order drill under screaming sergeants just reminded him of his father. Peter learned to throw back his shoulders and stamp his hob-nailed boots on the cobblestones in perfect imitation of the non-coms. Confined to barracks and feeling a great distance from his bunk-mates, he memorized long passages of '*Infanterie Greift An*' and 'The Grenadier's Guide', and cleaned his equipment again and again, taking pleasure in the routine polishing that took his mind off his resentment.

After six weeks his commanding office called him to his office.

"Private Oelrich reporting as ordered, Sir." He clicked his heels together.

Peter could see a records file before the Captain. Inside were various forms, one page with a red and black Gestapo tab, and a file of letters he recognized as being in his own handwriting.

"Private, you have not written home."

"Sir." Peter could see all the letters he had written there in the file.

"Your family is asking about you. I want you to write a letter home immediately. Go to the outer office. Bring it here when you're finished."

Peter saluted and went to the outer office. A Corporal supplied him with pen and paper. In ten minutes he took the letter to the Captain.

The officer read it, looked Peter in the eye and tore it up.

"Unsatisfactory. Two punishment tours. Try again."

Peter went back to the outer office and wrote another letter.

"Unsatisfactory. Three punishment tours."

When the letter was finally ready to be mailed, it read rather differently from the first draft.

Kaiserslauten, den 4. April, 1942

Dear Father and Hans-Jörg,

I am well and happy and about to finish my basic training. I am glad I found it advisable to volunteer. Army training is rigorous, but my fellow soldiers are cheerful and happy, and looking forward to an opportunity to serve their country.

I hope to get assigned to an engineering batallion where my F.I.T. training will be of value. Please ask Vreneli to write to me. You'll find her address and telephone number among my things.

Respectfully,

Peter.

Upon completion of training, Peter's company was shipped to Poland, but Peter was confined to the *Kaserne* where he moved into a cadre room. He saw his first comrades loading into trucks to go to the train station.

Several days later he was picked up by a lieutenant and a sergeant and travelled with them on civilian trains to France. They were replacements for a certain engineer battalion that had suffered some casualties during the invasion of France.

The new *Kaserne* was no different from the old. Peter and the sergeant were assigned to barracks and unpacked their belongings. Peter had no sooner made his bed than he was called to the Captain's office. On the desk he saw his file of records with its red and black tab.

"Private Oelrich, I see you have never been paid."

"That's right, Sir."

"And you've been confined to barracks or company areas."

"Yes, Sir."

"Mm...this educational background. What did you study?"

"Metallurgy, drafting, heavy and light..."

"Any bridge building?"

"Yes, Sir. We had to design military bridges. I did some component design on two German Army bridges: FT104 and 105."

The Captain slapped the file closed and tapped it on the desk.

"We don't have a Gestapo office here," he said. "This is a veteran line battalion and we run things Army style. You do a good job, and you will be treated like any other soldier. No confinement, no special duties. Your pay papers will be straightened out immediately."

"Yes, Sir."

The Captain slapped the folder again on his desk.

"All mail is subject to military censorship."

"Yes, Sir."

"We have an opening for a corporal assistant to the executive officer. I'm going to hold it open for you. Be careful, and you can do well here."

"Yes, Sir."

"Dismissed."

6

Corporal Peter Oelrich of the 7th Field Engineers Battalion of the German army at Landrecies in occupied France puffed a little as he pedalled his bicycle down the smooth road beside the canal. In accordance with regulations, he was wearing his coal-scuttle helmet, and his Schmeisser was slung crosswise over his back. There had been a spate of new orders since saboteurs or 'franc-tireurs' had killed a few isolated soldiers. All men who left the Kaserne alone were required to be armed and helmeted.

Life in occupied France was very boring. When Peter began to feel himself getting fat and loggy, he formed the habit of taking a bicycle ride in the country. It was a chance to get away from the military, away from the stolid and resentful Frenchmen at the bistro on the town square, away from the movies with their newsreels of the advance through Russia.

The canal, straight and peaceful in the cool afternoon, with plane trees neatly lining one bank, reminded him of one in Aarau—Argovie—where he had once gone with Vreneli. They had walked hand in hand, and he had kissed her. He could remember the rough cotton of her dress, and the fresh clean smell of her clothes and her hair as she held him.

The smooth flatness of the canal was broken by a military bridge—all iron girders against the sky. It was very German. Peter rode up on it and dismounted in the middle. He took the Schmeisser off his shoulder and hung it on the bicycle seat. He had never fired one, and he didn't like to carry a gun.

He sat down on the bridge, opened a flap of his cartridge belt, and took out some chocolate. It weighed less than ammunition. Besides, it reminded him of home.

It had been six months now, six months in the German army.

He still felt isolated. He had written to Vreneli and to his father, but no answers had come. He was unable to call home, unable to use the telegraph. He was still very much alone, but he was somehow beginning to feel more his own man than he ever had before.

He looked down into the placid waters of the canal. Trout were swimming upstream against the light current. He wished for a fishing pole. But then he looked at his watch, and with a sigh, put on his heavy helmet, slung his Schmeisser over his shoulder, and began the ride back to the only friends he had.

As he pedalled nearer town, the road became busy with military traffic. He was glad that the exigencies of riding his bicycle excused him from saluting the officers in the open staff cars that passed.

The barracks was deserted. Peter was putting his helmet away when a comrade came in.

"*Peterli! Gott verdeckel!* Where have you been? Get over to the office. We're pulling out!"

Peter grabbed a hat and buckled his collar as he ran. The wooden steps echoed to his heavy boots.

"*Oelrich!* It's about time," his officer said, full of smiles. "Pack everything. We're pulling out."

"Where to, Lieutenant Wolfschmidt? What's happening?"

"Shh—just between the two of us—Africa! We've got to pull the *asinus Mussolini* out of the fire!"

"*Nanu . . .*"

"File all these papers and get that cabinet ready to go."

"Yes, sir."

The lieutenant seemed very happy indeed to be getting away from dull garrison duty and back into action. He was stamping travel orders and filing requisitions, mostly in the wastebasket.

"They're bringing in a company of Volksgrenadiers to

replace us. *Volksgrenadiers!* Can you imagine!"

Peter cleaned off his drafting table and packed his drafting tools carefully into their cases.

"You're getting to be a foxy old corporal. You know just how to disappear when all the work comes in. Where have you been all day?"

"Out on the canal. There's a FT104 bridge there. About two kilometers north."

"That one! You know who built it? General Rommel himself. Stood in the mud with the troops under fire to get it built. Summer of '39. Best days of my life!"

"Who's Rommel?"

"Used to run the *Fuehrerleibstandarte*. Best tanker you ever saw. He used to fire broadsides from moving tanks. Completely contrary to standing orders, but it worked."

"Unwahrscheinlich."

They loaded their few vehicles with their drafting equipment, portable machine shops, and records while the batallion was issued with khaki uniforms and new brassards which bore the palm tree and swastika of the Afrika Korps. Then, under field pack with helmets and rifles and in their new uniforms, they bicycled, the entire battalion to a local airfield where Luftwaffe planes just in from Russia were to fly them to Tunis. Peter and the office staff prepared to emplane with Lieutenant Wolfschmidt and Captain Dreieck.

"Oelrich—get those ramps up to the Junkers. And make sure those bicycles are secured," the lieutenant said.

"Bicycles? Are we taking the bicycles?"

"What are you, a chocolate soldier? In this army we obey orders."

Peter went off to ask the noncoms to secure the bicycles.

"Wolfschmidt, are you putting that *petit Suisse* in charge of your duties?"

"He's a good man, Captain Dreieck. You should promote him."

"I wish I could."

Dreieck examined a dispatch from Gestapo headquarters in Paris. It had been handed to him just before the teletype was disconnected. He was ordered to detach Private Oelrich from duty and return him to Germany.

"Do you want me to file that, sir?"

"Never mind. I'll file it myself." Dreieck tore up the flimsy and filed it on the afternoon breeze.

"Let's load up."

They were crossing at thirty thousand feet over the Mediterranean. The air was delightfully cool after the heat of their departure. In their stiff summer uniforms, they were almost chilly. Captain Dreieck called a conference of his battalion staff.

"Oelrich—make notes and get them typed up."

"All right, gentlemen. We are being attached to the 164th Light Motorized Division and we report to General Rommel as soon as we can arrange forward transportation from Tunis. I am ordered to prepare our vehicles for desert service. Of course, they didn't tell me *how* to do it. Any ideas?"

"A metal mesh over the radiators..." Lieutenant Wolfschmidt suggested.

"That's a start. Wolfschmidt, take the Volkswagen tomorrow and scour Tunis for some wire mesh. Buy it, steal it—requisition it—but get it."

"Yes, sir."

"What about special tires for driving on sand?"

"Who the hell knows?"

"They say that driving on soft tires is one solution, sir."
They continued their conference until just before landing, Captain Dreieck watching Peter surreptitiously and listening to his diffidently offered suggestions.

The battalion looked absurd on their bicycles in

Africa. As soon as they got off the airfield and onto the coast road to Tunis, the velocipedes bogged down on the soft shoulders of the narrow desert road.

7

Herr Leutnant Wolfschmidt also got bogged down in arranging for accomodations for the troops. He wanted to delegate his responsibility to Peter, but he couldn't go on using a corporal to supervise sergeants.

"Oelrich, you speak French. Take the Volkswagen and start scrounging up some of that wire mesh in Tunis. And take your Schmeisser!"

Peter drove off into the streets of Tunis. He drove around the port area for a few minutes before getting lost in the Souk. A little coffee-house restaurant on a corner appealed to him as having the raffish air of a Swiss coffee house. There were a few uniformed French officers, some men in crumpled civilian clothes, and some dark-complexioned natives, all drinking coffee, playing chess or reading the newspaper stories of the El Alamein battle.

He parked the Volkswagen where he could watch it, sauntered on to the open cafe terrace and took a metal table. The triangular ash tray bore the legend 'Ricard'. He was glad to notice that the French francs in his pocket were good here.

"Un café noir, s'il vous plait."

He took his coffee to the telephone booth and checked the telephone book for manufacturing companies that might produce wire mesh. Then it occured to him to check under the name of Oelrich. Sure enough, there was a branch office of the family firm, in Tunis. A little engineering liason office, he presumed. Peter bought a *jetòn* and dialed the number.

"Allo, oui?"

"Bon soir. Ici Peter Oelrich. Avec qui est-ce-que je parle?"

"Peter Oelrich? Ici?"

"*Oui*. I am attached to the German Army here and I should like your cooperation. I want a list of all possible suppliers of wire mesh in Tunis. I want it delivered to..." he looked around for the name of the restaurant— "'Café des Sports,' Place Tebessa, in thirty minutes."

"But—who...Are you from the main office?"

"I have my identification here. You just compile that list immediately and deliver it here."

"Yes, sir."

Peter felt he was beginning to learn of a little of his brother's German arrogance. He went to sit at his table and keep his eye on his vehicle. He felt rather dramatically foolish in his new khaki costume with its palm tree brassard. He felt as if he was at a costume ball at the Baur au Lac, and that Vreneli would come through the door, dressed as an Arab Princess, the moment the orchestra started playing *La Mer*. He buried his face in a newspaper.

"Wonderful little cars, those Volkswagens."

Peter looked up. A young French civilian was looking at the markings on the vehicle.

"Should be all right in the desert. Air-cooled engines are practical here, I suppose."

"Just arriving? When are you going forward?"

Peter was getting suspicious of all and sundry.

"Who knows?" He looked at the Frenchman and noticed his carefully shined shoes, hat and gloves, and the chess set on his table.

"Like a game?"

"Oh, do you play? Yes."

"I'm not very good, I'm afraid, but I like the game."

They set up the pieces. The Frenchman regarded Peter's uniform, which was bereft of rank badges or distinguishing marks other than the brassard.

"May I introduce myself? Lieutenant Robert Jeannot, of the garrison."

"Oelrich. Afrika Korps."

They had a desultory game as they discussed the football scores and the El Alamein battle which was still raging up the coast.

"Rommel could go all the way to Cairo if he could get the gas," the Lieutenant said.

"I wouldn't know. Guard your Queen."

"Those Italians are of absolutely no value."

Peter bent over the board in apparent concentration, but his eyes were also on the lieutenant and on his own vehicle. Every time an Arab boy got too close to the car, Peter would stand up and make a threatening movement with his gun. He had begun to realize that he was not on a student ski trip.

"Monsieur le directeur Oelrich?" A harried and rumpled civilian sidled up to him, clutching a typed list.

"Oui," Peter stood up. "Excuse me, Lieutenant."

"Vous êtes le Monsieur Hans-Jörg?"

"No, I am his brother. May I see the list?"

"Oui, Monsieur le directeur."

Peter detested the asinine subservience of his father's employees, but after six months as an enlisted man in the German army, he was more than ready to take advantage of all the help he could get.

"Very good," he said, examining the typed but already crumpled list. "And a map of the city?"

"Oh, you didn't say anything about that."

"Then get me one, and bring it back here immediately. I have to leave shortly."

"Yes, sir."

The little man scurried away to the nearest bookstore.

"Now I see why your German Army is considered so arrogant, *Herr General*," the French officer said.

"It gets things done. Check."

The Lieutenant interposed a horse to protect his King.

"Are you attached to the *Kommandatura* here?"

"In a way."

"Then I shall be seeing you again. What is your rank?

We French also like to be...*comment dit-on...sehr korrect.*"

"General, will do, *mon Lieutenant*. Checkmate."

Peter thanked him for the game and said that he hoped to see him again.

"I'm often here in the evening, *mon Géneral.*"

8

Lieutenant Wolfschmidt was very pleased with the typed list and street map. The next morning they scoured the city for material to make their few vehicles desert-worthy. Among other things they found the machine shop set up by the German back-area Kommandatura. The courtyard was filled with captured British trucks.

While Lieutenant Wolfschmidt was examining the sand screens and oil filters in the trucks, Peter talked with the mechanics.

"We have forty of them! Captured at Alamein. We're supposed to set up a supply service to the front," the sergeant-mechanic said, examining Peter's new uniform. "I wish we could get rid of them. They're a pain in the ass to maintain."

"Maybe we could take them off your hands."

"Best thing that could happen to both of us."

"Trade you for a couple hundred bicycles."

"I wish I could."

On the way back to their temporary quarters, Peter broached an idea to Lieutenant Wolfschmidt.

"We'll take it up with the Captain," Wolfschmidt said.

When Peter brought up his suggestion, the smile on Captain Dreieck's face developed into a wicked leer.

"It's pure larceny, Oelrich. You should be ashamed of yourself."

"Yes, sir."

"But Rommel himself did it in France. Did I ever tell you about that, Wolfschmidt? We were short of bridging materials, so the General just ups and 'borrows' some from General Magnus. Old Magnus was mad as a hatter when he found out. But by God, we got across that canal."

"Perhaps if Oelrich picked out a few mechanics and went ahead..."

"A very good idea. Oelrich, just walk in—in a friendly sort of way—and find out which trucks are desert-worthy and gassed up, and then give me a call here. We can be ready and out of this command area in two hours. It might work. I'd like to see anybody stop the 7th E.B. as long as we've got loaded rifles in our hands."

Peter picked several men, made sure they loaded their packs into the machine shop truck but carried their rifles, mounted them on their bicycles, and rode into town.

When they arrived at the Kaserne, Peter sauntered into the vast courtyard and leaned his bicycle against a wall.

"Brought you a gift, sergeant," he said, pointing to his bike.

"They sell pretty well on the black market," the sergeant smiled.

"Maybe I could get you a few more. Let's take a walk. Which of these trucks are gassed up?"

"They're all in running order. We're just filling the backs with jerricans."

"Perhaps my men could help you. Maybe they'll learn something."

Peter's men infiltrated the parking area and helped to load the trucks, asking questions the while, and Peter slipped out to make a telephone call.

Twenty minutes later the entire Seventh Engineer Battalion mounted bicycles in battle order. They headed for Tunis rather than Alamein. When they arrived at the Kaserne, Peter nodded to Captain Dreieck.

"Sergeant," Dreieck said to the truck pool non-com, "I'm commandeering these vehicles on the behalf of the 21st Panzer Division. Oelrich, give him a receipt."

"Whatever you say, Captain," the non-com said. "But it might look better if your men were at port arms."

"Where do you want these bicycles?"

"Over by the paint shop, sir. I'll have to report this to

42

my commanding officer, of course."

"Of course. But not too quickly."

Within twenty minutes the happy engineers were out on the road to Alamein, out of the Tunis Kommandatura area. They were finally motorized.

"Oelrich, I'm promoting you to sergeant. I don't care what they say at the 164th. You motorized us."

"Thank you, sir."

Some weeks later, Hans-Jörg stood by his father's desk reading a letter.

"Africa! How did he get there?"

"I don't like it," his father said. "A man could get killed there!"

"We'll have a German war hero in the family." Hans-Jörg scratched his head. "But I don't like the way he's disrupting the office in Tunis. Why don't you tell them to ignore him?"

"He carries a Schmeisser."

"Little brother is getting too big for his britches." Hans-Jörg debated whether to call his Gestapo contact to see if he could get Peter back on the Continent. A war hero in the family was potentially more bothersome to him than a little brother in school. But still . . .

Peter had sent several letters to his family for Vreneli, and others to her address in Zurich and to the conservatory. He had never received an answer, and it was preying on his mind.

The letters from his father were curt and peremptory. The old man seemed to be irritated with him for leaving Switzerland, and his letters soon bogged down in business details.

Hans-Jörg wrote a few short notes congratulating Peter on his promotions and wishing him well. In one letter he mentioned Vreneli.

"I went to see your little friend, but she had moved, and left no forwarding address. It's a pity.

"Father is getting very old. He seldom comes in to the office. I try to get over to have dinner with him at least once a week. I don't know how he stands it, all alone in that old brickpile."

Hundred degree heat, humidity, sand flies, and skin rashes pursued Peter through the desert. The battalion laid mines by night, and tried to sleep by day. There was a shortage of everything, even including sergeant's stripes—not that Peter had any place to wear them. He went around in boots and a pair of khaki shorts held up by a new leather belt his father had sent him, together with a draft for cash on their Tunis office if he could get there again. Sewn in the belt were Swiss fifty franc gold pieces. They were not very useful in the desert.

The Battalion was being built up to strength through reinforcements from Germany. Captain Dreieck became a Major, and Peter became the battalion Sergeant-Major. He fitted up a truck as an office and bedroom for his commanding officer, and another as his own mobile drafting room with desks and beds.

Peter was adapting some fans he had scrounged from the Luftwaffe when Major Dreieck came by.

"Oelrich, I've got half the battalion out with dysentery or heat prostration."

"Yes, sir." Peter tried the blades of the fan.

"If we wait for supplies out here, we'll melt away. The division is short of three hundred vehicles. How would you like to drive into Tunis and scrounge up some vegetables and eggs? I'll give you every franc we can scrape up in the officer's mess."

"I'd like that, Major."

"Perhaps you'd better buy some civilian clothes. I wouldn't want to have you picked up by the Kommandatura."

"Whatever you say, sir."

Later that night Peter loaded up with jerricans and food and set off with Lieutenant Wolfschmidt on the long drive into Tunis. In their pockets were passes designating them as liason and authorizing them to buy or requisition materiel for the 164th Light.

The further they got from the front, the more eggs and vegetables were available. They slept by day and drove by night. When they crossed the border into Tunisia, Peter began to feel good.

"Lieutenant," he said, "I've got my own way of doing things. Why don't you just register in a good hotel and let me take care of business?"

"What do you mean, your own way?" Lieutenant Wolfschmidt asked.

"Confidentially, Lieutenant, my family has been doing business in Tunis for seventy-five years. We can get good prices on anything. And as far as the military is concerned, a sergeant can get a lot more information than an officer."

"Perhaps so."

"You're a fine soldier, Lieutenant. You've been out in that minefield every day. You deserve a rest. Let the enlisted men do the work for a change."

Peter dropped the Lieutenant off at the best hotel in town, put the truck in the hotel garage and went out with his little kit bag to find less conspicuous accomodations for himself in the native district.

After he had bathed and put on some civilian clothing, he felt almost human again. As he sauntered through the winding alleys looking for the *Café des Sports*, his feet felt as light as wings. The civilian shoes he had purchased were five pounds lighter than the jack boots he had been wearing for six months. Peter put his hands in his pockets in a decidedly unmilitary manner and began to whistle a tune.

When he found the cafe he called the local Oelrich office and gave lists of what he needed in the way of fresh produce and minor luxuries for the officer's mess. Then he got pencil and paper and sat down on the cafe terrace to write to Vreneli at her parent's address.

"Dear Vreneli," he wrote. "I hope this letter will get to you. I'm entrusting it to a local Oelrich office. It's hard to believe I'm back in civilization."

"Bon soir, mon général." Peter looked up. It was his acquaintance from the French garrison.

"Bon soir, Lieutenant. Asseyez-vous."

"Ah, you have been promoted to civilian, like myself."

"I wish I were," Peter answered.

"Not I, I'm a career officer."

"Just as I'm a career civilian, or would be if I could."

"All things are possible in this best of all possible worlds, as one of your German philosophers said."

"Philosophy is not my forte."

"Then it must be military tactics. May I have my revenge?"

"Wonderful. Let's get a chess set." Peter signalled for a waiter.

"You seem to have a good desert tan."

"Fresh air and tropical sunshine, Lieutenant—*Jeannot, n'est-ce pas?*"

"Yes. And—"

"Oelrich."

"A well-known name."

"It comes from an Alsatian village."

"Lorraine."

"Comme vous voulez."

"But your French has more the sing-song of the *Français Fédérale* than the harshness of Alsace."

"So they say. *J'adoube.*"

They played two games, and Peter lost them both. He began to wonder if the red Tunisian wine was going to his head.

A group of young men approached their table, and

Lieutenant Jeannot looked up with a smile.

"Bon soir, mes amis. Permettez-moi de vous pre-senter... Monsieur le Petit Suisse."

"How do you do?" Peter stood up to shake hands with them. They seemed to be Vichy officers in mufti. From the local garrison, he presumed.

"Monsieur Beaucaire."

"Enchanté."

"Monsieur Pierre le Gros."

"Une plaisir, Monsieur Pierre."

"My friend here is a loser at chess."

"But a winner at war games, I take it?"

"Pas mal."

"Alors. On y va?"

"We are going to *Pauv' Richarde's*. Would you care to join us?"

"What is *Pauv' Richarde's*?"

"The famous belly-dancing place! You've never seen it? Best in the quarter. A little basement, good cham-pagne—"

"Ils ont une chanteuse—quelle femme!"

"Parisienne."

"Ah no, sûrement de Grenoble."

Peter went along with them. He found them a great deal more relaxed than any group of German officers he had ever seen.

The bar was hot and smoky, with slow-moving fans stirring the night air. There were baccarat tables in the back room. A group of staff officers from the German Kommandatura was at a nearby table. They peered about nervously, and didn't seem to enjoy the Arab music that emanated from a band of drummers and wind players.

Some Frenchmen took their place on the bandstand and the lights were dimmed.

"Messieurs et dames: Nous avons le grand plaisir de vous presenter l'etoile des grands boulevards, Mademoi-

selle Marie Blancharde!"

Peter joined the applause, for the girl singer was very attractive. She didn't seem to sing very well, but her looks made up for it. She was small and her black hair was set off by a modish sequinned gown cut low in front. She sang the latest Parisian hits. After she had finished singing, she joined them at their table.

"Bon soir, messieurs."

"Adieu, Marie. Have a seat. You know everybody— except for *Monsieur le Suisse."*

"How do you do," Peter said.

They drank some wine and watched the belly dancer. She was an Arab girl with naked feet and hair hennaed down to her coccyx. Her performance grew wilder and wilder as the Arab musicians pounded harder on their drums. Peter noticed eyes bugging out at the German officers' table.

"Cochons d'allemandes," the girl singer muttered.

"Marie's boy friend was caught by the Gestapo," Lt. Jeannot explained. She's not very fond of Germans."

"I'm not exactly charmed by the Gestapo myself," Peter said.

"In fact, many of my friends are disenchanted with our Marshal Laval," the lieutenant said.

Peter concentrated on the shimmering navel that gleamed above the rotating sequinned hips. It was the first time he had seen a belly dancer, and the first time he had been near a woman in six months.

"Are you going to join de Gaulle too, *M. le Suisse?"*

Peter looked up. The lieutenant was frowning at Marie.

"I don't know much about politics, Mademoiselle," he said.

"Ooh la la. You're so formal."

"M. Le Suisse is very serious. And mysterious."

The gentlemen of the party broke off to go their several ways, and the girl singer moved on to talk with others.

Peter realized that it was getting late. His head swam with wine and perfume.

"C'est l'heure, mon Lieutenant."

"Oui, mon général. I trust you can find your way alone?"

"Yes. The air will do me good."

"Always a pleasure to see you. You have friends in Tunis. Please feel free to come to us if we can be of service."

"Vous êtes trop gentil."

"Good night. And you know where to find us."

"Yes. Good night, and thank you for inviting me along."

"You're always welcome."

Peter went out into the hot night. An ocean breeze sobered him as he wound through the narrow alleys.

"Backsheesh, Monsieur!" A little boy grabbed at him. Peter shied away.

"Psst . . ." Another street Arab stood in a dark doorway fingering himself and smiling, his white teeth gleaming in the shadows.

Peter's stomach crepitated and he lurched to the other side of the cobbled alleyway.

"Cherie. Viens avec moi."

A dark Arab girl opened her gown. Her face was veiled, but her stomach had hot shadows like the night itself. Peter gasped and slowed.

"Ah, un jeune soldat brave," the girl whispered, and guided his hand to her hot body.

"Toute la nuite?" she whispered.

She led him by the hand through dark alleyways and up odiferous stone steps to a hot apartment. She whispered to an old crone squatting under a dim red bulb.

The girl's room was lit by a tiny oil lamp. The shadows were hot, and moved with the flickering light.

Peter left before dawn.

Two days later Peter picked up the truck at Lieutenant Wolfschmidt's hotel, had it loaded, and drove it around to pick up his officer.

"Hello, Sergeant. All ready?"

"Yes, Sir."

"Then let's get out of here before the local *Kommandatura* starts checking passes."

"Yes, sir."

They drove off down the coast road.

"You look well, lieutenant."

"Wonderful. And you look like hell."

"La vie c'est dûre sans confiture."

Peter scratched himself a great deal in the next few days. The heat and the sand fleas drove him to distraction. Finally he went to a friend at the dispensary.

"I'm going crazy. I feel sand fleas on me even when there's nothing there. You've got to give me something."

The medical corpsman looked carefully at the hair on Peter's tanned chest.

"Have you been driving around the rear areas, Sergeant?"

"Why?"

"Take down your pants. Those are no sand fleas."

11

Peter was sweating and cursing in a Luftwaffe hangar as he tried to fit a defective airplane engine and propellor on the back of a captured flatbed truck. Outside, a Storch landed. It was a poor landing.

"Achtung! General Rommel."

"As you were. Go on with your work. Here, young man. Can I get someone to take a look at my ailerons?"

"Yes, sir," Peter said, signalling a Luftwaffe mechanic who was coming out of the office at a run, beer bottle still in hand.

"What are you doing?"

"Orders of Major Dreieck, 7th F.E.B., sir. He said the general was looking for a way to make a column of trucks look like a column of tanks from the air."

"Ach so!"

"It will be fine if it works. Better than dragging wire mesh. It'll blow up much more dust in this weather."

"Not bad. In fact, very good. Whose idea was this?"

"Mine."

"And who are you?"

"Oelrich, Sir. Sergeant-Major of the 7th E.B."

"Bist Schwäbisch?"

"Schwizer, General."

"This is the kind of thinking I like. Tell Dreieck to send in your papers. I'm promoting you to Lieutenant."

"Yes, sir. Thank you, sir."

"Macht nüt. Weiterfahren."

Peter kept many of his machinists out of the minefields that August by having them cut Perspex goggles, like Rommel's, out of discarded Luftwaffe material. All the officers in the division wanted to look like the general.

On the penultimate night of the month Major Dreieck

stopped by Peter's truck.

"*Leutnant Oelrich*! Big conference tomorrow with the general. I'm taking you along in case there are any technical questions. The general likes smart young officers, so get your best uniform ready. Shine your boots."

"*Ja wohl, Herr Major.*"

The Major inspected him after breakfast. "*Also gut. Losfahren.*"

They had to make a long drive to arrive at Rommel's open command tent before 8:30. All the Division Commanders were there with their aides. There was apparently something big cooking.

"Good morning, gentlemen. Did I get you up early?" Rommel's blue Maltese cross sparkled at his throat.

"Good morning, General" was echoed by all the khaki-clad officers.

"Well, gentlemen, tomorrow is the day. We head south tonight, gas or no gas. If we can capture enough petrol, we'll be in Cairo by Thursday. We have a hundred of the new long-barelled guns on our Tiger tanks and we have the advantage of surprise. Come—look at the map with me."

The general officers crowded around the map table as Rommel grease-pencilled their attack routes on the overlay. Peter stood back to regard them. They were young, lean and burned—the Italian foppishly handsome, the Germans thin and hungry.

"Littoria and Ariete here, on the left of the Afrika Korps, and then the light division. I want no headlights going through the minefields. Field police and engineers will have flashlight batons to guide you through. Dreieck, is that all arranged?"

"Yes, sir."

Rommel finished his instructions and wished them well.

"Gentlemen, either we reach the Suez, and Guderian reaches Groszny, or we'll . . ." he thumbed down. "I expect the best from you. You will lead your troops from the front vehicles, not from the rear."

Late that afternoon, before they went out to the minefields, Peter heard another echo of the same statements as the order of the day was read to the troops.

"Today our army sets out once more to attack and destroy the enemy, this time for good. I expect every soldier in my army to do his utmost in these important days of decision! Long live Fascist Italy! Long live the Greater German Reich! Long live our great leaders!"

12

The moon was a slice of yellow guiding his men through the minefields that night as Peter dropped them off and checked to make sure that their colored traffic policemen's night batons were in working order.

At the outer limits of the German minefields, Peter stopped his truck and looked back over the undulating desert. An eerie sound echoed from the German jump-off point. General von Bismarck had sent the band of the Fifth Panzer Regiment to play his troops off into battle.

Ich hatt' ein Kameraden,
Ein besserer find'st du nichts ...

Peter remembered seeing a newsreel. They had played that song when the battleship Bismarck had sailed in 1941. Those sailors were all dead now.

The huge Tigers clanked forward, followed by infantry and then Peter's engineers who loaded into the back of the trucks and drank cold beer. From the north there were already explosions and sporadic machine gun fire.

"Infantry ..." muttered Lieutenant Wolfschmidt.

"Heavy machine guns," said his radio operator.

"They must have hit mines already. Jesus!"

"Lieutenant—message from the Major."

"Here, hand me the earphones."

"Wolfschmidt. Get your ass up here! Bismarck is dead. Mines all over the place. We've got to clear them."

"Yes, sir."

They started north, driving carefully in the tracks of the tanks.

"Corporal Horner. Get out and walk in front. Watch for mines."

The corporal trudged in front of the truck, peering at the sand where one wheel of the truck would run outside of the tank tracks.

Star shells began to light the night. They all cringed with each explosion.

A line of tracer tore through the truck cab. Wolfschmidt's brains and blood splattered all over Peter and the driver. The truck ground to a halt. A British Hurricane was turning to make another pass further on.

"Everybody out. Fast. Spread out. Horner—look under the hood and see if you can get this truck running."

Up ahead another vehicle flamed in the night.

The corporal got the engine working again by wrapping friction tape around a punctured rubber hose. Peter pulled Wolfschmidt's body out and left it beside the track. Then he ripped off his shirt and wiped the blood and flesh from his helmet and from the truck cab and from Wolfschmidt's binoculars.

"Is that radio working?"

"Yes, lieutenant."

"All right, let's go. Horner, you drive. We'll walk. Spread out and walk in the tracks."

At midnight they came upon a command truck. A dead general was sprawled in the back near the shattered command radio.

"Horner—see if you can get this damned truck working. You men, lay out the general. Take his *Wehrpass* and identification. We'll let the Tommies bury him."

Just before dawn they came up to another command truck. Dreieck jumped out.

"Oelrich! It's about time. Where's Wolfschmidt?"

"Dead."

"Christ. They must have been expecting us. Hellish mess. Nehring's wounded. Bayerlein is in command. Your men all right?"

"Yes, sir."

"Get them out in front of those Tigers. Another eight hundred yards and we'll be through the British fields."

Peter turned. "All right, you heroes. Out in front of the tanks and take up those mines. And watch out for A.P."

Peter and the Major followed in the footsteps of the engineers and carried the disarmed mines back to the truck, walking back and forth under the glare of parachute flares. A mortar blew up their half-ton and fire lit the sweating figures as a pillar of smoke from the burning rubber rose into the shimmering desert air. Another Hurricane made a strafing run. Peter dove to the ground. Two inches from his nose a little three-pronged trip wire stuck out of the sand like a miniature palm tree.

"Oelrich, get off your ass!"

Dawn found them through the minefields. Peter took over the riddled command truck and found a workable radio in a disabled vehicle. On the way east into the sunrise they passed a burned-out Tiger tank. The stink of roasted flesh was sickening. Melted aluminum from the engine had formed in pools that shone like mirrors in the blood-red dawn.

When they passed a British machine-gun nest, Peter stopped to strip the bodies, getting a new khaki shirt and a pair of shorts to replace his blood-soaked trousers. Tea was still brewing over a field stove. It tasted delicious with the tinned cookies, and reminded Peter of après-ski tea at St. Moritz.

"Oelrich—" Dreieck's voice crackled over the field radio. "New orders. Proceed to point 37.5 on your field map. Do you have a field map?"

"Hell, no."

"Follow the tanks to Alun el Halfa."

"Yes, sir."

They headed into the sun. Peter fell asleep, waking up only to jump out of the truck during air attacks. At noon they opened tins of canned meat marked. 'A.M..'

"Asinus Mussolini."

"It's better than a bullet in the gut."

A sandstorm was blowing up, protecting them from air

57

attack. After taking his turn at driving, Peter sat again in the bloodied seat where Wolfschmidt had died as the half-track bounced and rocked northward in the trackless desert. He closed his reddened eyes and tried to get his mind off the nightmare he was living through.

He thought of his first trip with Vreneli to her home in Aarau. She hadn't really been aware of his family at that time. She knew his name, but it was not an uncommon name. She didn't associate it with the Oelrich factories. She knew him only as a student, rather typically Swiss-looking in his tweed jacket and loden coat, usually carrying books as he picked her up at the music conservatory to take her out for dinner at the student union or in a little student restaurant.

But Peter had already been getting rather serious about her. She gave him a warmth, a sense of belonging, a love he hadn't felt since his mother died.

Vreneli was always chattering about her father and mother, and her little sister in Aarau. Peter wanted to meet them, and he hinted that he would like to be invited to visit her family.

They had taken the Aarau train from the Zurich railway station one Saturday morning.

"Why did you take second class, Peter?"

"I thought you'd be more comfortable."

"A waste of money. Twenty francs extra for a little padding on the seats for just a few hours."

"And some privacy!"

"What did you have in mind? Don't you get fresh now. Somebody might come in the compartment any minute."

Peter had sat beside her on the lurching train seat, bouncing just like the half-track through the desert.

He had sat with her arm in his, looking out at the rolling mountains of home—Canton Zurich and then Canton Aargau... Argovia in Latin, for it had been a cavalry remount center for two thousand years since the days of the Roman legions.

He sat with her arm pressed to his side and felt that here was someone who belonged to him, someone who loved him, and respected him not for who he was, but for what he was—a plain but honest student in Switzerland—a nice young man with a nice girl at his side. He leaned over to kiss her behind the ear. She blushed and pulled away, but squeezed his arm.

Aargau was a little town. The landmarks protection laws had embraced it before modernization could alter the outlines of its medieval charm. Where the city walls had once stood to protect the village from marauding German soldiers there was now a wide cobblestoned boulevard, and inside the old walls were winding narrow streets and sixteenth century facades, with no advertising signs, no electric lines, no neon lights to ruin the "old town."

Peter and Vreneli walked from the railway station carrying their shoulder bags, and stopped on the corner of Vreneli's block to buy some cookies to bring home. It was only a few steps further to the house.

It was a fifteenth century house. Vreneli pulled an iron lever by the doorway, and Peter could hear a bell tinkling inside.

"*Ja, wer isch do?*"

"It's me, mother. Open up."

Mrs. Schmid unlatched the heavy door and put her arms around her daughter.

"Vreneli! How are you, dear?" Peter shuffled his feet uncomfortably.

"Mama, this is Peter Oelrich—my mother."

"How do you do." Mrs. Schmid took his hand. "Come in. I'm glad to meet you. We've heard so much about you. Come in."

Peter stepped into the flagstoned hall. The warm smell of baking apple strudel filled the house.

"Oh no, Mama! Peter just bought you some cookies."

"That's all right. They won't go to waste. Not with a

59

ten-year-old in the house."

They showed him his room. The ancient beams were low, and although Peter was only five feet seven, he had to be careful not to straighten up too fast as he unpacked his shaving things and his change of clothes. It was much too easy to crack one's head on low beams in these old houses.

Vreneli was in the next room, her little sister's room. Downstairs, Peter heard the doorbell tinkle again, and then the ripple of a piping childish voice, and the echoing thunder of a child running up the wooden stairs.

"*Vreneli, ciaou.* Where is he? Come on. I want to meet him. Mama made me take my piano lesson but I ran all the way home. Where is he?"

Peter came out into the hall.

"Peter, this is my noisy little sister. Anna, shake hands with Peter." The girl, small and blonde, her rosy cheeks flushed with running, was suddenly shy. Vreneli had to push her forward.

"How do you do, Miss Anna?"

The girl giggled and shook his hand. "We're going to play some Beethoven for you!"

"Oh, never mind, Anneli. Peter didn't come here just to listen to a concert."

"Why not? I've been practicing the sonata, Vreneli. Did you bring your good violin?"

"No, of course not. I've been playing all week."

"You have to hear me. Besides, Daddy will love it."

"We'll see." She patted her sister's head.

"Do you want to see Mama's loom?" Anneli asked.

"Yes."

The little girl took him by the hand and pulled him onto a porch. A big electric loom was there.

"It's Mama's hobby," Vreneli said, standing in the doorway. "Besides, it brings in some extra money. She had made hundreds of sweaters."

"Want to see how it works?" the little girl asked.

60

"Anneli, no! You know you're not supposed to touch it."

"Oh, Mama lets me run it now, sometimes."

"Never mind. Let's go downstairs. I'm hungry."

They went down the winding staircase. Its scarred wood gleamed with new shellac. The door opened as they came into the entry hall.

"Daddy!" Anneli jumped the last two steps and threw her arms around the gray-haired, sparse little man who was tucking a four-inch long key into his worn leather briefcase.

"Hello, darling. Hello Vreneli." Mr. Schmid kissed his elder daughter and put his arm around her shoulders.

"Daddy, this is Peter Oelrich."

"How do you do."

"How do you do, sir."

"Well. It's nice to have a house full. Come. Let's see if lunch is ready."

They went into the parlor after Mr. Schmid hung up his coat and put his briefcase down neatly on a table. At the rear of the little parlor with its upright piano, couch and chairs, there was a dining area with a table, already set, and a sideboard. Next to the sideboard was a doorway to the kitchen.

"Mother, I'm home. Is lunch ready?" Mr. Schmid pushed the kitchen door open and poked his head into the kitchen. "What are we having?"

"Fondue. Almost ready."

"Well, Herr Oelrich, how about a glass of wine?"

"Thank you, sir."

He poured five glasses from a bottle on the sideboard.

"Veltliner. Good Swiss table wine."

"*Prosit!*"

"*Zum wohl.*"

"Now don't you men start sipping on a lot of wine!" Mrs. Schmid came from the kitchen with a big

61

earthenware pot full of steaming melted cheese and put it in the center of the table. "I don't want you tipsy and cluttering up the house all afternoon."

"Never mind, mother. We have to make our guest welcome." Mr. Schmid opened a door in the sideboard and produced a bottle of Kirsch.

"Produit d'Argovie," he said, pouring a little in the fondue. "We make it right here in town. Does wonders for your digestion."

They sat down to lunch, spearing cubes of bread on long forks and dipping them into the fragrant melted cheese, blowing on the mouthsfull to cool them before eating.

Mr. Schmid was a high-school teacher of mathematics. It was not a job that paid well, but it guaranteed security and respectability.

"You have a wonderful family here, Herr Schmid," Peter said.

"Oh, we're nothing special, but we get along."

Anneli was chattering away about her piano lessons while Vreneli caught up on the local gossip from her mother. Peter enjoyed his fondue and envied the family life he had never known. In this tiny, warm house was an intimacy he had never experienced.

They finished their lunch with fresh apple strudel and tea, then Peter and the two girls went for a walk. Peter had Vreneli's arm in his, but took Anna's little hand as they crossed a street with tramcars, autos, and horse-drawn carts bringing huge wheels of cheese in from the country. From a church overlooking the old town ramparts, they heard organ music.

"Let's go in. That's Bach."

The church was empty and dark. Light gleamed through stained glass windows. From a balcony choir loft came the sounds of an organ. A white-haired man was playing complicated passages, stopping, and then playing again.

"It's Albert Schweitzer. He's playing here tonight, but it's sold out."

"Shh—Anneli. Be quiet."

They listened as the old man turned pages, played a few moments, and made marks on the music with a pencil. After a while they went out. Anneli ran and jumped up and down with childish exuberance.

A troop of Swiss cavalry came trotting by, variegated in their field-green uniforms, helmets bouncing on their heads.

They walked up another street that overlooked the Rhine. Barges, far below, were going up the river against the current.

"And that's where Daddy teaches." The high school was empty, a small building compared to the big ones at F.I.T., where Peter went to school. "I'm going to be going there soon," Anneli chirped. "Daddy's the best teacher they have."

"Oh, be quiet," Vreneli pressed her sister's head to her side to shush her, and leaned over to kiss her forehead.

After dinner that evening, Anneli insisted on accompanying Vreneli as she played some Beethoven. The little girl played piano well, Peter thought, and although Vreneli complained about having to use the three-quarters sized violin she had played as a little girl, Peter thought the music sounded wonderful. Mr. Schmid put down his paper to listen.

"Do you mind if I smoke a pipe?" he asked.

"Oh, Daddy. Not that stinky old thing."

"I don't mind at all, sir," Peter said.

The Schmids offered Peter their concert tickets, but Vreneli said that she would prefer to go to a new French movie that was playing nearby. It was about a German prisoner of war camp during World War I. Peter spotted Oelrich guns in one scene.

Still later they had a glass of wine and some cheese in Vreneli's mother's kitchen before going quietly to bed. As he lay silent in the narrow bed in the room where Vreneli had spent her childhood, and listened to the girls whispering in the next room, Peter closed his eyes. It had been a pleasant day. They hadn't done anything special, but there was a warmth and simplicity in Vreneli's parents home, a love that was lacking in Peter's life. He closed his eyes and thought that he would be very happy if he could settle down in a little town like this and live simply for the rest of his days.

13

The half track clanked and lurched through the desert. The sand got softer and softer, and the trucks bogged down as often as the tanks. They were making almost no progress when the weather began to lift. Above them, well within cannon range, was a sheer rock cliff. It suddenly burst into flame as massed British guns opened up on the immovable Tigers. Screams and explosions filled the afternoon.

"Dig in, you bastards. Scatter. Keep away from the vehicles."

The tanks opened fire on the ridge, but there was nothing to shoot at, nothing but muzzle blasts.

Bombers roared in from Suez, blasting their trucks, and towers of billowing smoke rose two miles in the air to mark the killing ground.

Peter dug a slit trench through soft sand and shale. Sweating, he took off his helmet and laid it on the rim. A bomb blasted him off his knees and a sharp fragment went halfway through the helmet. Peter examined the hot metal. Into the steel was stamped the legend 'Oelrich. Manchester.' Peter was pleased to know that the English were still licensing the family's designs. He lay down flat in his trench and took a piece of hard black bread from his cartridge belt. He washed it down with sips of cognac from his canteen.

The bombing continued all night. The men and vehicles were dispersed, but the screams never stopped. At dawn, Rommel drove up in his mammoth English truck. Shells were still flying.

"Who's in charge here?"

Peter sat up and put his shirt on.

"I guess I am, General!"

"You guess? Don't you know? Who are you, a Limey cook?"

"Oelrich. Leutnant, 7th. E.B."

"Oelrich, eh? Know anything about 88's?"

"Yes, sir, a little."

"A mile west of here you'll find three Flak 88's disabled. Flying shale. Get over there and fix them."

"Yes, sir."

Peter took two men and drove off in the mobile machine shop. He was glad to get away. Generals seemed to draw fire.

With sweat and a hammer, he got one of the 88's in working order after cannibalizing the others. No sooner did it begin firing than Major Dreieck drove up.

"Oelrich—load up and head west."

"West? What about Cairo?"

"Forget about getting to Egypt. Load up."

Peter looked at his bloody hands and greasy fingers, and wondered what he was doing in the desert. Many others in the Afrika Korp were wondering the same thing.

Two days later they were all assembled in their old camp. Peter was able to bathe and have a hot meal before he went back to duty securing the British minefields they had captured at the cost of so much blood.

They were on half-rations, laying mine fields with new model mines capable of blowing up a tank track. They worked twelve hours each night laying anti-personnel mines that spring into the air before exploding to fill the desert with flying steel pellets.

In the officer's mess Peter found a *Frankfurter Illustrierte* showing pictures of Rommel receiving his Field Marshal's baton.

"If he figures out how to run an army on sand and sunshine, they'll make him head of O.K.W.," Dreieck sneered.

The next newsmagazines had rotogravures of the street

fighting in Stalingrad. "What did the Marshal say?" Peter asked. "If we don't get Suez and the Caucasus, we're kaput?"

"Don't be defeatist. You could be shot for talking like that."

Their "Devil's Garden" of mines completed, the 7th E.B. was withdrawn from the southern part of the line and went into a new camp. They were still on half rations, with no vegetables for weeks. Peter hardly recognized his own thin face in the mirror, pale under his tan.

At the end of October huge artillery bombardments began blasting the camps and minefields. The British were building up again for another attack. Peter and Major Dreieck were at a forward command post overlooking the infamous Hill 28 one afternoon. A dark pall of smoke covered the British positions. A Storch observation plane landed in the flat desert back of the camouflaged command post.

"Marshal Rommel! I thought you were in Germany!"

"Hello, Dreieck. Is that Oelrich?"

"Yes, sir."

"How's that hill?"

"Can't see a thing from here."

Rommel climbed on a mound and examined the terrain with field glasses. His neck and hands were covered with running sores.

"Is that your truck, Major?" he asked.

"Yes, sir."

"I think we should get the hell out of here. Let's take a drive over to the flank and find out if we can see a little better."

They got into the command truck, and as they drove away, heavy artillery shells began slamming into the camouflaged headquarters. Rommel hardly noticed. "I saw the Führer Wednesday," he smiled. "We're getting all new equipment. The best. The new Nebelwerfer rockets and a 260 millimeter mortar. You have no idea what that man is doing for us on the home front."

"He's a great leader," Dreieck said.

"And absolutely fearless. When we entered Prague he stood up in the back of a Mercedes—no protection—and there were still armed Czechs everywhere. He's a real soldier."

They parked behind a dune and trained their glasses on Hill 28.

"Smoke..." the Marshal said.

The English were blanketing the hill with smoke generators while their engineers cleared paths through the mine fields.

"We're getting five hundred new smoke generators too. Do you have an officer you could send to Tunis to familiarize himself with the equipment?"

"We could send Oelrich if you wish, sir."

"*Nanu*. Then send him. And while you're about it, promote him to First Lieutenant."

"Yes, sir."

14

A few days later when there was a lull in the fighting, Peter was able to organize a night flight to Tunis in a command plane. Filthy in his uniform at the sleepy Tunisian airfield, he decided to go into town. He checked into the Hotel Splendide and soaked for an hour in the bathtub of his suite while he had his clothes washed, dried in the sun, pressed, and furbished with his new rank badges.

He had to take a taxi to the military airfield outside of Tunis to check on the new equipment. He had decided that it was more important for an engineering officer to carry a gun in the back areas than at the front, so over his shoulder was slung a fully loaded Schmeisser.

Tunisia was green and lush after the barren desert. Wild flowers grew by the sides of the road. The countryside was no longer shimmering with waves of heat as it had been when a much younger Oelrich had first arrived. The French guards saluted smartly as the taxi drove through the gates.

Engineering specifications were attached to the shipping manifestos on the new equipment. Peter inspected it and made sure it was properly stored to wait for trans-shipment to the front. The planes would have to go out at night to avoid the constant air harrassment.

He ate lunch at the Officer's Mess. The faces of some of the French officers looked familiar. Peter ignored them. He also kept away from the Luftwaffe officers.

At the end of the day he was exhausted. He hitched a ride back into town in a motorcycle side-car. It left him off in the native quarter. Within a few minutes he found the Café des Sports, pulled up a chair on the terrace, put his boots on one chair and his backside on another, took off his hat, and ordered a bottle of cognac. The shadow of his perspex goggles showed pale against his tan.

The men at the other tables stared at him with disdain. Since Rommel's initial defeats—or victories, depending on which wireless you listened to—German uniforms were apparently unwelcome here.

A detachment of German *Feldpolizei* marched past under the command of a young lieutenant, spruce and neat in his fresh garrison uniform.

"Halt."

The Lieutenant walked up to Peter's table.

"Papers, please."

Peter looked him up and down.

"Bug off, kid," he said softly.

"Leutnant, you're out of uniform and off limits. I'll have to ask you to come with me."

Peter stood up and looked the young man in the eye. His finger was on the trigger of his gun.

"I'm here under direct orders of Marshall Rommel. Don't fuck with me, kid."

His Schmeisser accidentally let off an air burst that startled a flock of pigeons from the roof of a neighboring building. The Lieutenant turned pale and stepped back.

"Ja wohl, Herr Oberleutnant. Gute nacht, Herr Oberleutnant."

"Ciaou, buebi."

Peter sat down and drained a glass of cognac as the detachment marched off in perfect order. A waiter picked up the shell cases and put them in an ashtray. Peter spit airport dust from his mouth.

"Bon soir, mon général."

"Hello, Jeannot." Peter stood up again and straightened his shoulders. *"Bon soir, mademoiselle."*

"You look like a Chinese Colonel in that uniform." Peter was wearing Italian boots, field-gray riding breeches, and an English safari jacket. His peaked cap with goggles lay on the table.

"Won't you sit down?"

"Thank you."

"Cognac?"

"Absolutely. Marie?"

The girl nodded sulkily.

"And what brings you to our fair city? Buying vegetables again?"

"I came to play a little chess. Sorry about the uniform."

"Our *petit Suisse* is becoming a hardened veteran."

The girl said nothing. She was very uncomfortable sitting with a German.

"You're all loaded up for a new campaign, *mon général*."

"Not really." Peter fiddled with his cartridge belt. "May I offer you some chocolate?"

"Sprüngli? Have you conquered Switzerland now, as well as Stalingrad?"

"Und der Schweiz nehmen wir im Rückzug," Peter quoted sadly. "Perhaps we'd be better off playing chess."

"Politics make strange bedfellows," said the Frenchman, raising his hand for a waiter. The sulky chanteuse ate her chocolate daintily.

"Would you care to join us for dinner before Marie goes to work?"

"I'd like to, but I have no civilian clothes with me. I wouldn't want to embarrass you."

"A friend of mine has an apartment near here. Perhaps we could borrow something. You're about his size."

Peter won a chess game and they finished off the bottle of cognac before winding through several streets as dusk fell on the city. In the distance Peter could hear a muezzin chanting nasally from a tower.

"Perhaps you'd better let me carry your gun, *Herr Oberleutnant*. You wouldn't want it to go off by accident."

"I put myself in the hands of our noble allies."

They knocked on the door of a second-story apartment. A peephole opened, and then the door. A young man, half clad in a French uniform, let them enter single file. In one hand he held a pistol.

"C'est rien, Pierre. C'est le petit Suisse."

They had Turkish coffee while Peter washed and changed into civilian clothes. He sat down on the couch and sipped some coffee. Then, slowly and painfully, he slid into unconsciousness.

When he awoke it was late at night. Lieutenant Jeannot was sitting with Pierre, who was still toying with a pistol. Peter's gun was nowhere in evidence.

"Did you have a good nap, Herr Oberleutnant?"

"Very good, thank you."

"I see Marshal Rommel himself signed your travel orders. You must be a very important man."

Peter looked down at his papers on the brass coffee table, and said nothing.

"You know, Germany is going to lose this war."

"That's very possible."

"The victors will not be kind to uncooperative soldiers."

"I must say, this is a bit much, just because you lost at chess."

Lieutenant Jeannot lit a Player's. "All of you Swiss are supposed to be mercenary. It might be very interesting to buy a report on Rommel's new weapons."

"I'm like the Vatican guards—incorruptible."

"But rather hung over."

"That's true."

"How would you like to take a little winter ski-trip to Scotland?"

"Perhaps one day. Not right now."

"It could be arranged."

"I'll think it over."

"Very well. Think it over."

It had been some time since Peter had thought of deserting from the German Army. He still didn't feel that the time was ripe. He did feel hungry.

"In the meanwhile," Jeannot said, "let's go out and play some baccarat."

"No more chess?"

"Not tonight."

Peter put on an ill-fitting tweed jacket and a tie, and they went out into the night. A walk in the fresh cool air was enough to clear his head.

Pauv' Richarde's was full of officers in mufti, officers in uniform, black marketeers, smugglers, prostitutes, and pimps. A Negro orchestra in white dinner jackets was playing American jazz. After he had had a few glasses of cognac, Peter bought the band a drink. "Cheerio, fellas," he said in English, toasting them.

"Ah merci. Mais nous parlons que Français ou Portugaise. Nous sommes Brasiliens."

"Excuse me. *Santé.*"

"A bas les boches."

Peter drained his glass. On the other side of the room he spotted the young lieutenant he had scared off that afternoon. Peter winked and raised his empty glass to him. The lieutenant reddened and turned his back.

That night, Peter walked Marie Blancharde back to her apartment. Just to hold her hand seemed somehow a guarantee against the deadly horsemen of war.

15

The front was aflame again with cannon fire and strafing runs. The Luftwaffe was not in evidence, except at night. And at night the enemy artillery was so active that the sounds of the explosions merged into a continuous roar that could be heard twenty miles away and seen as a false dawn from ten miles distance.

Peter reported to Major Dreieck, shouting over the noise of the bombardment.

"Rommel wants you," the major yelled.

"What now?"

"He thinks you're the local artillery expert. Get up to Hill 29 with your machine shop. You can take two men."

"Yes, sir."

Peter put on his steel helmet and drove toward the sound of the guns.

"*Leutnant Oelrich* reporting as ordered, *Herr Feldmarschall*."

Rommel was buttoned up to the *'Pour le Mérite'* in a winter uniform. His boots gleamed and his eyes glinted.

"Well, you lazy bastard. Did you have a good vacation?"

"Ja wohl, Herr Feldmarschall."

"*Wunderschoen.* Then get to work. Report to the C.O. of the 125th Panzer-Grenadiers. He has a screen of anti-tank guns. You keep them firing A.P. all night or I'll break your Swiss ass."

"Zum Befehl, Herr Feldmarschall."

Peter spent the night going from one gun to another as they were blown out of action, the flinty shale exploding like shrapnel and murdering ße crews. He cannibalized two guns and had to make a new firing pin for a third, but the dogs of war kept barking death until their muzzles glowed in the night. It was the Australians who were attacking, and by dawn the desert was red with Australian blood.

Peter drove back to the Seventh at noon, and passed out in the back of his truck, gritty and dirty in the afternoon sun. Dreieck shook him awake that evening.

"Oelrich, wake up. We're pulling out." Peter rubbed the sand from his eyes.

"Back to Merse Matruh. Here'a a map. Take the headquarters trucks and lay out a battalion area. I'll follow when I'm finished here."

"Ja wohl, Herr Major."

Things were quiet at the new camp except for Luftwaffe transport planes flying in equipment from Tunis or from Rome. Peter was again detached to demonstrate the new weapons and materiel to various units.

Tons of ammunition were coming in, and gasoline by the shipload, but the army seemed to be retreating ever westward.

The battalion was again laying a mine field, this time in front of Merse Matruh. Peter drew maps of their fields and laid out patterns according to the contours of the land. The coast road and the passable secondary roads were heavily covered by artillery.

Their kitchen truck had disappeared in the retreat, no-one knew how. Major Dreieck tried to borrow food and equipment from the 91st Panzer, but they too were short.

"Oelrich, you've got to go out and do some scrounging for us. We need food—vegetables, eggs, anything." They looked at the map. "The coast road is jammed. You had better try inland." The Arab village of Bir Khalda lay about thirty kilometers south toward the Solum depression.

"Try there. Take that English half-track that came in

75

yesterday and go overland."

"In this mud?" It had been raining off and on for a week.

"With a tracked vehicle you can make it all right. Just don't get in trouble. Things are breaking loose around Alamein. Did you hear about von Stumme?"

"I've been out in the mine field all day, Major."

"Stumme is missing again."

"Who's got the Afrika Korps?"

"Bayerlein."

"He'll make General yet."

"Look, Oelrich—take one man and the mess money and buy or requisition whatever you can lay your hands on. I'll put it down as a reconnaissance for the 90th Light. Take a radio and keep in touch. We don't want you pulling a von Stumme."

"Yes, sir. I'll leave after the sun sets."

Peter got Horner out of the machine shop truck. He had just been promoted to sergeant, and he would probably be anxious to earn his stripes.

"Get a radio and provisions and make sure that half-track is ready to go."

"Yes, sir. A couple cans of water?"

"We'll only be gone for a day or two. You figure it out. Food, blankets, ammunition for my Schmeisser, and for the twin fifties. Any British ammunition here?"

"Two thousand rounds."

"Good. I'll see you by the mess tent at seven."

Peter scrounged up some British tanker overalls to keep warm and cleaned Wolfschmidt's field glasses. He was waiting when Horner came with the half-track.

"Why is there no insignia on this bus?"

"Just painted it, sir. They wanted to wait 'till it was dry."

As the sun set they clanked away through the mud and the mine fields. The little camel tracks that led from oasis

76

to oasis finally disappeared. Peter navigated by compass and the stars.

They monitored radio traffic on all channels. The 90th Light kept getting panic reports from the coast road. As Peter and his sergeant got further south they began hearing the chatter of Italian on some channels, and then English. None of it made any sense.

Toward dawn they began finding camel tracks again. They led directly towards Bir Khalda. Peter stood up with his head and shoulders projecting through the roof of the cab. He tried the twin fifties.

"Beautiful, Horner."

"I cleaned them yesterday, Lieutenant."

"You're a good man."

"I have some grenades here too, if we need them."

They clanked on in to the dawn. The sun was hardening the track now and the going was faster.

"Sergeant, head for high ground. I want to have a look before we go into the village." A few more hills and they came to it. "Back off, Horner, and turn off the engine. I'm going up ahead."

Peter walked and then crawled to the top of the hill. Below, the little village lay steaming in the morning mist. A muezzin was climbing his tower to chant the morning prayers to Mecca. Peter surveyed the village. There were no signs of vehicles, no track marks or tire marks, but there were sheep pens and a mill, and fruit trees. Peter thought he could hear a goat bleating, and he could see the muezzin making salaams to the East.

He stood up and waved to Horner to bring the halftrack forward.

"It looks all right," he said when the Sergeant got there.

He hung a blanket over the twin machine guns so they wouldn't scare the natives.

"Put your gun out of sight, Horner." Peter stowed his helmet on the floor of the cab.

77

They banged and rattled into the village. Heads peered from windows—men with white skull caps and women with veils. Children appeared from around the corners of the buildings when they stopped, and approached shyly.

"This must be their first glimpse of the twentieth century," Horner said.

"Yes, maybe. Keep your gun out of sight under the blanket, but keep your finger on the trigger."

"Yes, sir."

Women appeared with water jugs on their shoulders. Like the children, they approached the half-track and touched it, giggling. They were surprised to find the hood warm to the touch.

When some men appeared Peter smiled and made the Arab gesture of respect. Taking out his well-filled billfold, he showed them money and used the Arab word for food, pointing to his mouth.

One of the men smiled and pointed up the village street. Peter cleared the children away from the front of their vehicle and they followed the man up the street and around a corner until they came to a grain mill. An old man in a fez and western trousers came out.

"Bon giorno."

"Bon giorno, signore," Peter was surprised to hear Italian.

"Comprare ... mangiare ..."

"Si, si."

"Oliven, tomate?"

"Si. Viene." The old man beckoned him to step down from the half-track.

They began bargaining. When he couldn't express himself, Peter drew pictures. The Arabs gathered around their spokesman and looked at Peter's collection of currencies. The Deutschmarks didn't interest them, but the French francs they would accept. Peter had only three hundred Francs left from the officer's mess and from his trip to Tunis. He took out the Swiss gold pieces he had removed from his belt the night before.

"Oro. Louis d'or. Napoleòn. Otto cento francs."

They examined his gold piece with interest and beckoned him into the mill. After comparing it with another they had secreted in a locked iron box, and weighing it, they were all smiles.

"Molto bene! Trés bien. Jolly good."

It took several hours to bargain for the food. Peter had an idea of the Tunisian prices for staples, but he knew that he had to bargain patiently and histrionically or the natives would be insulted.

"Lieutenant, I'm getting nothing but English on this radio. You better hurry."

"All right. Tune in on the battalion frequency and see what's happening."

He bought great bags of olives and tomatoes and barley, large sacks of oranges and dates, four live sheep and a goat. While they were tying the legs of the animals and putting them in the half-track, Peter monitored the radio. On several channels he heard English voices chattering back and forth about 'petrol,' and 'jerry' and 'bag of wogs'.

"Caffé, signore?"

"No, grazie. Andiamo."

Peter knew he was insulting them by leaving without having coffee, but he felt that the neighborhood was becoming distinctly unhealthy.

"Inglese, lei?"

"No."

"Francese, Italiano?"

"Suizzero."

"Si? Bella!"

"Grazie mille."

"Prego."

They drove off to the north, trailed for a while by a group of raggedy children. Peter monitored the radio and unveiled his guns again.

79

16

"Recco to 7th E.B. Do you read me?"

He got no answer on the battalion frequency so he tried the channel monitored by the 90th Light.

"Recco to 90th Light. Recco to 90th Light. Do you read me? Over."

Kiss my ass, you limey bastard.

"This is Oelrich, 7th E.B. I'm on special reconnaisance. What's happening up there?"

"Go ask Montgomery. I wouldn't give you the time of day."

Peter hung up his earphones. "Horner," he said, "I think we'd better turn in for the day. Let's get off the track and find someplace to hide."

They drove off into the hills and found a place where they could park their machine near the top of a hillock and hide it with a huge green camouflage net.

"Want an orange?"

They had dates and oranges for a late breakfast.

"I'm going to cover our tracks, Horner. Take the field glasses up to the top of the hill and keep watch, will you?"

Peter went back on their trail dragging a weighted tarpaulin to conceal their tread marks. The sun was getting strong. It was good flying weather. When he returned to the truck, the sheep were bleating loudly. He took another orange and went up the hill to Horner.

"Sergeant, you had better water the livestock, and then take a nap."

"Water them? How?"

"Pour some water in your helmet."

Peter lay down and scanned the horizon. In the distance he saw aircraft apparently heading in from Egypt. Behind him, down the hill, the animals stopped making noise. He found himself falling asleep, and had to tap his boots on the rocky ground to keep awake.

After an hour he went down to their little farm. Horner was sleeping under the tailgate of the half-track. The animals were munching on some barley Horner had put into Peter's new helmet. The other helmet still had some water in it.

Peter tuned in the radio to check the battalion and division frequencies. "Recco to 7th E.B. Do you read me? Recco to 7th E.B. Do you read me?"

"7th E.B. to Recco. Identify yourself."

"This is Swiss Chocolate. Swiss Chocolate. What's going on?"

"Stand by for the C.O."

An airplane droned over. Peter looked around and decided that his camp would be invisible from three thousand feet.

"Dreieck to Swiss Chocolate. Is that you, Peter?"

"Yes, sir. What's going on up there? All I hear down here is English voices."

"All hell's broken loose. We're getting bombed every hour on the hour. Did you get the stuff?"

"A whole truckload, and three sheep and a goat. The goat's for the 90th."

"Look, Peter. They want you to head east and make a real reconnaissance. They think the limeys are heading for Bir Khalda. Have you got a map?"

"Yes."

"Give me your co-ordinates." Peter reported his position as best he could.

"Head north and east to point J3. Report anything you see on the battalion frequency. Got that?"

"Yes, sir. You know, I was just going down to the corner to buy some groceries."

"Well, don't get caught."

"What am I going to do with these damned sheep?"

"Eat them, Peter. But don't get caught. If you don't see

81

anything by midnight, come home."

"All right, Major. See you tomorrow."

"I hope..."

Peter hung up the earphones and went back to wake up Horner. "We're moving out. Clean up that sheep dung, will you? I'll take in the camouflage net."

They tied up the sheep and goat and stowed them on their sides in the back again, and headed East, staying off the camel tracks. They drove just below the rim of the hills, making only a few miles an hour. Peter stood up by the guns with the binoculars to his eyes. The sheep were making so much noise that he turned on the loudspeaker to drown them out. It was a station in Alexandria and they were broadcasting something called "White Christmas."

"Listen to that, Horner. They're singing about palm trees."

"They can have them."

With a terrifying whoosh, a Hurricane fighter dived on them, but didn't fire. Horner jumped out and ran.

"Sergeant! Halt. Wave to them."

Horner dove behind a hillock as the Hurricane turned and headed back. Peter took off his hat and waved. The pilot banked and waved back.

"Come on Horner, let's go."

The abashed sergeant emerged from his hiding place and stumbled back.

"We look just like a Tommy lost on reconnaissance. Besides, they wouldn't shoot a bunch of sheep."

"Maybe he was just out of ammunition."

"I'm not going to say you're wrong. I was just too tired to jump out."

"How far do we have to go, Lieutenant?"

"Let's find a nice hill near that camel track and hide out until sunset. I've had enough of this."

They made another camp under the green netting and

set out the hobbled animals to graze again. The halftrack was warm in the afternoon sun, and beginning to stink of sheep dung.

"I knew I should have been a farmer," Horner said.

Peter took the first watch while the sergeant fed and watered the livestock, milked the goat and cleaned out the truck.

"Horner," he yelled down. "Why don't you make some tea, and turn that radio on."

Horner brought up a mug of tea and went back down to fiddle with the radio. Soon music was echoing up the hill. It was a beautiful domestic scene with music and tea and the sheep bleating from time to time. When aircraft came over, Peter just hid his binoculars under his jacket and relaxed. If they saw anything, they didn't stop to make a pass.

Finally it was Peter's turn to take a nap. He curled up under a blanket and passed out instantly.

"Lieutenant!" It seemed only a moment later that Horner was shaking his shoulder. "Lieutenant," he was whispering. "Tanks! A whole bunch of them."

Peter woke up slowly. "What are you whispering about?"

"Tanks, Lieutenant. Come on up and see for yourself. A whole damn division or two. I never saw so many tanks. Let's get out of here!"

Peter scrambled to his feet and ran up the hill.

Scores of heavy tanks were churning up the camel track, heading directly towards them. Peter recognized them as the new American Sherman tanks he had seen pictured at a briefing. They were moving slowly, pulling each other out of the mud as they bogged down. Peter could see that they would pass them on the camel track within two hundred yards down the hill.

"What a spot I picked," he muttered. "It's too late to try to get away. Horner, you'll have to stop those sheep from making any noise."

"What'll I do, shoot 'em?"

"God no. Cut their throats, and then bring up my Schmeisser."

"Why? You gonna get us killed?"

"We'll have to lay low. They haven't got any flank guards out and they're not even sweeping for mines. Now, get down there."

"Yes sir."

Peter watched their slow progress through his field glasses. The column seemed to be splitting to make a pincer movement around their hill, but then he realized that one group was heading north and the other directly towards him. He began counting tanks, making marks in his notebook.

Below him, Horner strung up the sheep and the goat by their hind legs over the side of the half-track and cut their throats. The blood splashed on the fresh tan paint as the animals writhed, but the noise stopped.

"Horner—bring up the map," Peter whispered loudly, gesturing. The sergeant scrambled up the hill again with map and gun.

"Can you operate that radio?"

"Yes sir."

"Get onto the battalion frequency and report. Seventy-five Sherman tanks heading North-northwest, direction Quasaba. Another sixty or more heading West for Bir Khalda at about five to ten miles an hour."

"Bir Khalda? That's where we just came from!"

"Yes. Go on, make that report and keep repeating it on battalion and division frequencies until it's acknowledged."

Horner hustled down the hill and under the netting. Soon Peter could hear the radio crackling. In the distance he began to hear the familiar clank of tanks on the move. He kept counting the tanks and trucks until the end of the northern column went out of sight. Then he crawled back from the rim of the hill and zipped down his overalls.

Horner came up the hill, swearing silently.

"I got them, Lieutenant. The major had me repeat it for him." Horner's arms up to the elbow were red with sheep's blood.

"You'd better get back under the netting. Take a nap."

"Want me to stand by the machine guns?"

"Never mind. If anybody starts shooting, we're both dead."

As Horner went down the hill, Peter tied his undershirt to the barrel of his machine pistol to make a white flag. He hoped they wouldn't send out flank guards, but he wanted to be prepared if they did.

Shivering in the cool of the afternoon, he zipped up his overalls and began counting tanks again. The column was approaching at a steady pace. As they passed below him Peter could read the British markings without his field glasses. A big white "2" was painted next to the tricolored cockade on each tank. When Peter finished counting, he tucked away his notebook and lowered his head.

The clanking went on for another half hour. He would hear fitful yelling in the distance as tanks bogged down and had to be towed out. Finally there was silence again. Peter stood up and stretched, keeping below the skyline.

In the front seat of the halftrack, Horner was sleeping peacefully. "Come on Sergeant, let's go home," Peter said, shaking his shoulder.

"Best thing you've said all day, Lieutenant."

They packed up the camouflage netting and threw it over the bodies of the sheep in the back. Once they got started heading across county back to Mersa Matruh and trying to avoid mudholes, Peter called in on the battalion frequency.

"Swiss Chocolate to 7th E.B. Swiss Chocolate to 7th E.B. Do you read me? Over."

"7th to Swiss. We read you, Over."

"I'll give you a recount on that bunch of camels

heading for point A5."

"Cut out the doubletalk, Peter. How many?"

"Seventy-three Shermans, ten half-tracks, fourteen trucks and ten jeeps. All Limey, marked with a 2."

"That must be Second Armoured Brigade. What about the other bunch?"

"Same as I told you before, but they were too far away. I couldn't see their insignia."

"All right. That is what we wanted to know. Are you all right? Come on home."

"I'm coming as fast as I can."

"Very good. You'd better hide out during the day."

"Yes, sir."

"I'll see you tomorrow then, Peter."

"Good night, Major."

Peter gave the compass bearing to Horner and fell fast asleep in the banging and clanking half-track.

17

Twice during the night they got stuck in mudholes, had to unload their produce, winch themselves out, and load up again. The last time they got stuck it was on the side of a small hill.

"To hell with this, Horner. Let's make camp and let the sun dry up some of the mud before we go any further. You put up the netting and I'll wipe out our tracks."

Peter made a tarpaulin drag weighted with sacks of oranges and covered up their tracks for a quarter mile. He knew the tracks would be like an arrow pointing to them if any aircraft observer was alert. When he got back, Horner had breakfast waiting.

"Dates with goat's milk, and hot tea."

"Perfect, my dear Horner. Like a honeymoon breakfast."

The warm tea and the warm sun cheered them up. Horner took out a pipe and lit it from the flames of the field stove.

"You married, Lieutenant?"

"No. Are you?"

"Yes. Wife in Düsseldorf. Two little girls, six and eight."

"You're a lucky man."

Horner puffed on his pipe.

"Rosa was the best thing that ever happened to me," he said.

"I've got a girl."

Horner puffed on his meerschaum.

"She hasn't written to me at all. I don't know where she is."

"Well, who knows? She may be in war work or something where she can't write."

"I doubt it."

Horner put out the fire and rolled himself up in a blanket. Peter stared at the red sun rising like a fireball from the desert hills until his eyes were burning sockets glued to the binoculars. Then it was time to change lookouts and get some sleep.

It was late afternoon when they breakfasted and listened to the radio. The 90th Division traffic sounded like a general rout was in progress. The battalion channel was silent. Loudest of all was the chattering in English and Italian. Peter decided to keep radio silence.

Before the sun had set they clanked off towards the coast, taking turns driving and keeping watch. Peter was driving when the two armored cars came roaring from behind a dune.

"Englisch," Horner whispered.

"Hide those helmets under a blanket. Pretend you're asleep."

He stopped the half-track and waited. Two British soldiers came out and approached them, machine guns at the ready, keeping well apart.

"Where are you chaps còming from?" one of the Tommies asked in English.

"Second Armoured," Peter muttered. "You?"

"Twenty-second. What do you have in the back there?" He approached the rear of the vehicle.

Peter shrugged.

The Tommy leaned over and felt dead bodies under the camouflage netting. Then he noticed the sheep's blood that had dried on the side of the truck, and Horner's arms holding the blanket to his body, his sleeves still streaked with blood.

"Oh," the Tommy was suddenly quiet in the presence of death. "Where are you heading?" he asked, less belligerently.

"Coast road," Peter answered in as few English words as possible. "And you? I thought you were at Quasaba."

"We were, but then we got a report that there's a whole Wog division at Bir Khalda. French or Italian. The natives reported it. Hundreds of tanks."

"Yes. Big battle."

"Oh," the Tommies put up their guns. "I'd better report this to the Brigadier. You stay here, and I'll be back."

The Englishmen got into their armored cars and roared away, waving. Peter waited a moment, and then drove off slowly in the opposite direction, hiding behind the hills, crossing the fresh ruts of the English tank tracks, and then heading Northwest again. Night was falling.

Horner didn't move. "Can I open my eyes now?" he asked.

"All clear."

The sergeant sat up and peered around.

"Where'd they go?"

"Bir Khalda."

"They having war games down there?"

Peter didn't answer. It took all his concentration to keep out of the mudholes and on the sides of the hillocks without turning over.

"I didn't know you spoke English, Lieutenant."

"I don't. Not worth a damn. But I got by, I guess."

"Just when I was looking forward to some American beefsteak and those California palm trees you were talking about."

"Those were Limeys. The only palm trees you'll get are on your armband."

It was three in the morning when they passed through the sparsley mined outposts and got to their battalion area. The false dawn of distant artillery was lighting the eastern sky. Dreieck came out of his command truck fully dressed and rubbing the sleep from his eyes.

"Peter! You made it." He put his arm around him and slapped his back. "Horner. We're glad to see you."

"I thought we were goners, Major."

"Well, you fellows turn in, and I'll get a detail to unload for you. You look like you've been in a battle."

"We almost were."

Peter reported the latest troop movements and then went to his truck where he fell on the bed. Only in the late afternoon did he wake up enough to take off his boots.

18

Peter slept through the day and into the night. Twice he had to get up and move his truck to higher ground, for torrential rains were turning Merse Matruh into a quagmire.

There were fresh eggs with black bread, and chicory-flavored coffee for breakfast when Peter splashed through the mud to the little house where the 7th E.B. had set up an officer's mess.

"Good morning, Oelrich."

"Morning, Major."

Dreieck was morose and sullen as he sopped up his fried eggs with crusts of bread.

"It's total insanity. The whole front crumpled up. Tenth Corps has been wiped out. Trento Division, Bologna Division finished. The Ninetieth is down to three battalions. Everyone's running as fast as they can get gas—sixty miles of vehicles."

"Are we pulling out?" Peter asked.

"Who knows? Rommel's meeting with the division commanders, but I'm not invited. We've got a new chief of engineering—General Beulowius. Crazy as a hoot owl. He just sent orders to gather up three truckloads of scrap metal."

"What for?"

"Christ only knows. When you finish your breakfast you get somebody started on it. And inspect all the vehicles. I want everything in working order in case we have to run for it. Cannibalize anything that won't move and abandon it."

Peter finished his fried eggs and used bread to sop up the olive oil they had been fried in.

"Good eggs," he said contentedly.

"That mutton was pretty good too. A little high, perhaps."

"Aged in the truck."

"We're the only outfit in the whole army with fresh meat and vegetables."

"Tomorrow the world."

"Don't get smart, Lieutenant. You'd better get to work on those trucks. I've got to go see the general."

Peter got his sergeants together and assigned the new troops to gather scrap iron. He took all the older men and set them to putting all their vehicles in top shape.

"Anything that's going to break down, take it over by the headquarters and have Sergeant Horner look at it. Horner, if they won't make it, you condemn them and strip them of anything useable."

Peter got the men started on their work. Mid-morning found him bent over a Volkswagen in front of the headquarters truck when Major Dreieck drove up with a small, bustling Major General.

"Achtung," Peter shouted, bringing his men to attention and getting grease on his forehead as he saluted.

"As you were," said Dreieck. "*Herr General*, this is our famous 'Swiss Chocolate' who sent the whole twenty-second Armoured down to fight the battle of Bir Khalda."

"Oh, yes. The Tommies should make you a Brigadier if you're going to order their divisions around."

"Just luck, sir."

"What are you doing here?"

"Cannibalizing these trucks, sir. We're abandoning them."

"Very good. Make sure you booby-trap them."

"Booby-trap, sir?"

"Yes. From now on you booby-trap everything. Let me show you." The General grabbed a tarpaulin, put it on the ground and crawled under a truck.

"A pound of explosives here, and the whole engine blows apart, killing everybody within ten feet." The

92

troops gathered around to watch the spectacle of a major general grovelling in the mud.

"Wire it to the ignition, or make a trip wire to a wheel, or a pressure plate under the driver's seat."

As the General showed them how to turn the abandoned vehicles into death traps for the British, his eyes sparkled with demonic glee.

"You will be the last troops to pull out—all the way up the coast. When the 90th Light comes through your lines, you set all your booby traps and pull back to the next position. Tow the vehicles to likely spots. Booby-trap the houses, the toilets, the kitchens, everything."

He wiped the mud from his breeches and snickered. "We'll make them bleed for every mile, the boobies. Come—let's go inside."

The officers went into Dreieck's command truck and sat down at the map table to study detailed topographical surveys of the coast along which they would be retreating.

"I'm sending you thirty thousand mines today. You have to lay out fields everywhere as we go."

"Thirty thousand? We had half a million at Alamein."

"You'll have to make do. For every minefield you put in, you must lay three dummy fields with scrap metal. Lay them out just like the real thing. Any piece of iron that's big enough to set off a mine detector. And put in anit-personnel trip wires. We'll splatter them from here to Cairo." He rubbed his hands together with an insane grin.

"Get to it, Peter—we're pulling out of here tomorrow noon at the latest. I'll do the booby-trapping. You start laying the mine fields."

"Yes, sir."

Peter took Horner and another sergeant and began plotting their real and false mine fields, arranging for men to put in the mines and scrap metal, and putting up signs to warn the 90th Light as they retreated through the abandoned positions.

It was a long hard day and all the men were glad to

come in out of the mud at the end of it to wash up and have a good dinner. It was dark when Peter finished his mutton and stewed tomatoes, had another glass of the local red wine, and headed for his bed.

From the sergeant's mess came the sound of yelling and breaking glass. A cook staggered out, holding his hand.

"What the hell's happening in there?" Peter asked.

"Horner. He's crazy drunk and breaking up the furniture."

Peter strode through the door and shouted, 'Achtung'. The soldiers came to attention, Horner swaying slightly.

"What are you doing, Sergeant?"

"He's completely nuts. Look what he did!" one of the mess attendants complained. Three bottles of red wine had been thrown against a wall and their contents were dripping down into a lake of wine and broken glass.

"What's the trouble, Horner? Come with me. Come on."

He put his hand on the sergeant's arm and led him outside.

"What happened? What set you off? I've never seen you drunk before. What's the trouble? Maybe we can help you."

"It's my wife." Horner pulled out his billfold clumsily and showed Peter pictures of two pigtailed girls and their mother.

"Dead. All dead. The whole house bombed out. The whole street. I just got the letter. The whole street disappeared. Goddam Americans. Tons and tons of bombs. And Goering said they'd never bomb Germany! The fat Field Marshal. Those fat stupid Americans sitting up there at sixty thousand feet pulling levers and eating chocolate bars! My whole life is gone. Those beautiful girls! And I could never go through it all again. Everything finished."

"Take it easy, Horner. Let's sit down." Peter put his arm around the man's shoulders and tried to calm him.

"Overnight," the Sergeant babbled uncontrollably. "It's all gone. All those years of diapers and crying and spitting up and going to the doctors in the middle of the night. I could never go through it again. Look at them . . ." He flipped open his billfold again, scattering cards and papers in the mud.

"Look at them. Beautiful children. Rosa would braid their hair every morning before school. And smart! They'd cuddle up to me every night, one on each side, and I'd read Grimm's fairytales to them. *Griselda and the Prince*. All gone.

"And Rosa. She always worked so hard. Morning to night. Those children never lacked for anything. Not like when we were kids. They had good warm food and clean clothing every day. And now they're all gone. Goddam Americans. What did we ever do to them? Why are they mixing in our war?

"Dead—all three of them. And the house and all the way up to the corner. All gone . . ."

They went up to the highway and walked up and down by the minefield tapes until they were exhausted, and then slogged back to the battalion area. Horner was subsiding into shock.

"Why don't you turn in, Horner? Try to forget everything, and get some sleep. There's nothing you can do. I'll try to get you some leave and a pass to Tunis. I'll take you there with me if they send me again. You'll have to get this off your mind."

"I'm all right, Lieutenant. Just leave me alone. You go ahead and go to bed. I'll be all right. I'm sorry about the Sergeant's mess. I'm sorry about everything. I'm sorry I'm alive."

"Turn in, Horner. Get some sleep."

"I think I'll walk some more. Thanks for trying. There's nothing you can do. Nothing anyone can do."

"All right. I'm going to go to bed. You'd better do it too, pretty soon."

"Good night, Lieutenant."

Peter watched him sloshing off through the mud and up toward the coast road, shaking his head and talking to himself.

After explaining the situation to Horner's bunkmates and making sure no weapons were available there, Peter went to bed. Sometimes it seemed that the war had lasted forever, and would never end. His student room in Zurich, the cold tram rides and the drafty classrooms seemed to have existed in another time, another age, on the other side of the moon. He fell asleep thinking of Vreneli.

19

When morning came the rains had ceased. Peter pulled on his sodden boots and slogged through the mud to the officer's mess. He didn't notice that the other officers stopped talking when he came in, and conversed only in low tones thereafter, leaving him alone.

Dreieck poked his nose in while Peter was finishing his eggs, then again when he had finished his coffee.

"Good morning, Major."

Dreieck sat down. "Did you hear about Horner?" he asked.

"No. I left him about midnight. Is he acting up again?"

"Dead. Went for a walk in the minefields."

"How is that possible? He knew where those fields were. He laid them. They were all clearly taped. Even at night you couldn't miss them."

"All I know is he was blown all over the field. Someone's got to clear it up."

"Not me. He was a friend of mine. And I'm the guy who got Wolfschmidt's brains splattered all over my helmet."

"All right. I'll take care of it. You get the trucks loaded and ready to go. I'll clear the tapes and signs when the 90th comes through. You'd better be ready to move right after lunch."

The next several days were a nightmare of fatigue as they laid minefields and dummy minefields by the roadside, on the roads, and on the secondary roads as they retreated ever westward. The battalion was dispirited by Horner's suicide and the steady attrition of their men through accidents and air raids.

Peter was dealing only with minefields, but he would

hear the other officers chortling with glee over their booby-trapping exploits.

"We wired this piano in the parlor. They won't discover it for months, but as soon as someone plays a certain key, the whole damn room will blow. It's in the best house in town. They're sure to be using it for a headquarters..."

"A five thousand pound bomb with a pressure plate right in the middle of the runway. A truck won't set it off, but as soon as they land a transport plane—*kablooey*! It'll take half the Libyan desert to fill in the hole."

"A little battery acid on the trip wire. In a couple days it will release and blow the whole wall. And we plastered up the wall and put dust on it, so you can't see a thing."

Peter was too tired to be disgusted.

"Oelrich," Dreieck was beckoning him to come out of the minefields they were putting down. Rommel was with him, apparently on an inspection tour. Peter brushed off his overalls and stepped carefully through the minefield until he got to the walkway indicated by white tapes, then strode quickly over to salute.

"Good morning, Lieutenant. How many mines have you put down this week?"

"About ten thousand, *Herr Feldmarschall*."

Rommel smiled, and the blue Maltese cross glittered from an opening in the checkered civilian scarf he wore over his bandaged throat.

"This is the famous Oelrich, *Herr Feldmarschall*," Dreieck said.

"*Ach so*. The hero of Bir Khalda. You're familiar with the new Flak 41, Oelrich?"

Yes, sir."

"I thought you were." He turned to the major. "Your young man helped design our new high velocity guns. And his father manufactures them for us."

"He never told me anything about that."

"Never mind. I have my own sources of information. Dreieck, I'm taking him away from you. I'm attaching

98

him to my headquarters staff."

"You can't do that, *Herr Feldmarschall*. He's the only veteran officer I've got left. All I have to do is give him an order, and it gets done."

"You'll survive, Major. Oelrich, report to my headquarters at four this afternoon. Pack up your gear. And change uniforms! You look like an Italian bootblack."

"Yes, sir."

"That's all. Keep up the good work, Dreieck. You're doing a wonderful job." Rommel got into his staff car and sped away.

Dreieck was dejected. "Jesus Christ, Peter," he said. "How did you arrange that?"

"I don't know, Major. I have no idea what he has in mind."

"You're just showing your true colors. A slacker!" Dreieck chuckled.

"I wonder what he wants of me? We don't even have any of those new guns in Africa."

"Who knows?"

Peter brushed off his grimy overalls. "Can I take my truck with me?" he asked.

"No. I'll need it. You can go over in my Volkswagen and send it back with my driver." The major was getting positively sentimental. "I wish you the best of luck, Peter. We're going to miss you."

"Same to you, major, but I'll be back as soon as I can. I hate to leave you with this bunch of greenhorns. They'll blow themselves up."

"Yes . . ."

Peter packed up his few personal effects and said goodbye to his messmates. There were only a few left from the original battalion that had flown in from France those few long months before. All the rest were dead, or invalided home to Germany, or captured. Peter had avoided becoming too friendly with the new men after Wolfschmidt had died. There was no sense in making friends only to have them blown apart the next week.

20

Peter reported to a *Wehrmacht* Lieutenant by the name of Berndt.

"The Marshal is not back yet. Put your gear down over there." The lieutenant looked him up and down, and apparently approved of his uniform. "Sit down. I don't know how long he'll be. He's out inspecting the 90th Light."

"I wonder what he wants me for?"

"No idea."

"It might have something to do with the new Flak 41."

The headquarters lieutenant was as prim as a schoolmaster. "I do not make it my business to outguess the C. in C.," he said, "or to talk about military secrets." Peter wasn't used to rear-areas types. He sat down on his luggage to wait.

A phalanx of cars and trucks drove up in front of the modest house that served as headquarters. Lieutenant Berndt stood up, so Peter did too, and they came to rigid attention as Marshal Rommel strode in accompanied by a covey of captains and colonels.

"So. Anything new, Berndt?"

"Situation report from 21st Panzers, sir, and a Lieutenant Oelrich to see you."

Rommel glanced over and took a moment to remember Peter.

"Ah—yes." He looked at his watch. "Wait here," he said.

"Yes, sir."

Ten minutes went by, and then twenty and thirty. Smart young officers went in and out of Rommel's office, and Peter could hear the Marshal ranting from time to time over the telephone at one recalcitrant commander or another. Peter sat, and then he stood in the doorway and watched the sharp staff drivers waiting by their cars. A theatrically handsome young Italian officer was chewing on a pepperoni. Storch liaison planes were being hidden under camouflage netting at a neighboring airfield.

"Berndt, where's the evening report? Is it ready?" Rommel stepped out of his office and glowered.

"Oh yes, Oelrich. Come in. Come in."

Peter went into the office and stood at attention while the Marshal studied a report, amended it and signed it.

"Berndt," he yelled. "This will do. Send it off." He looked at Peter as if seeing him for the first time.

"Oh yes. Sit down, Lieutenant." Rommel closed the door and returned to his portable field desk. He toyed with a file for a moment. Peter could see that it contained some of the red and black Gestapo tags he had never yet seen in North Africa.

"So, mein lieber Herr Oelrich," the Marshal began. "I have been finding out about your very interesting, if untypical career in the German Army."

Peter said nothing.

"You did some design work on the new Flak 41."

"Yes. When I was a student. Just components."

"Marvellous weapon. And you didn't see fit to mention it to anyone."

Peter waited for the marshal to continue.

"You are a lucky man," Rommel said. "I like that." He chuckled. "Dreieck has been telling me about some of your exploits. The battle of Bir Khalda! And those damned bicycles!" The Marshal laughed, and then turned serious. "I don't think you have much of a future as a career officer. On the other hand, for certain jobs..."

"Yes, sir?"

"You apparently have a way of getting along in Tunis without being too conspicuous. And you get things done without finding it necessary to talk about your affairs to all and sundry."

101

"Yes?"

The Marshal seemed to be slow in getting to the point. "Berndt just came back from seeing the Führer. We're being re-supplied. Everything new—the best Greater Germany can offer. We're getting the first dozen of the new Panzer VI, and the entire supply of the new high velocity cannon." Rommel's eyes sparkled. "We're also getting a new General in Tunis. Von Arnim." Rommel smoothed back his short gray hair. "Von Arnim is one of the old school. You don't know Army politics, of course. Arnim is a few years older than I, but I outrank him. It makes things difficult sometimes.

"I want someone in Tunis. Someone I can depend upon, and who is discreet, and has no ax to grind."

"Yes, sir?"

"I'm sending you. Find yourself a place to stay, and keep away from the garrison. You can wear civilian clothes if you want to. In fact, it might be better. I want you to keep yourself informed. Find out when those Tigers come in and where they're being kept. Inspect those Oelrich guns. You can take a B.O.Q. room at the airport and report to my chief of staff where you are. But I expect you to find out what is going on in Tunis. And stay away from von Arnim. Is that clear?" He stared at Peter sternly as if he expected him to read between the lines of his orders.

"Zum befehl, Herr Feldmarschall."

"Look here, Oelrich," the marshal said. "There's not too much I can do for you in the Army, but this war is not going to last forever. If we both survive it, we may be able to be of help to each other. It does no harm for a man in your business to know his neighbors."

"Yes, sir."

"Berndt," the marshal shouted. The Lieutenant came in and stood at rigid attention. "Make out a *carte blanche* order for Lieutenant Oelrich, and separate orders also to act as Luftwaffe liason at Tunis."

"*Carte blanche*, sir?" The lieutenant raised his eyebrows.

"You heard me. All officers are instructed to co-operate with Lieutenant Oelrich who is engaged on a special mission for the *Oberkommando Nordafrika*—signed C. in C."

"Yes, Herr Feldmarschall." The lieutenant withdrew slowly as if hesitant to follow such an unusual order.

"He's a good man," Rommel laughed. "Personal friend of Goebbels. He's running the office for a few days. His predecessor is suffering from a severe case of lead poisoning. Those pencil pushers don't understand how to get along in the field. They expect the enemy to come to attention and present arms."

Rommel chuckled as if sharing a joke with Peter. "So tell me about the battle of Bir Khalda. You spoke English with the Tommies?"

"Not very well, I'm afraid."

"*Unwahrscheinlich!* Two whole divisions chasing each other around in a monsoon, and fifty kilometers away from the action! Wonderful!"

21

Peter picked up his gear and took his new orders and passes over to the neighboring airfield. One glance, and the operations officer put him on the next plane to Tunis. At the military airfield there, Peter asked for a room in the bachelor's officer's quarters, had dinner at the officer's mess, and went to bed. The events of the last months seemed to flow past him like a stream of flying steel, flowing blood, and dying screams.

The dawn awakened him in spite of his habit of working nights and sleeping during the day. He rang for the Luftwaffe corporal who was in charge of the barracks.

"Good morning. I am Lieutenant Oelrich. I'd like you to draw me a hot bath, get some breakfast brought over here for me, and clean up my clothes. I'll want my Class A uniform right after breakfast, and my civilian clothes a half hour later." He gave him a fistful of French francs and smiled.

"*Ja wohl, Herr Oberleutnant! Sofort. Zum befehl, Herr Oberleutnant.*"

The corporal crashed his boot heels together, saluted, and almost ran on his way to start the bath.

Peter soaked the minefield mud from his body and stared at his hands, veined with grease, the fingernails broken and grimy. He decided that the glories of war did not greatly impress him.

Breakfast was waiting when he returned to his room. He slipped on some clothes and enjoyed his eggs and some real coffee as he watched the corporal steam and press his uniform and shine his boots to glistening perfection.

The November sun was shining warmly as Peter went across the tarmac to find the commander's office. To the Officer of the Day he presented the orders designating him as a liaison officer, and requested that he be allowed to send a note to Marshal Rommel advising him that he had arrived and could be reached through the Luftwaffe B.O.Q., and suggested that he would like to make a courtesy call on the commanding officer. He was received almost immediately.

"Good morning, Lieutenant. Have a seat." The Colonel was all smiles. He studied the brief one-paragraph order in front of him.

"Your orders are unusually succinct—for Berndt. He usually likes to write in rounded periods that Goebbels can quote."

"Yes, sir." Peter waited for the Colonel to come to him.

"I wonder what Rommel wants with a liaison here."

"Actually, Colonel Schmiedhofer, I think he ran out of iron crosses. This is a sort of paid vacation. I've never had a leave since I've been in the service. I have no specific instructions to speak of, so you won't be bothered with me. As a matter of fact, I'm going to take a room in town also, so you probably won't see much of me."

"Well, that is unusual. You—you aren't 'Swiss Chocolate'?"

"You have the advantage on me, Colonel."

"Oh, never mind. Just a wild story we heard. Well, Lieutenant, enjoy yourself. If we can be of service to you or the Marshal, just ask."

"It's an honor to have met you, Colonel."

"Nice to make your acquaintance, Oelrich."

Peter saluted, walked out, and went back to his barracks.

"Corporal," he said as he changed into his freshly steamed and pressed civilian clothes, "how can I get a taxi into town?"

"Just go to the main gate, sir. They always have some hanging around the gate. Charcoal-burners, some of them."

"Thank you, Corporal. I won't be here very often.

Corporal, would you recognize Marshal Rommel's signature? You've seen it in the papers and on placards haven't you?"

"Yes, sir."

"I'm going to show you an order signed by Marshal Rommel." He spread out the thick headquarters bond topped with eagle and swastika. "This is highly confidential. I haven't shown it to anyone on the base."

"Yes, sir." The Corporal was impressed.

"I'm going to take a room in town. If there are any messages for me here, I want you to communicate with me. I'll give you addresses and telephone numbers, if any, when I return. Can you do that for me?"

"Yes, sir. Whatever you say."

"And if anybody else questions you, you don't know anything."

"Zum befehl, Herr Oberleutnant."

Peter adjusted his tie and strolled to the main gate. Visions of Horner in the minefield kept coming to him, but he blotted them out of his mind.

When he got to the harbor, he walked. The beaches were cluttered and big ships rode to anchor, but the air was fresh and crisp. Peter looked out across the blue sea blowing with whitecaps and stared in the direction of Europe, of home, and wondered what he was doing in Africa.

He wondered how the whirlwind year of war had singled him out to tear him away from Vreneli, from his tall, talented and intelligent older brother, from his curmudgeon of a father, and to bear him away to become something he had never dreamed of being—a man of action instead of reflection, a leaf in the whirlwind instead of an observer of the weather of war.

He wondered why his father or his brother could not have rescued him from the peculiar fate that had singled him out from all the thousands who crossed the Swiss border daily, singled him out for involuntary servitude to

106

a country he could hardly respect, with men who shared a philosophy he rejected, on a continent he would gladly have traded for a solitary mountainside.

He saw a ship being unloaded far out in the harbor.

Great cranes were lifting huge packing cases from the depths of the hold. Peter looked about the harbor area and spotted a likely looking house, went to it, and knocked.

"*Bon jour, Madame*. I'm looking for a room to rent in this quarter. Do you know of any?"

"*Monsieur est allemande?*" she asked suspiciously.

"I'm Swiss, Madame. I'm with a little engineering firm near the Place Tebessa."

He found a nice room overlooking the harbor, and reminded himself to bring in Wolfschmidt's binoculars from the base. He would have a clear view of the harbor from behind the linen curtains of his modest room.

After a quiet lunch of snails and *sole meunière* at the Café des Sports, Peter again looked up the address of the local Oelrich office and strolled over there.

It was on the second floor of a sunwashed building on a quiet square. Peter opened the glass doors and walked in without knocking. Four draftsmen were bent over drafting tables laden with plans and blueprints.

"*Oui?*"

"I'd like to see the manager."

"Whom shall I announce, please?"

"*Monsieur Oelrich.*"

"*Mais oui, Monsieur.*"

The draftsman, an unhealthy looking young French colonial, almost ran to the office to get the manager.

"*Monsieur le directeur Oelrich*! Hello. What a surprise to see you."

"Good afternoon, I take it you received a letter from my father?"

"Yes, sir, *Monsieur le directeur*. We are at your service. Anything you wish. Come in to my office—*your* office if you wish. What can we do for you?"

Peter glanced at the work on the drafting tables.

"For the French Navy."

They were working on parts designs for ammunition hoists and a new breech block mechanism.

"Where are you getting your steel?"

"Flown in directly from the Ruhr. We get things manufactured locally."

"Wonderful."

Peter went into the office.

"I'd like to write a few letters home. Can you get them through?"

"Of course. Have a seat. Take my desk. Here's paper and a pen."

"You're very kind."

"Not at all, *Monsieur le directeur*." The office manager bustled around emptying ashtrays and closing windows. "I see you are not in uniform."

"That's right."

Peter wrote letters to his father and brother, and to Vreneli, sealed them up and gave them to the office manager. He hoped they would not end up in Gestapo hands, as had so many before.

"Are you going to be around for a time, Monsieur?"

"Yes. I'd like you to get me an automobile. Could that be arranged?"

"Yes, sir. You can take mine temporarily." He handed over the keys to his Citroen. "But gasoline—that's not so easy."

"That's all right. I can get access to other supplies."

"If you'll be here for a time, I'm sure the Governor would like to meet you."

"I really don't know how long I'm going to be here. Here's my address." He wrote down the address of his rented room by the harbor. "Please regard this as highly confidential."

Peter went out and tried the Citroen, and then went

shopping for a dark blue civilian suit and some shirts. At the Luftwaffe base he picked up his binoculars and left his address with the corporal in charge of quarters. Then he had his gas tank filled with aviation gas and drove back into town.

After he changed clothes for the second time that day, he found a little restaurant where he could have some lamb with rice, some of the white *vin du pays*, and Turkish coffee; and he listened to the news being broadcast over the little radio that blared from behind the zinc-topped bar. The announcers were almost hysterical as they described the landing of one hundred thousand American soldiers at Casablanca.

Peter tried to imagine what one hundred thousand Americans in Sherman tanks would do to the remnants of the Afrika Korps. His imagination could conceive of one hundred thousand land mines, of a hundred thousand bridge components, but a tenth of a million American gangsters, chewing gum and carrying tommy guns in violin cases, was beyond his ability to envisage.

Pauv' Richarde's was jammed full, noisy, hot and smoky in spite of the cool night air outside. Peter sat at the bar sipping on a Vermouth cassis and listening to Marie Blancharde sing nostalgic songs of the boulevards of Paris.

"Bon soir, mon général."

"Hello, Jeannot. Will you have a drink with me?"

"Volontiers." The Lieutenant sat down. "My you're formal," he said. "All in black." Peter had purchased a black silk tie to go with his white shirt of Egyptian cotton and his new suit and polished oxfords. "Are you in mourning for the Italian Army?"

"I'm afraid I have had no contact with them, Monsieur Jeannot."

"The Americans will have to build glass-bottomed boats if they want to inspect the Italian Navy."

"And the French Navy."

"*Touché*. Tell me, are you ready for that little skiing trip to Scotland? Ski season is almost upon us."

"Not yet, I'm afraid." Peter remembered where he had been exactly a year before. "By the way, *mon ami*, I wonder if you could get a letter through Switzerland for me. My fiancée. Somehow my letters seem to go astray. Could you help?"

Jeannot reflected for a moment. He had no way of knowing what actions Peter's letters might initiate, but he thought it might be a good way to put Peter in his debt, and with no apparent risk.

"I'd be glad to try. If you wish, I'll introduce you to the manager here, and you could go into his office and write it out."

"That would be very kind of you."

"A simple gesture to a brave ally."

Peter stepped into the office and quickly wrote out three almost identical short letters to Vreneli, saying signing them simply "Peter" and asking her to write back in care of the people from whom she received the letter. He addressed them to her Zurich address, her parent's address, and in care of the Conservatory.

"Here they are, Jeannot. I didn't seal the envelopes. I asked her to write back in care of your friends."

"I'll do what I can for you, *mon général*."

"You're very chivalrous, Monsieur Jeannot."

They drove back to the Café des Sports for a late coffee after Marie Blancharde got off from her work. Squads of German soldiers from the Kommandatura made the cobblestones echo with the sound of jackboots. Peter tapped the new leather case he had bought to carry his special orders from Rommel. He hoped he wouldn't have to show them again.

22

Peter spent the next morning watching the harbor through Wolfschmidt's field glasses. The large Italian ship well out in the harbor was still unloading huge packing cases. From the size of the cranes, Peter could calculate the weight of the cases.

While he was composing a note to Marshal Rommel, his landlady came upstairs with a heavy cream-colored envelope. It contained a formal invitation to dinner with the French Governor of Tunisia on the next day but one.

Peter put it aside and drove out to the military airbase. His note to Rommel was included with the afternoon dispatches, sent daily by air. Peter's note contained a few innocuous comments and casually mentioned that some friends of his had received ten big packages of Swiss chocolate and were putting them in cold storage.

For the Governor's dinner Peter purchased a tropical white dinner jacket, and a black tie to conform with the invitation. His habitual Swiss economy made him decide not to get a full tuxedo. He could wear his black suit trousers and an ordinary white shirt.

The parking area outside the Governor's mansion was filled with German and French military vehicles, Citroens, Mercedes-Benz open cars, and even an old Rolls-Royce.

Peter presented his invitation and went to look for his hostess.

"*Ah, oui, Monsieur le directeur Oelrich.* I believe I met your father once."

"*C'est bien possible, Madame.*"

"Come, let me introduce you to my husband, and some of his dull military friends, and then I'll show you some of the young ladies. It's so seldom they get to meet presentable young men these days."

"You're very kind, Madame."

She towed him by the arm to a group of men resplendent in white tie and tails and dress uniforms. Miniature medals gleamed on their chests. The French dress uniforms were outshone by the high-collared Wehrmacht uniforms and the brilliant Luftwaffe blue.

"M. le directeur Oelrich—mon mari le Gouveneur, le Général von Arnim, le Coronel Schmiedhofer, le Coronel René Dupin..."

"Enchante, messieurs."

Peter shook hands with the Luftwaffe Colonel, looking him straight in the eye. They pretended not to know each other.

"You are here with the Army, Monsieur?" the Governor asked.

"I'm here in connection with some engineering problems, sir."

"Ah," von Arnim smiled, his monocle sparkling. "You're familiar with our new supplies in that case."

"Yes, General. I trust they arrived in good order?"

"Quite. A little trouble with assembly, I believe, but..."

"If we can be of assistance...I helped design some of the components."

Von Arnim looked doubtful about trusting a civilian with his precious tanks.

"Oh, I can vouch for Monsieur Oelrich," Colonel Schmiedhofer smiled mischieviously. "He comes well recommended."

"Please, Colonel," Peter raised an admonishing hand.

Von Arnim was not to be stopped. "We are having a bit of trouble with assembly. If you'd like to look at—the equipment—I'll send a pass around to your hotel."

"You could send it to our local office. We maintain an office here to service some of our French accounts."

"Excellent. I'll have a pass sent around in the morning, Monsieur Oelrich."

"One is always glad to be of assistance, General."

At the earliest opportunity Peter extricated himself from the profusion of high brass and clinking medals and wandered around among the bare shoulders and seductive eyes of the French colonial ladies. Now that his main business was transacted, he felt rather shy, as he had felt many times at formal dinners in his father's house.

He saw one group of young people of his own age who seemed to be having a good time.

"Monsieur Pierre!" It was Captain Jumel.

"Non! C'est le petite Suisse! What a surprise to see you here!"

"I'm a world traveller, Monsieur Pierre."

"This is an excellent season in which to travel."

"You're absolutely right."

Peter had a butler rearrange the place cards so that he would be opposite the convivial French Captain at dinner.

The cuisine was extraordinarily good, the wines of vintage rare, the conversation difficult. It was hard to keep from talking about the war and the landings at Casablanca, and Peter was not exactly a veteran of the *grandes boulevardes*.

"Are you any relation to M. Jean Oelrich?" the old lady on his left asked. She seemed to be the wife of a purveyor to the French garrison.

"Yes, Ma'am. He's my father."

"How charming. I met him when he came through here with the Kaiser in 1912. What a glittering entourage that was! We won't see its like again—although the British with their red trousers—*Ooh la la*, such handsome young men!"

At the other end of the table, General von Arnim was sparkling.

"Ex Africa semper aliquid novi," he smiled.

"Who said that?"

"Pliny. I believe he was with one of the earlier occupying armies."

Colonel Schmiedhofer joined the conversation with

one of his favorite new anecdotes. "Did you hear about that funny fellow Rommel has over in Cyreneica? 'Swiss Chocolate' they call him. The story is all over headquarters. It seems that..."

Peter turned to Pierre Jumel with a smile. "I saw Mademoiselle Blancharde the other night."

"So I heard. She is rather taken with you—or would be if it weren't for..."

"I thought she was Jeannot's girl."

"Just friends. Comrades in arms, you might say. War makes strange bedfellows."

"Don't remind me."

The next day Peter picked up his pass at the Oelrich office and drove out to the dockyard area where the new high velocity cannon were being warehoused and partially assembled.

Here were the new guns that could make Rommel the King of the Desert again. Peter studied the cargo manifests and the plans that came with them. Minor improvements had been made in the last year, but it was essentially the same gun that had so excited his brother in 1940, a deadly weapon upon which to build a thousand year Reich. He was able to help with their assembly.

"Monsieur Oelrich, would you like to see something incredible?"

The captain in charge of the military warehouses took him down to an isolated building the size of an aircraft hangar. It was guarded by *Feldpolizei* in full battle gear.

"You won't believe this, Monsieur Oelrich." The captain took him inside. Twelve huge tanks were being assembled there. Each was sixty tons of mechanical monster.

"Our future in Africa!" Apparently the captain didn't think Peter would be able to make a military appraisal of what he was seeing, or perhaps he was just overpowered by a desire to show off his charges. "The most powerful weapon in the world!"

"Very impressive, Captain. Thank you for letting me see them." Peter doubted if this dozen could stand up to five hundred Sherman tanks.

That night Peter sent off another harmless note to Rommel saying that all his friends had arrived safely from the continent and were recuperating from their trip. He was sure that the marshal would want to meet them soon.

23

With no responsibilities or duties other than to keep an eye out the window for any signs that the new military equipment was being hidden away by von Arnim for some coup such as attacking the Americans, Peter began to lead a quiet and uneventful life.

Unlike his student or army days, he no longer had regular assignments to occupy his mind, and he began to catch up with the great changes that the kaleidoscopic events of the last year had brought not only to his outer life, but also to the inner man that was emerging from the chrysalis of youth.

Vreneli's love had brought him out of the cold emotional shell of his childhood to realize a want and need for warmth, a warmth that had never been present in his family after his mother had died. His emergence from his drafting rooms onto the stages where important affairs were decided made him realize how much he had been held back by his father and brother, whether intentionally or through neglect. His fleeting contacts with Rommel and von Arnim made him realize that his true desires were different from those of his family, and that he himself did not need to hang back in the drafting rooms of life. He too could take an active role and form not only his own future, but help to form the world itself in the image of his imagination.

As he sat in his quiet room staring through the binoculars, or had his solitary luncheons at a local restaurant, or played desultory chess games with the officers of the garrison, or sipped Algerian wine at Pauv' Richarde's, he turned these ideas over in his mind.

Lieutenant Jeannot had disappeared from view for a time, and Peter got into the habit of taking Marie Blancharde home to her apartment when she finished work. And then they sometimes met for a meal at the Café des Sports—Peter's lunch, Marie's breakfast—and they would drive up the coast to a little beach she knew where they could swim and lie in the warm winter sun.

Marie was still a sulky and morose woman who seemed to have a smouldering hatred for all things German. She often tried to pump Peter for information about his duties or his army experience. He could usually ignore her questions, or turn them aside. Finally, however, he had to put it to her.

"Marie—spying can be a very dangerous game, and not one for amateurs. There is no Gestapo here, but the German Army itself is not exactly noted for its gentleness with spies."

"I don't care. I hate all Germans."

"Don't you think they realize that? I see you sitting with them in Pauv' Richarde's every night, pumping them for information. They're not dumb. They can figure out what you're doing, and how you pass the information along. Even Jeannot, and Pierre. One of these days you'll all get arrested, and shot."

"And what about you? What kind of a double game are you playing? Are you serving God or the Devil? There is no middle way."

"Oh, come now. Germans aren't all that bad."

"That bad!" Marie sat up on the beach and glared down at him. Her voice was rising. "Don't you know what they're doing on the continent? And have been doing for years now? Mass murder, pillage, rape!"

"Marie. I've never raped you, have I?"

"You're tarred with the same brush. You're wearing the uniform and you'll pay the price. Do you know what they're doing to the Jewish population of Europe—and the Gypsies, the Slavs?"

"Idle rumor. The Germans are a civilized race, if a bit mad..."

"You have no idea. You're as stupid as they are. Do

you know what they did to me in Paris? I was appearing at the Gaiêté with my fiancé, one of the best known singers in Europe. Jean Levesque. Part Jewish. We came home one night—boom—they hit him in the mouth with a rifle butt and threw him in a truck like garbage. And then four of those monsters took me upstairs and raped me, one after another. Beasts of the field! And then the next day when I tried to tell my story to the police, or the newspapers, even to your army—nothing! They wouldn't even admit it had happened, much less do anything about it. And Jean—it was as if he had disappeared from the face of the earth. All of a sudden no one knew him or ever heard of him.

"I went from authority to authority, from newspaper to newspaper, tramping through the rain like a crazy woman. I guess I was crazy. And then when a booking agent offered me a chance to get away, I boarded the first boat out of Marseille.

"But I'm going back. I swear to God I'm going back. And I'll get my revenge. I want to see Germans hanging from every lamp-post in Paris."

Peter took her hand to comfort her, to calm her.

"Get your filthy paw off me, you Fascist pig, you murdering..."

Peter jumped to his feet as something snapped inside of him.

"You dumb slut! Do you think you're the only one who has suffered in this war? I've never pulled a trigger in my life, but I've had the blood and brains of the best comrades any man could know splattered all over me until the whole world turned to blood and flying steel. Do you know what it's like to be bombed and shelled for twelve hours running, never knowing when the next moment is going to be your last, and you'll scream your life out and your guts are falling out on the sand? I didn't ask to get into this mess. I had nothing to do with Germans or Germany until I was caught up in this madhouse. It's war, Marie. It's not a picnic at the *Jardins des Tuilleries*."

"But there's a difference. You're on the wrong side." She walked away.

Peter turned and faced the sea, and then he sat down and lowered his head in onto his arms. His emotions were in a turmoil, and he didn't really understand what was going on inside of him, what had caused him to rant and rage against his fate for the first time in his life.

The sun burned down on him. After a time he felt Marie's hands on his shoulders.

"*Pauvre Pierre, pauvre Marie*—poor world."

"Let's go back to town."

24

Jennot showed up again. He came to Peter's room overlooking the harbor.

"Hello, Robert. How did you get my address?"

"I make it my business to know things. I have something for you."

It was a letter bearing French stamps. Peter glanced at it and lost his breath. He recognized Vreneli's handwriting.

"Have a seat, Jeannot. Here—some cognac."

Peter took the letter and went over to the window to read it in the sunlight.

My darling Peter,

I hope you get this letter. I finally got one from you, and it was wonderful, but censored by your Army. I gave several letters to Hans-Jörg for you, but I can see from what you wrote that you never got them. I'm going to write you anyway because nothing like you has ever happened to me, and just to imagine that I'm talking with you again will fill my night with something warm. At least something.

I was terribly hurt that you joined the Army to get away from me. There was no need to do that. You didn't even know I was pregnant. I was so happy. Nothing would have made any difference to me. I would have loved to have your baby—any remembrance from you. But Hans-Jörg just laughed at me. He is a cruel man. Perhaps you are too. I don't know. I don't know anything anymore.

So I left Zurich and went home to Aarau. Mother and Anneli were very kind. They are so good to me. I teach a little bit, and work in the bakery on the corner every night, and I work very hard. It helps me forget.

The baby is no more, and you are no more, and I'm so alone, in spite of Mother and Anneli. My father is a fine man, but I can't talk to him. It's not like being with you.

Oh, Peter. Have you changed? Have you forgotten me?
I will never be the same. I think of you every day, every
night. I love you so much.

Vreneli

Peter looked up. Jeannot was watching him intently, silently. In a state of shock, Peter read the letter again. He began trembling so much that the onion-skin paper rattled in his hand.

Jeannot quickly poured a tumbler full of cognac. "Here. Drink this."

Peter gulped it down, hardly knowing what he was doing.

"Read it," he said.

"I have."

"*God*. I must get to her."

"There's no way you can. Not until this war is over and the *boches* are defeated. You're a casualty of the wars, the same as she is, the same as your child, the same as Marie's fiancé. There will be no peace for you. There will be no separate peace."

Peter's next days seemed to pass in an alcoholic fog as he went through the motions of living while his mind and emotions were elsewhere. The Frenchman listened to him. Marie held his hand. They tried to convince him to desert to the enemy. They listened to his drunken babbling about his brother and his father and their great exploits for the Greater German Reich.

At one time or another during those days Peter sat down to write a reply to Vreneli.

Dearest Vreneli,

Great God in heaven. I feel like I have been caught up in a sandstorm, a storm of war. I had no idea of leaving you . . . ever. I was forced into the army, and not allowed

121

to write to you. The letters I wrote you didn't get. If only I had known that you were going to have a baby!

A child of my own—the last of the Oelriches or the first of the Swiss Oelriches. If only I had known, I would have risked anything and walked home from France just to tell you…

But here I am, separated from you by a vast sea, and by how many armies? How could I get there? I hate what I'm doing and I hate what I've done. I only want to be with you—forsaking all others, forgetting everything else.

What was our baby—a boy? A girl? What happened to the poor little thing? Maybe you thought it wasn't right to bring a child into this world. It is a cruel world.

What will become of us? I only know I want to be with you, and I can't. I can only say—wait for me. Don't forget that I love you. Don't forget the love we had. Hope for me that we can have it again if this terrible war ever comes to an end.

I love you

Peter's letter went through Vichy and ended in the hands of the German military censors who, following a security check, gave it to the Gestapo. An S.S. officer handed it to Hans-Jörg Oelrich. Peter's brother read it in his office overlooking the Rhine. He found himself beset with worries and responsibilities. He could take on no more. He dropped it carefully into a wastebasket.

They kept Peter away from Pauv' Richarde's and away from any place where he might meet Germans. When Jeannot had to disappear again on some confidential mission, it fell to Marie to collect Peter and pour him into his car and get him safely to his room. She never quite knew how it happened one night when she had gotten him to his bed and taken off his shoes and loosened his belt and necktie. He threw his arms around her and buried his head on her breast and began to cry.

"Poor Peter," she said, stroking his hair. Then, somehow she began to cry too. And then with feverish haste, they tore at each other's clothes and made love in tearful rushes of cruel lust.

Sobered by the shock of it, silenced after all the talk, they straightened their clothing, only to be taken again by that rushing need for love in the midst of death, for creation in the middle of destruction, and they removed their sweaty coverings and made love again and again until exhaustion overtook them with blessed sleep and surcease.

25

The knock on the door came at midmorning. Peter struggled to consciousness, removed himself from beneath Marie's heavy body, and padded to the door to stop the infernal noise.

"Herr Leutnant, Herr Leutnant." It was the Luftwaffe corporal from the air base. "I've been trying to get here all morning. There's a Captain Berndt . . ." He looked inside at Peter's dishevelled room where Marie's clothing was flung on the floor and her naked foot protruded from the unmade bed.

"Oh . . ."

"Yes, what are you saying? A Captain Berndt?"

"He says he's going to wait there until you show up. He keeps asking questions."

"Wait for me downstairs. Better yet, wait right here on the landing."

Peter closed the door and slipped into the first clothes that came to hand. Marie was still sleeping, her mouth open and one arm hanging over the side of the bed.

Peter closed the door quietly and went downstairs with the corporal. The landlady looked at them with loathing.

"You drive," Peter said, giving him the keys to the Citroen.

They went into the back entrance of the B.O.Q. and the Corporal helped Peter get into his stiff uniform and glistening boots. When Peter emerged into the bright sunlight he blinked and tried to keep his hands from shaking. Berndt was waiting impatiently by the front door.

"So, Lieutenant Oelrich. Finally you are here."

Rommel's aide had been promoted to Captain. Peter saluted.

"Good morning, *Her Kapitän.*"

Berndt looked him up and down. "Is this how you perform your special duties?"

Peter tried to ignore his headache and keep his hands from trembling. He hoped Berndt couldn't diagnose his horrendous hangover from his appearance.

"I have a message for you from Marshal Rommel."

"Yes, sir."

Berndt stared at him with disdain. This wasn't the officer material from which he and Goebbels could create myths. He didn't know what Rommel was cooking up, but he didn't much care for his chosen confidante.

"You are to remain in constant touch with the Feldpolizei here. The Marshal will be sending a large truck convoy. You are to maintain yourself in a constant state of readiness to comply with the orders you receive from the commander of that convoy. Do you understand?"

"No, not really."

"Well, neither do I. But I have delivered my message."

"Ja wohl, Herr Kapitän."

"Heil Hitler!" Berndt stalked away to his waiting plane.

Peter walked stiffly back into the barracks and sat down by the window of his silent room. The corporal was already pressing and hanging up his civilian clothing.

"Can I get you anything, *Herr Oberleutnant?*"

Peter looked down at his trembling hands.

"Breakfast. Some toast, eggs, coffee." He reached for his billfold to give the man some money. It would be his first meal in several days.

Alone again, he stared out at the desert of Tunisia. Silent again after all the talk and torment of the last days, he tried to make some reasonable plans.

He slept most of the day, put on his stiff Wehrmacht uniform and heavy boots and walked to the Officers' mess for a solitary dinner, nodding only to Colonel Schmiedhofer who was sitting with a group of staff officers at a table. Peter walked back to his barracks, and then walked up and down some more to try to get his thoughts in order. He seemed somehow to be a different man than the one he had been a few days before. His stiff uniform and boots seemed to make him think differently, more logically, less emotionally.

26

Peter was sitting at his table in the room overlooking the harbor when Jeannot walked in unannounced.

"Hello, Robert."

"Hello, Lieutenant. I presume that is your rank today." Peter was sitting stiffly in his uniform.

"Yes."

"Peter, what are you doing? You have no interest in serving the Germans. They've ruined your life."

"Perhaps so."

"Then come with us. We're going to England. I can't tell you how, or when, but we're finally going to be able to do something to serve our country."

"Ah—your country. And what is *my* country?"

"You should know better than we. Put it this way, Peter. This is your last chance to get in on the winning side. You can be of service to the allies. And perhaps they can be of service to you—help you. This is your last chance."

"Not yet, Robert. Not yet."

"You're making a mistake, Peter. I can only hope you'll change your mind. Do you know that beach where you and Marie went swimming?"

"Yes?"

"If you want to join us, go there. There is a deserted lighthouse out on a sandspit just one kilometer north of there. Wait in that lighthouse."

"You're trusting me with your life when you tell me such a story."

"Yes."

They sat in silence for a moment. And then Jeannot stood up.

"*Adieu*, Peter. Oh—I forgot to tell you, Marie sends her love."

"Thank you. Goodbye, Robert."

"I hope everything turns out all right."

Peter raised his hand in farewell, and Jeannot slipped through the door as quickly as he had entered.

The next evening just after dusk, Peter's door opened again. This time it was a *Feldpolizei* officer, and with him was Major Dreieck. He seemed like an apparition from another world.

"Hello, Peter." He peered around nervously, his eyes red-rimmed and squinting.

"Wait downstairs," he said to his escort. He paused until he heard the boots descending, and then turned to Peter.

"Rommel's orders. We're supposed to pick up those cannon and one tank for a demonstration. I've got the whole battalion under arms, just outside of town. Whole battalion! There's just sixty of us left."

"God, what happened?"

"What didn't! Where are those damned cannon?"

"Look," Peter said, handing him Wolfschmidt's binoculars and pointing out at the harbor.

"See those warehouses? Just past the gate. The first three are where the 88's are kept. Then the next to the last—the big one—has the Tigers."

"Look, you come with us. I'll blast any goddam rear-area ass who gets in our way. My boys will stop at nothing. Let's get those cannon and get the hell out of here."

Peter buttoned his tunic and put on his peaked cap. He looked as correct and stiff as a general's aide.

"We'd better figure out something. The marshal won't like it if we have to go in shooting..." He picked up his new brief case of Moroccan leather and they went down to the car. On their way through the blacked-out streets, Peter thought up a plan, drew maps, and explained his idea to Dreieck.

"All right. All right. But if it doesn't work, I'm going to start blasting."

"It will work."

The truck convoy was parked beside a service road, pulled over and blacked out, with not a soldier showing. It included one of the biggest flatbed trucks Peter had ever seen.

"Where did you get that thing?"

"Flown in from Berlin—in pieces."

"I hope it's big enough. That Panzer VI weighs maybe sixty tons."

"You get us in. We'll get it out."

"You understand me then, Major. Exactly five minutes."

"Ja, ja. Komm' doch!"

Peter took a soldier driver and got into his Citroen. He led the convoy through back streets to the great Avenue Foch overlooking the harbor and the coast road which was to be their exit, and signalled for them to stop at the top of the hill overlooking the harbor so that he could point out the warehouses and the main gate to them. Then he shook hands and proceeded on alone with just his driver. "Exactly five minutes," he said in parting.

At the guardhouse by the entrance to the warehouse area he pulled up and got out, still immaculately turned out and carrying his briefcase. The sentries came to attention.

"Officer of the Day. Get him. Hurry. And turn out the guard."

Peter waited nervously, slapping his gloves against his thigh, his boots glistening and his peaked cap bright with gold braid. The braided golden fourragère that denoted his attachment to the marshal's staff hung from his left epaulet.

A garrison officer ran up, still buttoning his tunic. *"Ja, Herr Oberleutnant?"*

"Captain, here are my credentials." He showed him the

129

laissez-faire order from Rommel.

"The Field Marshal is coming in exactly three minutes for an inspection. Have your guard turned out on both sides of the road and prepare to present arms."

"*Ja wohl, Herr Oberleutnant*. Guard . . . fall in! Double time! Form two columns! Space yourselves properly!"

The officer ran hysterically up and down the ranks getting his soldiers properly aligned and pulling at their uniforms—adjusting a button here, a cap there. Peter stepped inside the guardhouse and pulled the telephone wire from the wall.

"All set, Captain?" he asked, glancing at his watch. Peter was beginning to hear a growing roar of engines as the huge trucks came barrelling down the hill to the harbor at speeds they could never have attained on a level road.

The captain stood in the middle of the road. "All set, Lieutenant." The roar was increasing, and suddenly the convoy flashed into view around the last shallow curve of the harbor road.

"I'd get out of the road if I were you, Captain." Peter said in a friendly tone.

"Wait. Stop! They've got to stop at the gate!"

The captain was gesticulating, still trying to wave the trucks to a halt when the roar became overpowering, and he had to jump aside while the huge trucks zoomed past at fifty miles an hour, their drivers grinning with insane glee as they jammed on their brakes.

The scream of brakes was deafening as the huge trucks took hundreds of feet to stop, the biggest flatbed back by the huge warehouse that housed the Tigers, the others cannonading off each other with ear-splitting bangs, or skidding sideways to slam against warehouse doors. The armed *Feldpolizei* in front of each warehouse were jumping aside for dear life, and the engineers were springing from the sides of the trucks, laughing, and opening the doors to the warehouses.

130

"What are they doing? Where is the marshal?" The Officer of the Day was screaming. "You're all over the area!" He went on piping as if his breeches were too tight as his troops, still at rigid attention with their guns present arms, gawked at the screeching trucks and shouting engineers that had turned their quiet back area into a sudden roaring madhouse.

"What's happening? Where's the marshal? Who are they?" The captain's voice was going right through the stratosphere.

"Oh, that's just the 21st Light Recco Squadron. That's the way they are. Excitable."

Winches were screaming, and truck tractors roaring and backfiring as eleven huge flatbeds jockeyed simultaneously for position and cargo tractors pulled the long cannon in line to be loaded and red-faced sergeants shouted intermingled directions and profanity at the drivers.

"Where's the marshal? I've got to report this! You must be crazy!"

"Oh, Rommel will be along directly. They just have to get things ready for him. He likes things done fast and right, and devil take the hindmost. He will expect you to be standing at the head of your guard here. He drives rather fast himself. He used to be a skier, you know. He likes speed, and the 21st is one of the fastest and best field units in the Afrika Korps when it comes to preparing for inspections. They may be noisy, but they know exactly what the marshal wants and how he wants the equipment lined up."

The captain was torn by indecision. The truck engines, which had quieted for a moment as the cannon were being lashed to the flatbeds, began roaring again as the drivers backed and filled to point towards the front gate again.

"I've got to report this to General von Arnim. This is no way to run an inspection. This is totally unprecedented. I . . ."

He strode into the office and reached for the telephone. Still as impeccably correct as a General Staff aide, Peter followed him, opening his brief case.

"Hello, hello. Give me the Kommandatura. Give me the General. What's the matter with this thing? Hello . . ."

Peter took a Schmeisser out of the briefcase, snapped the stock into place, and pointed it at the Captain's stomach.

"You shut your mouth or I'll blow your goddam belly open. *Come to attention*, you bastard, and *close your mouth*. Do you think we're on maneuvers here?"

Trucks were roaring past the guardhouse picking up speed as they headed for the fastest road out of town.

"You saw the marshal's instructions. You're supposed to co-operate. And if you don't you'll be blasted right out of your breeches. Now, by Christ, you turn around and face the wall. Your backside's a hell of a lot better looking than your front side. Pushing a pencil in a guardhouse is not very good preparation for dealing with combat troops. When we get orders, by Jesus we carry them out, and God help the man who gets in the way."

The last trucks were roaring by, already picking up speed, when Peter heard the lighter sound of the Citroen pulling up. Still talking, he pulled the clip out of the Schmeisser and laid the gun down on a desk. Walking backwards, he stepped out the door, came to attention and saluted the doorway, and then turned to get in the open car door.

As the Citroen roared past the smartly aligned guards and onto the coast road, Dreieck exploded with laughter.

"Not a shot fired!" he yelled. "Those door guards were so astounded that we picked their rifles off their shoulders like apples from a tree. Great Christ, what a show! Here, have a drink, you crazy mountain goat! Von Arnim is going to bust a gut when he hears about this."

"That captain still doesn't know what hit him. I told him we were the 21st Light." Peter gulped some brandy as

132

the Citroen screamed around a kiosk and jockeyed to get to the front of the column.

"God knows what he'll tell von Arnim."

"And not a shot fired!"

"We locked those guards in a little storeroom the size of a toilet. It'll be a week before anyone finds them."

"You should have been a commando, Major."

"Or a Chicago gangster."

The convoy roared through deserted side streets as Peter led them through town and out onto the open desert. The moon was rising. Dreieck straightened up and looked out, and then signalled his drivers to slow down to what was a more normal speed when pulling such heavy loads. They turned onto a secondary road and stopped to inspect the column, view the breechings, and tie down any steel cables that had come loose, as well as to report to Rommel's headquarters by radio that the mission had been accomplished. By the time he got back into the car, Dreieck had turned morose.

"A lot of good ten popguns are going to do us. I tell you, Peter, those damned English keep coming on like the advancing sea. There's no stopping them. There are thousands of them coming at us, and we have nothing left. We can lay a hundred mine fields, and pull back, but they just keep coming on."

Peter glanced at the driver.

"He's all right. Christ, he knows what's happening as well as everybody else does. We're going in the bag, all of us. And those that do will be the lucky ones who don't get shot first. Did you hear about our great leader's 'Stand or Die' order? 'No retreat,' he says. Insanity! We'll stand or die to save Italy, and they'll stand or die to save Germany; and Germany will stand or die to save Adolf. We'll all die or go in the bag. There's no other way. We're doomed. Like the Bismarck! Like the Trento, the Bologna, the Tenth. Like Alamein. A half million mines and the best army in the world, but we couldn't stop them."

Peter let him continue, neither encouraging him nor stopping him. He wondered what had happened to the ardent and loyal officer who had come from France less than a year before. Dreieck was over thirty, an old man as fighters are judged. The continuous fighting retreats, the endless bombardment, the murderous casualties had finally taken their toll.

27

It was an immense and featureless plain. They had driven all night and into the dawn, leaving the coast road and heading south into an area as deserted as the surface of the moon, guided only by their compass and the stars.

Peter put his hand out of the window and signalled the column to stop.

"Major," he shook his shoulder. "Major Dreieck!"

"Where are we?"

"I think we're lost."

"Christ. Can't you read a map anymore?"

Peter looked at the only landmark in sight, a deserted French Colonial mud fort. Doors like barn doors hung open, banging in the desert wind.

"This can't be it."

Dreieck rubbed his reddened eyes and studied the map.

"That must be it."

"This is a 1927 Legion Survey Map!"

"Nevertheless, that's it." The Major unfolded himself stiffly from the Citroen and started yelling at the troops, who were beginning to peer over the sides of trucks and out of the truck cabs.

"All right, you glorious Hitler Youth, out of the trucks. Let's show some Strength Through Joy here. You had a good night's sleep. Now get the hell in that fort and clean it up for the marshal. The sooner we get this range set up the sooner you can sit on your ass. The 21st will be here ready to shoot by ten so you better get those bunkrooms cleaned out before they grab them. Let's go. Kitchen trucks first. Herrlingen, crank up that radio and get me the chief of staff."

Peter closed his open mouth, aghast at the speed and energy which this veteran troop could summon to meet any emergency. Already officers were stretching their legs and breaking out the surveying instruments to set up an artillery range. Already the kitchen trucks were lighting stoves and preparing a hot breakfast.

Dreieck returned from the communications truck, still kneading the kinks out of his muscles.

"Bayerlein says the 21st will get here by noon and the marshal will try to make it by three. Think you can get those guns set up by that time?"

"You give me a range, and I'll shoot those guns."

"You'll have to practice dry loading, and get the boys from the 21st to zero them in."

"There's nothing complicated about the mechanisms. I'm going to get started situating the guns now. I can eat later while they're being put in."

Peter laid out gun emplacements and consulted with the veteran officers he knew concerning the down-range targets and radio reporting of the hits. By eleven o'clock all the guns were emplaced, for there was no need to dig in or prepare protected positions.

As the advance group from the 21st Panzer drove up with ammunition for the guns, Peter went to inspect the Tiger VI, the first in Africa. The cannon with its new flash suppressor was as long as a telephone pole, and a lot stronger. Peter had to spend an hour studying the plans before he began to understand the arcane modifications Krupp-Berlin had introduced on the guns, as they did on every series.

By the time Marshall Rommel's Storch landed at three-thirty, the battalion had prepared an artillery range as good as any peacetime installation, and the Twenty-first's best gunners had already tried ranging shots and zeroed in the weapons.

"*Dreieck, du alter Schafseckel*, you did it again!" The Marshal was as jovial as a warlord in Valhalla. "*Peterlein*. Good to see you back."

"Do you know Colonel Dinkelhofer from the 21st, Sir?"

"Hello, Dinkelhofer. Ready to shoot?"

"*Ja wohl, Herr Feldmarschall.* Wonderful weapons."

"The best gun in its class anywhere. Wait until we pull some Shermans in on a screen of these."

"You won't have to. Their range is incredible."

"By God, we'll get to Cairo yet."

Peter withdrew from the charmed circle. He had heard those words before.

"Come on, Dinkelhofer," the Marshal smiled. "Let's go look at your loading drill."

Peter went to find the mess truck which had set up in the courtyard of the old fort, now cleaned up and sporting a swastika flag snapping red and black in the winter wind.

They had set up a mess hall in the old mud-walled fort. Peter slipped ten Reichsmarks to the mess Sergeant.

"Swiss Chocolate! Good to see you back, Lieutenant."

"Glad you're still cooking. Do you have anything warm for me?"

"Of course, of course." The fat and jolly Bavarian bustled around to find something good.

"Do you know, we've been serving continuously ever since we got here. No peace for the wicked. Breakfast. Lunch for those big dopes from the 21st. Lunch for our men, and now they want a regular banquet laid on for the Marshal tonight. And all I've got to serve is some stringy old goat meat."

"Throw some cognac in the sauce and they'll never notice. The marshal's not a fussy eater."

Peter had a good lunch and went out to watch the action again. The top gunners of the 21st were operating like veterans with the new weapons, and Rommel was up in his plane observing hits and monitoring the range officers as they tried single shots at various distances.

Dreieck was pacing up and down and watching the loading drill.

"You can't beat a country that can pull weapons like this out of a hat in the middle of a debacle. Wait 'till they get these at Stalingrad."

"I'll wait. But will the Russians?"

137

Dreieck looked at Peter and frowned. "Why don't you go take a nap? The marshal has invited you to dinner. And get that uniform straightened out. You look like you slept in it."

Peter found a bunk in his old machine shop truck and entrusted his uniform to a new corporal he had never seen before.

"Take this over to the mess sergeant and see if he can get somebody to steam it, and maybe press it."

"Yes, sir, *Herr Oberleutnant*. Lieutenant, were you the sergeant who traded the bicycles for trucks? I've heard that story a million times but I never thought it was really true."

"Yes, corporal. Now you polish up these boots for me and take care of my uniform, and I'll take care of you. Don't forget to wake me up for dinner."

Quickly learning again to ignore the outgoing artillery, Peter pulled a blanket around himself and fell sound asleep.

28

The corporal woke him up when the marshal had returned. Peter stretched and dressed himself, shivering in the cold. In the battalion kitchen truck he was able to scrounge up some water with which to shave.

The guests were assembling for dinner in the fort's old mess hall, eating off tables made from the main gates of the fort, which had been put on trestles and covered with blankets. Candles guttering in wine bottles lit the scene, and the drinks flowed freely.

Peter was seated next but one to Rommel, who was jovial with stories of his last flying trip to Rome.

"No heat in the hotel! We had the best suite in town, and I thought we were going to freeze.

"But the *Duce*! Now there's an old fighter! Speaks German pretty well, too. He asked me about my medal." The marshal's eyes sparkled as he touched the *Pour le Mérite* at his throat. "I had to tell him I got it in the Italian campaign." The officers laughed.

"And the *Reichsmarshal!* You should have seen his uniform! He designs them himself, you know. Six stars! Kesselring says I'm bad enough with my plaid scarf. He should see Goering."

"Have you seen the pictures of Montgomery in that silly hat? He looks like a constipated *poilu*."

"Slow as a march hare. They'll sack him too."

"So, *Herr Oberleutnant*," the Marshal smiled to Peter, "Did you get a chance to see my charming colleague von Arnim while you were enjoying Tunis?"

"Yes I did, sir. I believe he thought I was a French civilian. He himself gave me a pass to inspect the 88's."

"He thought he could hide those guns away for his own offensive," Dreieck said from the other side. "Wait 'till he finds out you had an officer watching out the window every minute since they arrived."

"They can't outfox the old desert fox. That's what Churchill calls me, you know." The officers laughed sycophantically.

"Tell them about 'Swiss Chocolate', Dreieck," the Marshal said.

Peter blushed as he listened to his adventure recounted for the tenth time and embellished with details he had never before heard.

The high brass laughed and stood up to let the attendants clear the table for coffee and cognac.

"Could I see you for a moment, Marshal Rommel?" Peter said.

"Of course, my boy. Let's get a little air out in the courtyard. Come." He took Peter by the arm and walked with him out the door.

The clean sand of the courtyard was freshly raked; it gleamed white in the cold light of the waning moon. Sentries paced the rotting boards of the balcony. The swastika still snapped above them on an improvised flagpole.

"What can I do for you, my boy?" Rommel asked.

"It's my girl friend, *Herr Feldmarschall*. She's having an awful time. I've got to get back to Switzerland, even if its only for a few days. We must have couriers going in and out, and steel coming up from the Ruhr to our factories. If I could only get even a few days to straighten things out with her, marry her, and get some money for her to live on. She thinks I've deserted her."

"Impossible, my boy. I'm sorry, but it's totally impossible. I don't know what you did to the Gestapo, but they're after you. If you set foot on the continent, they'll get you. Himmler spoke to me on my way in to see the Führer in October. He wanted me to arrest you and send you back under guard. But I told him I needed you—and they're afraid to fiddle with me."

"Great God! What did I ever do?"

"I don't know, but as long as you're with me, you'll be safe. I'll keep you with the Seventh or on my staff, and if I go back, you go back. Could you ask for anything better?"

Peter said nothing.

"This is war, my boy, not a football match. A good many people are suffering. At least you're alive and well." The marshal smiled and patted Peter on the back. "Come now. Cheer up. I have a little surprise for you."

He took him inside again, walked up to the glittering group standing around the banquet table, and summoned an aide.

"Gentlemen, your attention please," the Marshal raised his voice. Opening the box presented by his aide, he took out a black and gold Maltese cross.

"It's a pleasure to present at this time on the behalf of Führer and Fatherland, for outstanding services to the Afrika Korps, the order of the Iron Cross, second class, to *Oberleutnant Peter Oelrich* of the 7th E.B., the hero of Bir Khalda!"

The officers and even the mess attendants applauded and smiled their bravos as Rommel slipped the ribbon around Peter's collar and adjusted the medal at his throat.

"Thank you, *Herr Feldmarschall*," Peter said softly.

"It's the best I can do for you right now," Rommel said," but you stay with me, and there'll be a captaincy, maybe a majority within a year."

29

The Twenty-first pulled out with their new guns and flatbeds right after dinner. Rommel flew back to the coast. The 7th E.B. stayed behind to clean up the fort and get a good night's rest, and Peter Oelrich stayed with them.

Peter walked up and down in front of the courtyard in the moonlight, his glittering cross bobbing at his throat.

"What's the matter, Peter? Can't sleep? That's not like you." Dreieck was out for a last look around before turning in.

"I slept all afternoon, Major."

"Well, you turn in. God only knows what tomorrow will bring. We're pulling out before nine. Just pray that rain will ground the planes."

"Yes, sir."

"And—congratulations, Peter."

"Thank you."

"We've come a long, long way."

"Yes, sir." It wasn't like Dreieck to get sentimental.

"Remember Wolfschmidt, and those stories he used to tell about the *Parteitag* in Nuremberg?"

"Yes," Peter smiled. "He was some cutup."

"Well, Merry Christmas, Peter. And good night."

"Merry Christmas, Major."

Things were quiet except for the sentries. Peter found his battered Citroen and checked the trunk for the old burnoose he had purchased to wear at the beach, checked the glove compartment for his road maps, loaded some jerricans and iron rations in the back, and then turned in for the night.

The next day, alone in the Citroen, Peter brought up the rear of the column as they drove north. When they got to the coast road and turned east to head for the front,

Peter hung back further and further until he could hardly see the rear truck through the misting rain; and finally, as the convoy curved around a circling bluff, he stopped, turned around, and headed for Tunis on the secondary roads.

He avoided the military checkpoints, and skirted around Tunis itself when he got there at dusk. As night fell on the seaport, Peter came again to the coast road, driving slowly, and found a place to go off the road onto the beach. There, in the dunes, he abandoned the car and started walking west on the silent beach hearing only the roar of the ocean.

He dropped his hat in the surf, and then his belt, and his tunic, and finally all the rest of his uniform piece by piece as he walked along at the edge of the water leaving footprints in the sand, knowing that they would be washed away before another December sun had risen.

Oberleutnant Peter Oelrich was no more.

30

In the board room of the *Oelrich Fabrik* in Basel, Hans Oelrich stared blankly through the grimy windows at his factory chimneys belching smoke over the Rhine. The old man's hair was whiter than ever, and his red pate showed through its sparse covering.

He didn't turn his head as the soundproof double doors opened to admit his eldest son, resplendent in a Chesterfield coat, gray Homburg, and gray mocha gloves. Hans-Jörg tossed his hat on the boardroom table and strode across the room briskly, slapping his gloves against his thigh.

"What is it, Papa? What are you moping about? We just got another order for five thousand proximity fuses. Is that bad?"

The announcement of the award of Peter's Iron Cross had come in from Berlin on the same day as the message from the Reich Chancellor's office. Hans Oelrich handed over the crumpled telegram with trembling hands.

The Chancellor's Office of the Third Reich regrets to inform you that your son, Peter Oelrich, is missing in action and presumed dead. His services to the State and People will always be remembered.

Heil Hitler!

"Well. A German war hero. In our family."

"Perhaps he'll show up. Captured, wounded—something."

Alone in her tiny room in Aarau, Vreneli Schmid watched the snow falling on the river below her window.

From a shelf smiled the picture Peter had given her. A single tear ran down her cheek as she hugged herself in the cold.

31

Three Frenchmen and one woman walked up the sandspit toward the abandoned lighthouse in the light of the waning moon. When they got close, they saw a white figure emerge onto the beach.

"Behind the dunes, Marie, quick." They drew pistols and spread out on the beach. The barefooted man enveloped in a white burnoose walked toward them slowly, his hands empty and visible.

"Halt! Qui va la?"

Slowly the man pulled back the cowl of his burnoose.

"C'est le Suisse."

"It's a trap!"

"Shoot him, and let's get out of here."

"Bon soir, Messieurs," Peter had said, raising his hands. "I'm all alone. How are the chances for a little ski-trip to Scotland?"

"Search him, Pierre." Lieutenant Jeannot scrambled up to the lighthouse, pistol at the ready. "Empty," he shouted.

"What about the dunes? They could have a whole squad hiding in the grass."

"There's not time to worry about it, Jumel." Jeannot looked at his watch. "Break out the boat, Marie," he shouted.

"Stop yelling," whispered Pierre.

"Either they're here, or they're not. But if they are," he said, turning to Peter, "you'll be the first to die, you Nazi bastard."

"Hello, Peter."

"Hello, Marie."

They launched the unpainted old rowboat and took turns rowing out to sea on the compass bearing Jeannot gave them from the stern.

Peter was shivering in his light robe.

"You look like Jesus on his way to the cross," Marie said. "Poor boy, you're freezing." She put her arms around him to keep him warm. *"Mon Dieu,"* she said, "you don't have a thing on under there!"

"No socks, either," Peter's teeth chattered.

"Hey, cut that out, you two," Jeannot laughed from the stern. "The English will think we're running a seagoing bordello here."

H.M.S. *Seraph* surfaced promptly at three A.M.

"I have an extra passenger, Captain," Jeannot said.

"Come on. Plenty of room."

The submarine officers hurriedly sent them below and then riddled their rowboat with bullets before they submerged.

32

For the first time in years, Peter felt that he was among friends with his French fellow officers. He felt relaxed and convivial, and he wasn't about to give up his new freedom until he had to. As for the submarine officers who were taking them to England, they couldn't tell one Frog from the next. As far as they were concerned, this bunch of foreigners was incomprehensible, interchangeable, and intolerable. They were happy to disembark them.

Once landed, things became more organized as they lined up to be documented and assigned.

"*Pierre Jumel. Capitaine. Quatorzième Régiment de Chasseurs.*"

"*Robert Jeannot. Lieutenant, Deuxième Dragons.*"

"*Robert de Bourgival, Sous-Lieutenant. Deuxième Dragons.*"

"*Peter Oelrich. Oberleutnant. Deutsche Afrika Korps.*"

"*What?* What the hell did you say?"

"I am Lieutenant Oelrich of the German Africa Corps, Seventh Field Engineers Battalion, attached to the Marshal's staff."

"Step this way, please."

Royal Marines surrounded Peter and took him to a detention room. They stripped him of the borrowed naval clothes he wore, and shouted, "Aha!" when they discovered his iron cross on a ribbon around his neck.

Within hours, military intelligence staffs all over England and Scotland were advised of his presence. Peter faced many hours of interrogation, again and again.

"A deserter," they would cry.

"Let us just say—I unvolunteered myself. Excuse my bad—*Englisch*. I was never very good with language."

"Why should we trust you?"

"Why not? I just want to get the war over, same as you."

"Your family is making cannons to kill us with."

"And there are Oelrich guns in your Liberty ships too, not to speak of proximity fuses."

"What do you mean?"

"Ask your Board of Munitions, or whatever you call it."

"Why did you volunteer for the F.F.I?"

"I did not. My French is almost as bad as my English. Why should I commit—self-murder?"

"Tell us about the indoctrination courses for the Africa Corps."

"What indoctrination? There is none. They are just ordinary *Wehrmacht* units."

"You're lying to us."

"You are the victims of your own propaganda. Or that of the Germans."

"You're one of the Germans."

"*Keineswegs*. The first thing I want to do when I get home is find a canton that will take me for Swiss citizenship."

"Perhaps we can help you. We're going to win, you know."

"Yes, I know. So help me. That's my total war aim: to get Swiss citizenship and go back to building bridges and railroads."

"You're going to be on the winning side, no matter what. Is that it?"

"It's a Swiss tradition. Our best export is manpower."

"Mercenaries."

"Nanu..."

Peter's interrogation was taken in relays by ever more exalted officers. It was a British Colonel who seemed to be the most influential among his many interrogators. Peter confided in him.

"Colonel Smythe, I came here for one reason. I must

149

get to Switzerland. My girl friend thinks I deserted her. I want to marry her and get some money for her to live on. Send me in. I'll do anything."

"Absurd! Perfectly absurd. What would you do, sabotage your own factory?"

"Anything you say. I've got to get to Vreneli."

"Out of the question. Even if we did, everyone knows you. And the Swiss would probably deport you for serving in a foreign army."

"I'll take my chances. Just send me."

"Don't be asinine. You're going into prison camp— right here. Say—did you know von Ravenstein?"

"Yes."

"Maybe you could talk to him a bit, and tell us what he has to say?"

Peter scratched his head. "Maybe..."

Colonel Smythe made a note to pursue the subject further, and then went on to other matters.

"What can you tell us about Rommel's tactics?"

"Tactics? I know nothing about tactics. I'm an engineer."

"And just what did you engineer?"

"All...bloody all. Bridging, weapons, railways, the 'Devil's Garden',—what all was needed."

"What do you know about rockets?"

"Nothing. Except the *Nebelwerfer*. Power is not my forte."

"Nebelwerfer—what is that?"

"The multiple rocket. It throws—you call it a mortar—we..."

"That must be that new thing they used at Kasserine Pass. You know that *Werfer* thing?"

"I'm an engineer. I was Rommel's expert in these things."

"Can you draw one?"

"Of course. Almost a blueprint."

"We want you to draw one for us."

"Just give me the drafting tools."

Their interest quickly changed from Peter's motives to his expertise as they debriefed him on the latest weapons information, materiel disposition and personnel. Somehow it did not seem reprehensible for Peter to give engineering information. Much of the information was not really secret, and by its nature could not be since all weapons produced in quantity were soon captured.

Peter spent almost three weeks at drafting tables doing mechanical drawings of the *Nebelwerfer*, the new high velocity 88, the monster mortar which had not proven its value to Rommel, and other technical details with which he was familiar.

And then he spent another two weeks writing or dictating everything he could remember of his German army experiences, and suffering endless interrogations on every meeting he ever had with Rommel or the other high officers in Africa. No detail was too small for his inquisitors.

"He said he'd seen the Führer on Thursday."

"Then if that was Tuesday, and we know he was in Rome on Sunday, where did he see Hitler?"

"I don't know. He didn't say."

"You're sure it was Thursday?"

"Yes. I told you. I remember it clearly."

"He saw Hitler on Thursday. Where?"

"I don't know and I don't care."

"Don't care? You're not very patriotic."

"Of course not. It's just happenstance I'm a German citizen. I never lived there, and I don't much like Germans. I'm not patriotic about England either. Why should I be?"

"Then what do you believe in?"

"Minding my own business. Why don't you try it? Actually, the only country I could get patriotic about is Switzerland. They have no dreams of worldwide conquest."

"Is that a reflection on the British Empire?"

"Comme vous voulez."

"Then why did you volunteer to fight against Germany?"

"I didn't. I volunteered for nothing. I just wanted to get away from the killing. I have never killed anyone, and I don't want to."

"Some soldier!"

"I was a very good soldier, and in the front lines, I may say—not hiding in an office."

"Then why won't you fight for what you believe in?"

"I have not desire to kill anyone, not English nor German."

"We're giving you good food and a good place to stay and warm clothes to wear, and you won't do anything for us?"

"Is that bothering you? You English must have half a million of pounds belonging to my family. Sequestered funds—blocked monies for using our designs. Release some to me—then you make a profit."

"What are you talking about?"

"Ask, and you'll find out."

"I think you're a spy."

"You've got nothing but spying on your mind!"

"Then why did you volunteer for the F.F.I.?"

"I didn't. I just happened to run into a group of Frenchmen."

They kept going around and around, Peter and the Englishmen. English officers could understand a German being violently pro-German, or violently anti-German, but they couldn't imagine a German who was non-violent. Neither could they understand how a German could become friendly with a bunch of Frenchmen. No proper Englishman would do that unless he had an ulterior motive. They kept looking for ulterior motives.

The Americans, however, who were privy to the interrogations but also had their contacts in Switzerland, accepted Peter at face value. They made their inquiries at the other end of the line. They discovered that there really was a Vreneli Schmid. Peter had been asking permission to contact her and to contact his father ever since he arrived in England. The British had refused to allow any messages. They were afraid that some incomprehensible and unforeseen plot might be set in motion by any communication whatsoever.

And the Americans discovered that Hans Oelrich was indeed manufacturing German guns on Swiss soil. General Donovan of the American O.S.S. put some questions to his British counterpart.

"Those guns were used to kill American boys in Africa. They'll kill more in Europe. Why haven't you put a stop to it?"

"You Americans don't understand. Switzerland is a neutral country. We can't tell them what to do."

"I understand that you're letting them continue to manufacture guns with which to shoot you..."

"My dear General. They are also making proximity fuses for His Majesty's forces."

"You could get proximity fuses from the United States. By air if necessary."

"At twice the cost, no doubt."

"What difference does that make if it would save lives? All we would have to do is drop a couple thousand-pound bombs on that factory, and we'd save hundreds, even thousands of lives."

"We would never consent to the bombing of neutral territory. That wouldn't be playing the game."

"We are not over here to play games. I've studied the aerial surveys. That plant isn't even camouflaged! It would be the easiest thing in the world to drop a few bombs by accident."

"And kill a few hundred Swiss."

"Since when does that bother you? You're ready to kill off this Oelrich fellow, but you're not willing to bomb a factory that's producing guns to kill *you* with."

"Quite a different thing, old chap. You Americans just don't understand European politics."

Chapter 33

Colonel Smythe had consulted his superiors and obtained approval of his plan to have Peter enter a V.I.P. prisoner-of-war camp to spy on captured German officers. Peter was not pleased to be spying on his former colleagues. It was a risky and dishonest, but he felt it would be best to appear to co-operate.

So he found himself once again in the uniform of the German army, now an ill-fitting hodge-podge of other men's clothes with boots too tight and tunic too loose. Only the Iron Cross at his throat was his own.

The prisoner-of-war camp on an isolated estate in Buckingham seemed quite luxurious to Peter. He was brought into the great dining room just at dinner time, and his escort, an overage British Major, paused with him at the doorway, and announced him in quite passable German.

"Gentlemen, you have a new colleague just in from Africa, *Oberleutnant Peter Oelrich*."

Peter took a seat and waited for his dinner to be served. Looking around, he found that he was one of the lowest ranking officers present. There were half a dozen colonels and several Italian generals, all in remnants of their own uniforms, some even in complete field gray with rank badges and the ribbons of their decorations. In one corner he spotted von Ravenstein presiding over a covey of field officers.

"Well, Lieutenant, welcome to England," said a morose major. "Where did they bag you?"

"Merse Matruh."

"Merse Matruh, *Sir*. Being a prisoner does not excuse bad manners. We are still officers."

"Yes, sir."

"This camp is mainly for field grade and above. I wonder why you are here?"

"I was Rommel's ordnance expert. Perhaps that's why."

Peter ate his meal in silence after that charming exchange. He had little to contribute to a conversation that seemed to be a continuation of other conversations begun in regimental messes all over Europe sometime in the Kaiser's era.

As he savored his tea and biscuits after dinner, and watched the officers drifting out to the smoking room, he was conscious of General von Ravenstein leaving his group and approaching the table where he was seated. Ravenstein was in a plain tunic without rank badges, but his uniform was neatly buttoned and pressed to perfection, and his boots shone. Peter stood up and clicked his heels together.

"Good evening, *Herr General*."

"Good evening. You're in from Africa?"

"I've been in transit and in interrogation camps for many weeks, *Herr General*."

"You look familiar."

"I had the honor of serving with the General at Alamein and afterwards. Oelrich, sir. 7th E.B."

"Oh yes. Dreieck's young man. Do I detect something new?"

Peter touched his Iron Cross, and smiled diffidently.

"The marshal was kind enough to give it to me just before I was captured, sir. For 'the hero of Bir Khalda' he said."

"Congratulations. And how was the old boy?"

"Well enough. He got out in time, at least. No one seems to know where he is right now."

"The British would give a lot to know."

"Yes, sir."

"Well, my boy. Drop in at my cottage for tea

tomorrow. You can fill me in on the desert war."

"Zum befehl, Herr General."

"Good night, Lieutenant."

The white-haired old gentleman walked briskly from the room.

The next afternoon Peter asked one of the guards how he could find General von Ravenstein's quarters, and was directed to a tiny cottage across the garden from the main house. It was four o'clock, and tea was being served to the General by a British sergeant in a white coat.

"Come in, my boy. Come in. Have a seat and tell me all about yourself. How do you like your tea? Sugar and lemon?"

Peter sat down and gawked at the luxury in which the British were keeping their prisoners. When the sergeant had left, von Ravenstein smiled.

"A batman, I believe they call them. Of course, it's not like the old Deathshead regiment, but there's nothing like tradition."

At the General's urging, Peter trotted out the story of his capture which he had concocted and rehearsed with the help of the British intelligence officers.

"And how about you, General? How did you get caught up?"

"Quite by accident. You know how it was. You could go out on a flank for a few miles and—in the bag. I almost got away with a disguise. I pulled off my insignia and dropped them in the sand, but then they took me to meet Auchinleck, and you know—automatically—I saluted and put out my hand and said 'von Ravenstein, General,' and the cat was out of the bag. Otherwise they would never have known who I was."

"Bad luck, sir."

"Did they ever find out what happened to von Stumme? Was he captured? We were at Spandau together."

"Oh yes. And it's an unlikely story. He was put alone in the back of a command car, and he had a heart attack. Fell out and it took them two days to find him. His driver didn't even know he had fallen out."

"A sad ending for a fine soldier." The general brushed at his hair, and then smiled. "The little corporal must have had apoplexy when he heard."

Peter glanced up in surprise to hear Hitler referred to in that way.

"Oh, don't be shocked, young man. There are no Gestapo men running around telling tales. We're all gentlemen here, and gentlemen don't tell tales."

Peter wondered what possible use his reports of von Ravenstein's conversations would be to Colonel Smythe.

The next day, as transcripts of the conversations picked up by the battery of microphones that were hidden about the General's quarters lay open on Colonel Smythe's desk, the Colonel too wondered of what value they could be.

"I tell you, Sergeant," he said to the typist who brought him the transcript direct from the translator, "either those two fellows are sly foxes, or we're wasting a lot of time listening to them. I sometimes think we'd be better off just shooting the lot of them and then getting on with the war."

"Yes, sir," the sergeant said, secretly blessing the luck that had put him in this clerical job far away from the shooting.

Chapter 34

In London the Allied Interservice Assessment Board was meeting.

"Commander Fleming, Commander Montagu, Colonel Smythe—General Donovan. The rest you have met, General."

They covered various items of their agenda with equanimity and even humor. A certain strain intruded into the proceedings with the question of what to do with Peter Oelrich.

"This Nazi Leftenant."

"Swiss."

"You Amis don't understand Europeans. These Swiss are completely mercenary. Bleeding us dry. I wouldn't trust this *Oar-lick* with a bow and arrow, much less with a net of trusted agents."

"He could be valuable for some jobs."

"He could be a double agent."

"I shouldn't care to entrust him with any knowledge. Let's put him in a P.O.W. camp, or just drop him over the side."

"Keep him on tap. Send him up to Scotland. He'll be isolated there. No chance to escape or contact anyone."

"His Majesty's forces will not accept him. And the French don't want him."

"I'll put him in our Army. Give him training courses until the war is over. If we never use him, that's okay too."

"Why are you so keen on this bloody turncoat?"

"I've had our men in Zurich and Basel check him out. It may be that he was a hostage to guarantee delivery of Oelrich guns to the Germans. Perhaps now they can be persuaded to stop. With the U-boat menace finished, we don't need their guns any longer. But if *we* can use him as a hostage to stop delivery of the Oelrich guns and timers to the Germans, it will save a lot of lives."

"Send the blighter up to Pemberly, or Ringway, or a weapons course if you want to. But don't put him where he can damage us..."

Chapter 35

"A chantoosy?" Colonel Smythe's fluting accent was redolent of a class-conscious disdain which was quite lost on Marie Blancharde. "Why should you want to risk your pretty little neck fighting the *boches*?"

"I've told you, *mon Coronel*, I want revenge. My fiancé was taken from me and thrown in a truck like a bag of garbage. I want to do anything I can to fight the Germans and free my country—and perhaps free Jean if he's still alive."

"And yet, I understand, you had a very cosy relationship with our Nazi friend—this Oarlick."

"He's just a boy, Colonel. I travelled thousands of miles to get the opportunity to fight for my country. And I risked my life in Tunis getting information for you. Ask Lieutenant Jeannot. Surely you cannot deny me the privilege of joining my friends on the continent to fight our mutual enemy."

"Our F.F.I. friends are very costly. We cannot risk a whole spy net on anyone in whom we have the slightest doubt."

"How can you doubt my loyalty? I'm here, aren't I? What can I do to prove to you that I am sincere?"

The colonel rubbed his hands together as if washing them clean after shaking hands with this picturesque representative of the Paris slums. The interview was taking just the turn he had wanted.

"You are rather friendly with that Nazi. The Amis are sponsoring him, but frankly, we think he's plotting something, and we'd like to know what it is. Now, if you were to take up with him again..."

"Spy on him, you mean?"

"Well, my dear—you've done it before. If it turns up nothing, then there is no harm done. On the other hand, if you find something, what better way to prove your willingness to fight the *boche*?"

"I was a *petite putaine* for M.I.-5, is that it?"

"It's up to you, my dear."

"And if I do, will you promise to get me into France with the F.F.I.?"

"Certainly. I'll send you on the same training courses with this Oarlick. When the time comes, you'll be all ready to go."

Marie smoothed down her hair. "I'll do it," she said, "but you must make good on your promise."

"Done and done, my dear."

Chapter 36

Peter was removed from the Buckingham estate in a police van and confined for several days in a walled hospital-like structure near London. There, still in his ill-fitting German uniform, he was summoned to an office for an interview. His British armed guards left him at the door. Peter knocked.

"Come in."

He opened the door and saw an American officer sitting at a table with another soldier who seemed to be an enlisted man. He went in and closed the door, and decided not to salute. He wasn't sure of the man's rank.

"Have a seat. I am Colonel Briggs, and this is Sergeant Feuer."

"How do you do."

"Now, Lieutenant, let me lay my cards on the table." Peter looked around for some cards.

"Oh, by the way, if you don't understand my English, Sergeant Feuer will translate. Now—I have read all the interrogation reports, and we have made discreet investigations in Switzerland. I have some news for you. Your father and brother are well and still making guns for Hitler."

"Yes?"

"And we are reliably informed that you were reported as missing and presumed dead, and your family so notified."

Peter looked a question at the sergeant, who proceeded to translate the sentence into a good Berlin German.

"And then, one of our people informed your brother that you are indeed alive and here in England. We were not able to contact your father directly. He doesn't leave his house much, and we couldn't take chances."

"Is he all right—healthy?"

"Yes, apparently."

"May I ask—did anyone contact my friend Vreneli?"

The Colonel thought about that one for a moment.

"Yes. We checked her out. She's in a village called Aarau. However, we didn't contact her. In your own interest, the fewer who know about your presence here, the better."

"Vreneli—she is the main reason I left Africa. I have to get in touch with her. I . . ."

"Yes, yes. I've read your interview with Colonel Smythe. Now . . . our main interest in you, Lieutenant, is in getting you to somehow help us to get your family to stop making those damned Flak guns."

"All right. That seems straightforward. You know my motives, and I know yours."

"There is another factor—the British. They mistrust you. They would just as soon put you in a P.O.W. camp."

"I wouldn't mind going into a prison camp if I could write to Vreneli and make sure she got my letter. Isn't that a privilege you allow to any prisoner?"

"Lieutenant, I think you can do more than that. You say you want to help finish the war. Very well—will you undertake a mission in Germany?"

"They would shoot me if they caught me."

"Yes. But you would be helping the war effort."

"Your war effort. I have my own war aims—to get back to Switzerland. Why can't you send me there?"

"I don't think we're quite ready for that. Would you be willing to write a letter to your brother and father asking them to stop manufacturing 88's?"

"Don't be absurd. What good would that do? It would just brand me as a traitor to Germany."

"Will you do it?"

"No. I fail to see the sense in that."

"Well then—you didn't answer my question. Will you volunteer for a mission in Germany? For instance—we would like to know what Rommel is doing right now."

"It would depend on the mission. Frankly, I don't much care for shooting or getting shot at. Why should I? I'm an engineer, not a soldier."

"You're a hard nut, Oelrich."

Peter looked at the sergeant, who translated the phrase into pungent Berlin slang. The Colonel got up to pace the floor and look out at the walled-in rainswept garden.

"I'll tell you what, Oelrich. Instead of sending you to a P.O.W. camp, we'll let you enlist in the U.S. Army. That way the British can't touch you. You'll be under our protection, and also subject to our court-martial laws. If you double-cross us, you can be shot for treason. Make sure he understands that, sergeant."

The sergeant translated.

"And we'll send you for assessment and training for a mission in Germany. If and when the time comes, you will be allowed to volunteer, and you'll be assigned to non-combatant duty if you don't volunteer. Do you agree to that?"

The sergeant translated again, and Peter signified his assent.

"Now, because of your experience and training, I propose to enlist you as a master sergeant in the U.S. Army. Do you agree to that?"

"Wait a little," Peter said. "I've already been a sergeant, and didn't much like it—no offence, Sergeant Feuer. Why should I take a rank lower than *Oberleutnant*?"

"You're not going to be in the Afrika Korps."

"All the same, if I'm going to be of service to you, I should have the rank suitable."

"Very well. First Lieutenant, then."

"So. Einverstanden."

"He says he agrees."

They finished their conversation and laid plans for Peter's future. That afternoon Peter borrowed a sweater and trousers from Sgt. Feuer and went with him to a huge warehouse in London where he was issued with complete

American uniforms. That evening he went before the United States Ambassador to the Court of St. James, swore allegiance to a country he had never seen, was inducted into the U.S. Army, and immediately promoted to first lieutenant's rank. The Ambassador was confused as to why this new American citizen, wearing a uniform without rank badges or insignia, needed an armed interpreter at his elbow.

The next morning First Lieutenant Peter Oelrich, Army of the United States, an armed sergeant still at his side, entrained for Pemberley and a six day assessment program.

Chapter 37

There were twenty of them in an old country house which had been set up as a military establishment somewhat less luxurious than the one in Buckingham, but equipped with an officer's mess and bar, armed guards, and conference rooms.

There were tests of every kind—psychological, psychiatric, intelligence tests, language tests, tests of physical skill. For the written tests, Peter was segregated and supplied with a non-com who translated the tests into German. Otherwise he made do with his French and his rusty schoolboy English. They went through some of the tests in groups. A part of the group spoke French as a native language, and Peter elected to stay with them.

At the end of the day they would bathe and change into their Class A uniforms (which were French, British and American) and have cocktails before dinner. Peter discovered that one of the Free French officers spoke German.

"How is that?" he asked.

"I'm from Alsace," the man answered. "And you?"

"Oh, a lot of Americans speak German."

"Is that right? Where are you from?"

Peter eyed him suspiciously. For security reasons, all of the prospective students had been ordered to use false names and conceal their past.

"Oh, I'm from various places" he answered. "But I went to school in Switzerland."

"Really? So did I. Rosey, near Gstaad. Do you know it?"

"Of course."

They discussed Swtizerland, and Peter recognized that the man did indeed know something of the school which his brother Hans-Jörg had attended.

Throughout the week of tests, he found it very comfortable to be able to relax and speak German with his Alsatian friend, but still he was on his guard at all times, for he suspected, quite correctly, that the man was a plant, sent by the British, to spy upon him.

There were tests for leadership, tests for teamwork, tests to determine stability under pressure, and always his "friend" to confide in.

The tests confirmed what Peter could have told them about himself. He was self-reliant, a loner; unshakeable under pressure, a good leader if he had to be, but one who preferred to work through others.

After that it was radio-telegraphy school, the parachute school at Ringway, the small-arms courses, spy training in secret inks and coding, endless courses. Most courses were given in the Northwest Highlands of Scotland, a dour and rain-soaked part of Scotland isolated by a chain of lakes and canals called the Caledonian Canal.

The only people allowed to cross the canal were locals, military personnel, and certain subversive agents who had been spotted but not arrested.

Peter had asked time and again that his superior officers contact Vreneli Schmid. He was not discontented to keep his survival a secret from his brother and father, but he hated to think of Vreneli pining away in wartime Zurich, and perhaps meeting some lonely American flyer or exiled Hungarian Count. Somehow, even the Amis didn't trust him not to be sending some special message, one that could hurt them.

Peter was vaguely aware that he was being followed whenever he left Scotland. His spy training, however, was not in vain. On his next trip to London he went to the Savory Grill, ordered a big dinner, and disappeared out the kitchen door. He changed taxis several times, then went to a post office and bought a simple postcard. He purchased some international postal coupons and put them together with the postcard in an envelope addressed to the Red Cross in Lisbon with a request to remail it to Zurich. He could only hope that it would arrive. The message was simple:

Dear Vreneli:

I wanted you to know that I still think of you. I'll never forget our stay in the sanitorium in St. Moritz. When this terrible war is finally over, I hope to see you. I hope you'll be waiting for me.

Hans Castorp

Chapter 38

The following week Peter was sent to a survival course in Scotland where he learned about orientation, map reading, compass reading, the edible herbs of Northern Europe, and the trapping and cooking of small wild game. He also began to get some physical conditioning. It left him sore and dispirited, for he was out of shape after so many weeks in various camps and schools.

He travelled again that weekend, alone on a train to Scotland, but he felt he was being shadowed every minute. Only when he crossed the Caledonian canal to report for a test in his survival course skills did he begin to feel free. Wearing his pinks and trench coat, and carrying a B-4 bag full of fatigue uniforms and boots, he reported to a military headquarters which had obviously been converted from a country hotel. They scrutinized his written orders carefully.

"Yes, Lieutenant. You have room twenty-eight for the night. The rest of your survival group is already here. You can meet them in the lounge at five P.M. Is that clear?"

"Thank you."

Peter took a shower and changed clothes, and spent a few hours reading the *Manchester Guardian* and the *Officer's Guide* before going down to the lounge to meet his fellow survivors. The lounge was a little room separated from the lobby by curtained French doors. Peter knocked and stepped inside.

"Jeannot! Marie! Quelle surprise!"

"Le petit Suisse! Et en uniforme Americaine! Incroyable!"

"Pierre! Comment ça va?"

"Are you the group I'm training with?"

"Yes. The survival nonsense."

"How did you get an American uniform?"

170

"What have you been doing?"

They ordered wine and caught up on their various adventures. Marie had been taken into the Free French army as a second lieutenant, and had completed a radio-telegraphy course. She expected to be dropped into France and serve as a clandestine radio contact for a Maquis group.

Pierre and the two Roberts had been given courses in organizing resistance nets, and had been given guerilla training.

"How about you, Peter? Are you going to get to Switzerland?"

"Who knows. I'm just trying to survive right now."

"Did you take that stupid course at Pemberley like we did?"

"Yes. Fell in the pond. Did they have that pond that was supposed to be full of sulfuric acid when you were there?"

"Yes. I fell in too. I thought I was going to freeze."

"And those sergeants. Spies, every one of them."

"The English are suspicious of everybody who didn't go to Eton."

"You must play the game, old chap."

They had an uproarious dinner. Not good, but uproarious. Someone found a cottage piano, and Pierre played as they sang folk songs and Army songs, and even French Foreign Legion songs in execrable German. Peter and Marie sat to one side, holding hands.

"Marie—chante une fois."

"I can't sing. I haven't practiced for weeks."

"Come on. You have to be better than we are."

"All right." She let herself be coaxed, and chose a haunting song of the *grands boulevards*. She sang it pitched very low, and very slowly, to accommodate to Pierre's amateur piano playing.

It reminded them all of Paris, and then of home. They became very quiet as Marie's haunting voice, a touch of

171

their youth in that faraway, very foreign country, spoke to them in verse, in accents of melancholy, of that which they missed, and wanted, and needed.

"Thank you, Marie." They were suddenly sober and quiet, and each of them kissed Marie on the cheek as they left to go upstairs to their solitary rooms.

"Good night, Marie."

"A demain."

"Seven-thirty."

"It's good to see you again, Peter."

"Yes. Good night, Marie."

Chapter 39

In the lobby at seven-thirty in the morning—a rag-tag group of disorganized, half-asleep Frenchmen as far as appearance went—they were met by an excitable little Welshman and a huge redfaced sergeant, both in the uniforms of the Royal Fusilliers.

"*Eh bien—bonjour, Marie. Tout prêt pour la grande exercice militaire?*"

"*Bon jour. Je n'ai pas dormi deux secondes ensemble. J'avait dans ma chambre...*"

"*Monsieur le Général. Bon jour!*"

"Sergeant, will you call this—*bunch* to attention!"

The sergeant filled his lungs with air, crashed his boots together and bellowed so loud that the glass panes in the windows shook.

"At—ten—HUP!"

"*Que-est-ce qu'il veut, ce petit idiot?*"

"*Moi, je voudrais avoir du café, avant de commencer a ces jeux, moi.*"

"*Je n'ai pas mangé, moi non plus.*"

The Welsh major was fairly hopping up and down with anger at this flouting of his authority, and his curly red hair glinted like copper coils charged with electricity.

"Who's in charge here? Who's the leader of this group? I thought you people were supposed to understand English."

The plump and easy-going Captain Jumel took pity on the Major.

"*Alors, mes enfants*, make a nice line for the Major, and let's see what he has to say. Come on Peter—Marie."

They straightened themselves out into some semblance of military order and stopped talking. Pierre saluted. "Captain Jumel, at your service, Major."

"Well. That's better. I take it you're ready to go?"

"Of course, Major."

"Sergeant, read them their orders."

The sergeant read in a sing-song voice from a clipboard.

"This exercise will test the survival skills you have learned in your previous week's training. You will be required to surrender your identification papers, all weapons and supplies, including pocket knives, all weapons, and all of your moneys. You will be taken by boat to a spot where you will be landed and required to live off the land as best you can and to rendezvous with your conducting officer in exactly seven days at the place where you landed."

"What was that all about?" de Bourgival asked.

"Didn't understand a word," Marie said.

"All right, gentlemen, and you, Miss," the Major was beginning to enjoy himself. "The sergeant will put your personal effects into manila envelopes which you will sign with your name and rank and deposit with our clerk together with your luggage."

"Major—just a minute. Can't we have at least a gun and a knife to skin game? This is carrying things too far."

"Absolutely not." The Major smiled at their apparent discomfiture. "You must learn to live off the land just as you would behind the lines in France or Spain."

"I'd rather be in the Pyrenées any day," Marie muttered as she put her purse into a manila envelope.

"Not even some matches to build fires?" Jeannot asked plaintively.

"Positively not. This exercise is designed to teach you something, and we want to simulate field conditions as nearly as possible for your own good. It will be excellent training."

The Frenchmen made a number of voluble remonstrances which only served to give the major a certain disguised sadistic pleasure. After they handed over their luggage and envelopes to a waiting non-com, he herded them into a truck, down to the waterfront, and into a motor whaleboat that chugged out into the Scottish sea.

Crowded together into the small cabin of the boat, they peered out at the bleak islands and the flinty mountains that overlooked wild and desolate shores.

"Too bad it's not ski season, Peter."

"I thought you were the tour guide."

"Don't worry about it. We were expecting something like this."

Jumel peered out the tiny porthole. "Is that the Sound of Rum?"

"What is the sound of rum?"

"Looks like Muck to me."

The whaleboat let them out on a deserted rocky shore. They had to wade ashore over sharp rocks, getting their feet and boots wet.

"So long, chaps," the major said. "Have a good time. We'll meet you here a week from today." He was positively enjoying himself now as he envisioned what they would look like in a week: hungry, clothes torn by brambles, sneezing with colds, their hands cut and scraped from digging for roots or trying to snare rabbits.

"That'll fix the bloody muckers," he smiled as the boat pulled away. His bull-roaring sergeant laughed.

"Eh bien." They sat down in the sun, took off their boots and hung up their socks to dry. Jeannot seemed to be the natural leader of the group even though he was outranked by Jumel.

"Eh bien. Let's figure out where we are." He pried off the heel of his combat boot and extracted a compass from it.

"The well-equipped officer," Peter said.

"We've been expecting something like this." Jumel smiled, pulling out the lining of his hat. He brought out part of a detailed map of Scotland which went together with one from de Bourgival's jacket lining.

"We all went through the course together," Marie explained, "and we thought they might strand us like this, so we're prepared. We pooled our money and changed it into big bills," Marie retrieved three twenty pound notes from her brassiere and put them into her emptied pockets.

"I trust you'll allow me to make a contribution," Peter said, pulling off his belt and extracting, with some effort, a Swiss fifty franc gold piece from the tiny slit in the leather after working it down carefully from the middle of his belt.

"Wonderful. But can we change it?"

"Gold is like a magic spell. It works anywhere in the world."

"Well now. Things are looking up. Now if we can only find our way back to civilization. Where the devil are we?" They bent over a map filled with strange place names that stuck in Gallic throats like haggis.

"Acharacle. Mallaig. Eigg. The sound of Eigg."

"If that was Muck, then we must be north of Eigg."

"I thought I saw the loom of land over the west."

"Maybe that would be Teangue."

"No, we're up by the Isle of Skye."

"Perhaps we could try for Kyle."

"That's too big a town. Someone could report us to the authorities."

"Who cares? This is supposed to be a survival test. I'd rather take a chance on surviving in a good hotel."

"We don't have enough money for a good hotel and twenty-one meals anyway."

"With Peter's contribution we do."

After considerable discussion while their socks dried, they decided that they were on the Sound of Arisaig, and they walked overland until they came to a country road. A rubber-tired farm cart pulled by a huge shaggy horse was coming up the road. It was driven by an old crofter who looked as forbidding as the Scotch mountains themselves.

"Peter—you speak the best English. You talk."

Peter waved at the man, who peered at them suspiciously from beneath bushy eyebrows.

"Good afternoon. Is this the way to Arisaig?"

"It is."

"It is a big town, Arisaig?"

"It is not."

"I wonder if we could ride with you?"

"You may."

They climbed into the cart. It already held two stoats, three sheep, and a crate of eggs. Peter sat beside the driver. The craggy old man was puffing on a pipe and staring stolidly at his horse's backside. He was so obviously a rough man of independent opinion that even Marie quit talking and rode in silence.

"How big is Arisaig?" Peter asked.

"Four churches."

Peter digested that one, but didn't bother translating.

They went along in silence for several miles. Then the old farmer grunted a question of his own.

"You English?"

"Swiss."

"Oh." He puffed on his pipe. "I was afraid you might be foreigners."

Peter let that remark, too, drop to the straw-covered wagon bed.

"Hup, hup, hup, hup..." A squad of Highlander recruits in full battle dress double-timed toward them with Enfields at port arms.

"Faites rien!" Jumel ordered, and they ignored the soldiers. The squad went on by, only their officer sparing a glance at the cart.

"Fine lads," the farmer said.

"Yes, sir."

They finally came within sight of Arisaig, which appeared to be an unpainted little village of a few thousand inhabitants. Jeannot tapped Peter on the arm and nodded his head at the roadside.

"We'll get out here. Thank you very much." They jumped out nimbly, for the farmer didn't stop the cart.

"Headquarters be over there," he pointed vaguely to the west.

"Thank you again."

"Well," said Jeannot. "What headquarters? We'll get picked up by the military if we stay here. Too many soldiers."

"And we have no papers."

"Let's reconnoiter the side streets. Maybe we can figure out something," Jumel phrased his order as a suggestion.

They split up and walked down a side street, two on one side, three on the other. The streets wound unpredictably. At one turning Jeannot raised his hand and reversed course. They all turned around and started walking back the way they had come, and heard a military truck cross the road behind them.

They came to a cobblestoned street that overlooked the harbor and the ten or fifteen buildings that constituted the hub of the little market town.

"There's a hotel."

"Let's try it. Perhaps we can get some afternoon tea." Trying to avoid having their non-existent papers checked by authorities or nosy officers, they went through an alleyway to get into the two story wooden building.

It was a nice old lobby with a stairway leading upstairs, a dining room to one side, and a worn wooden desk, not unlike that in the converted hotel lobby they had left that morning, except that it was not a headquarters clerk, but a nearsighted old Scotswoman who peered at them from behind the counter. Jeannot pushed Peter forward.

"Good day, Madame."

"Good day," she answered grudgingly.

"Could we get something to eat?"

"Tea is sierved at four in the pooblic bar. Not a moment before. Ye'll have to wait."

Peter looked at Jeannot and Captain Jumel, who nodded slightly.

178

"We should like to get accommodations for the week. Five rooms—baths, et cetera."

"Are ye with the schools headquarters?" She threw back her head and stared at Marie through the bottoms of her glasses. Jeannot shrugged his shoulders.

"In a way, Madame."

She gave another severe glance at them and then responded in the Scottish brogue that sounded almost Swiss to Peter.

"Na, cum'," and she requested payment in advance, and insisted that the register be signed. Jeannot beckoned to de Bourgival.

"Lieutenant Count Robert de Bourgival and party," she read from the ledger book that served as a register. "Very good, your Grace," she accepted a twenty pound note from Marie and rang a bell. From the bar came a buxom young girl wearing an apron over a plaid skirt.

"Take his Grace up to rooms 21 through 26, Fiona, and show them the bath. A shilling charge for hot baths, gentlemen. And a hearty welcome to the Arisaig hotel."

"Have ye no cases, y'r Grace?"

De Bourgival looked to Peter, but it was Jeannot who answered.

"No luggage."

They tramped up the creaky stairs and were shown their rooms and as well as the community bathroom with its old-fashioned tub on claw and ball legs. De Bourgival got the sitting room.

"First bath is mine," Marie said, traipsing off with the maid.

They went to their rooms, hung up their jackets, and then reassembled in de Bourgival's sitting room to remove their boots and massage their feet.

"I saw another squad of trainees out my window," Jeannot said.

"What can that schools thing be?"

"We'll either have to hide all week or get out of here," Jeannot said grimly. "If they catch us, they'll just start us

179

over again in some even more God-forsaken spot."

"Be that as it may, I'm going to have something to eat before I think about moving on."

"The army marches on its stomach."

"I hope we can buy some cigarettes."

De Bourgival was studying their tiny map again. "If we could get down to Oban, I might get a place for us. The Duke of Inverness has a home there. He used to go hunting chamois with us in the *Alpes Maritimes*."

They looked at the map.

"It doesn't look so terribly far—if we could just avoid getting our identities checked. Once they find out we're foreigners—and one with a sauerkraut accent, and floating around with no identification, they'll escort us straight to a military jail."

"Or a drafty castle somewhere."

"Top of the morning, Messieurs!" Marie came in, fresh from her bath, with light slippers instead of her military boots, and wearing a plaid skirt instead of her fatigue trousers.

"Brava!"

"Beautiful. Where did you get that?"

"The eternal feminine!"

"Do you like my little Scots-girl costume? I bought it from the maid."

"That's where our money is going to go!"

"I hope we can get some more, somehow."

"It's three-thirty, gentlemen. Shall we adjourn to the public house?"

They pulled on their heavy brogans and clumped down the stairs. As they tramped through the lobby, the proprietress stared with surprise, and then with disapproval, to see that one of her soldiers had turned out to be a lady, or at least was wearing a kiltie.

Off the lobby was a dimly lit but cheerful bar-room with a table being set for tea and a bartender already on duty. There were no customers.

They took a corner table and sent Marie to the bar where she peered out at the bottles and beer taps in dismay.

"Yes, Ma'am?" The old barman in his white apron looked at her with an appreciative eye for femininity.

"Perhaps . . . five of the Glen Fiddich."

"An' Soda? Water?"

"Soda water."

"Sit ye doon, lassie. I'll fetch them for ye."

Marie smiled uncertainly, returned to their table, and explained that no cognacs or aperitifs were visible.

"Here you are. Ten shillings tuppence." He put down the tray. "*Och nay*, I canna' take a twenty pound note. I'll put it on tick."

He didn't seem disposed to step away from the table after serving their drinks to them.

"An' which of you would be his Lordship, if I might ask?"

They looked at each other, and Jumel pointed to de Bourgival.

"Might I ask where ye may be from, your Lordship?"

Peter spoke for him. "That is a top secret," he said.

"Ahh—'tis a shame. All our young boys here are far away as well, with nae family, nae friends. They're up in Sutherland, or doon in Africa. 'Tis a cruel war."

The maid bustled in with a tray of sandwiches and smiled at them shyly.

"My daughter, Fiona. Sixteen, she is, and a fine buxom lass."

"Your daughter!" Marie said. *"Sa fille."*

"Yes indeed. Fresh out of school and a great help in parlous times. At the desk is me wife."

"Will you have a drink with us, sir?" Jumel smiled.

"With pleasure." The old man stepped over to the bar to pour himself something. Before he returned, they put their heads together.

"To your good health, gentlemen, and to the young

lady." The old man raised his glass, and they drank together.

"My name is Peter Oelrich," Peter said. "And what is yours?"

"Thomas McLaughlin is my name." The proprietor of the tiny hotel shook Peter's hand.

"And this is Lieutenant de Bourgival, Lieutenant Jeannot, Lieutenant Blancharde, and Captain Jumel, all of the Free French Army."

"Welcome."

"We should like to confide in you. We are on one of those silly training exercises for the English. We should like to spend the week here, and we don't want to get caught up by the local soldiers or anyone else."

Mr. McLaughlin seemed to digest that information slowly.

"Tell me, do you know if the Duke of Inverness keeps his house open at Oban?" de Bourgival asked.

"Nae—do ye know him, your Honor?"

"Yes. He and my father were good friends before the war."

"Shall I see if I can put through a trunk call for ye?" They all looked blank.

"The telephone is right out in the lobby. We have all the modern conveniences."

"Oh—yes. A call. That would be very nice."

"But feerst, let us have another dram. This one is on me."

McLaughlin bustled about getting them another round of Scotch whisky while shouting out to his wife to have her start the time-consuming process of making a long distance telephone call to the next county.

As they had their buffet luncheon, trying the watercress sandwiches and the herring and the tea and the scones, local inhabitants drifted in for their tea or half-and-half. De Bourgival was called away from flirting with the blushing Fiona to speak to the Duke of

Inverness, and McLaughlin was kept hopping to serve his guests.

"I would suggest—if you don't mind," he said, "the military gentlemen start to come in at about sixish."

"Oh thank you. We will make it a point to be out by then."

"'Tis is a good thing you know the Duke," McLaughlin said. "I was just about to report you to the constabulary as German spies. But now—we Scots enjoy fooling King George."

"Mr. McLaughlin, another favor. Is there a bank here in Arisaig? We should like to change some money. A Swiss gold piece or two."

"Sure and there is a bank. But there are also currency restrictions, you know. We don't get much foreign money up here, not since the war." He examined the gold piece Marie had taken from her pocket.

"But I am friendly with our banker. I'll take it to him meself, if you like."

"Wonderful. We would appreciate that."

De Bourgival came back in from the lobby. *"Messieurs et dame,"* he announced with a smile. "I have accepted an invitation on your behalf to the Duke's house. Overnight. He's sending a car for us tomorrow."

"De Bourgival, you're a blessing!"

"Let's have a party."

"We haven't had one since last night."

"Monsieur l'hôte!"

"Mine host, we say," McLaughlin smiled, now feeling even merrier.

"We should have a banquet tonight. And you and your family must come. What could we have?"

"Grouse, of course. Scotch grouse is famous the world over. Even in London!"

"Grouse it is!"

"And champagne."

"No!"

"In my cellar I have just a few bottles left. We used to get them for the Duke when he would come up here in his boat and stop for luncheon."

"We'll have a feast!"

That evening was one which the McLaughlins were to turn into an Arisaig fable in the many years to come when they told it at their little hotel bar. They laid on the feast in de Bourgival's sitting room, keeping the spitted grouse warm over a peat fire in the tiny fireplace, serving the last of the prewar champagne chilled from the sideboard. They ate from a trestle table covered with a bolt of Inverness plaid that matched Marie's new skirt and that worn by Fiona McLaughlin.

A gramophone played vintage prewar HMV records, and Fiona taught Marie the Highland dances, the two young women bobbing and stepping so prettily that soon de Bourgival and Jumel removed their heavy boots and tried it too.

"The girls look so nice in their kilts," Peter smiled.

"'Tis the Clan Invernary plaid," said McLaughlin. "We make it here with our own wool and vegetable dyes. Our Highlanders wear trews of thim."

"And what are trews?"

"Wha, ye dinna know trews are trewsers! Wha' min wear if they dinna wear a kilt. Our boys wear them with their dress uniforms. I should know. Our tailor has a whole houseful. He canna sell thim for the Highlanders canna wear their likes in wartime."

"Have him sell us some! We don't want to wear the same clothes all week."

"We'll design our own uniform. The First French Highland Regiment!"

Chapter 40

The next morning—it must have been about ten o'clock for McLaughlin was just dispensing a few eye-openers in his pub—a Rolls-Royce saloon of majestic proportions drove up in front of the Hotel Arisaig, and an ancient chauffeur in uniform came around to open the door for the Duke of Inverness. Children gawked.

"Mrs. McLaughlin, isn't it?" the Duke asked in the lobby.

"Oh, your Grace, I dinna think ye would remember me."

"How could I forget the prettiest lass in the Highlands? Is young de Bourgival about?"

"Right up the stairs, your Grace. He's expecting you. Fiona—take his Grace up to the Count."

"What a pretty little gosling!"

"My daughter, your Grace."

"No! How the years pass us by!"

Fiona blushed and took him up the stairs. The Duke knocked on the door, and music immediately started from inside the room. Fiona opened the door for him.

"Attention!"

Lined up and identically trousered and kilted in Invernary plaid, with their fatigue jackets topped with blue caps decorated with plaid, the five came to attention as de Bourgival saluted.

"First French Highland Detachment at your service, sir! The Duke's Own."

"Robert!" The Duke doubled up with laughter, and they all began to laugh.

"We have a bottle of champagne for breakfast. Let's drink a toast."

Fiona was still standing at the door while de Bourgival introduced his friends and spoke to the Duke. He

185

beckoned her over, whispered in her ear, and patted her backside as she scampered away.

"Robert," the Duke was saying, "I'm just glad to have a chance to entertain you and your friends, and if you want to bring the young lady along, so much the better. I am only sorry it took a major war to get you here. How is your father?"

Fiona was back, beaming with pleasure because her mother had given her permission to join the party overnight at the Duke's house. While she ran to get a few things, they drank their champagne and tramped down through the lobby to the car.

"Take good care of my little girl, your Grace," Mrs. McLaughlin cried as they got into the huge Rolls.

"She'll be back tomorrow, safe and sound. Don't you worry."

The huge chauffered Rolls with the coat of arms on the doors, filled with rollicking French Highlanders, breezed across the bridges and through the military checkpoints almost without stopping.

The Duke's house at Oban could have been more properly called a mansion.

"A bit overgrown, I'm afraid. Wartime, you know," he smiled apologetically. "We've closed off both wings and sealed up the windows."

Weeds were growing in the gravelled driveway and through the flagstones of the courtyard, but the entrance hall was warm and glowing, the guest rooms cool, the library rich with leather-bound books and panelling that shone.

"Bourgival—come into the gunroom. I wish your father could see my collection." He pulled out shotguns with inlaid stocks and showed them proudly to Jeannot and Bourgival. "Can't get shells, of course. Been loading my own."

The Duke was in residence alone, with only a cook, butler and a footman to help in the house, so dinner had

186

to be simple—salmon, mutton, and some vintage claret—but it was served in the state dining room on silver and gold.

"Does the old buggers good to polish some silver," the Duke said testily.

After the port had been passed, de Bourgival whispered into Marie's ear. Once she had understood, she stood up, quite delighted.

"Your Grace, Miss McLaughlin, gentlemen—as the lowest ranking officer present, if not the youngest, it is my duty, I am told, to break with tradition while, *au même temps*, initiating a new one. *Gentlemen, the King*." All drank to His Majesty.

The Duke rose to the occasion.

"On the behalf of Miss McLaughlin and myself, I propose a toast to General Charles de Gaulle."

Jumel was next. He stood up pompously.

"As ranking officer, I have the honor to propose the *premier* toast to—*The First French Highlanders*."

Jeannot mystified them with his proposal. "Gentlemen: a toast to—William Tell. He fought against foreign oppression."

Peter seemed to be next in line, and he was at a loss. He rose to his feet and stammered

"I have an English toast I heard some years ago..."

"*A bas les Anglais!*"

"*Malbrouck va-t-en!*"

They confused him by shouting him down, and he retaliated by imitating a stodgy Swiss professor beginning a boring story.

"I am reminded of '*unser Shakespeare*' He said, 'all the world's a stage, and all the men and women merely players. And one man in his time, plays many parts...'"

He had their attention. "This is the newest of many uniforms I have worn," he said, and then he seemed to have lost touch with what he had in mind. "In any case—my toast was—'to absent friends'."

In that far northern climate the night was still dim with daylight after dinner, and though the drawing-room was lit by candles, the doors overlooking the great park were open and looked out over the vast lawn, now populated with a few sheep grazing among the statues.

Marie sang to them, accompanied by Pierre on a magnificent inlaid grand piano which was dreadfully out of tune. Then, to the music of His Master's Voice, led off by the Duke, the gentlemen danced with each of the ladies in turn; and the girls found the right record to perform their Highland Fling.

"De Bourgival," the Duke said, "Did you see that new American film—that 'Waterloo Bridge?'"

"No. We haven't seen many American films lately."

"Never mind. They used an old Scots song in it, and the fellow danced with his girl in a cabaret while they put out the candles. Rather than draw the blackout curtains, that's what I'd like to do tonight."

He put a record on the old Victrola, and signalled to his ancient butler to begin snuffing the tapers. The music played—the words in their strange dialect were vague and misty to the young people in their new plaids, but the sentiment survived all transfiguration.

*"Should auld acquaintance be forgot,
And the days of auld lang syne..."*

"I'm getting old, de Bourgival, and I don't know whether I'll ever see the Alps again." The Duke walked slowly toward the door, de Bourgival at his side. "We had wonderful days together, your father and I."

"Yes, sir."

"And I'm glad you and your young friends were able to come here so that I could thank you again for all the happy memories."

"It's been like old times, your Grace."

The Duke turned at the door, and his eyes were glistening. "You young people stay up, and enjoy your

188

youth while you can. I'll bid you a good night. And God bless you."

"Good night, your Grace."

"Thank you."

"Bon soir, bonne nuite."

"Good night, my friends."

> *"We'll take a cup of kindness yet,*
> *For auld lang syne."*

The rest of their week of survival was an anticlimax after that night at Oban. They returned to Arisaig and spent their time quietly in peaceful pursuits. Peter and Jeannot played long games of chess. Jumel taught them all to play *pokair*, a new American game he had learned in England. Marie and Peter took long walks in the dusk of the midsummer night and saw the aurora borealis shimmer in silvery majesty.

Before they left their oasis of peace, they solemnly packed up their kilts and trews in a package entrusted to the McLaughlins, to be picked up by whichever of them might survive to come back to the highlands, and they had a final toast in Glen Fiddich:

"To the First French Highlanders."

A taxi delivered them to a point within easy walking distance of the beach where they were to rendezvous with their Welsh Major. Immaculate in their freshly laundered fatigue dress, they walked carefully over the rocks.

The whaleboat chugged in from the Scottish sea. The Welsh Major nudged his red-faced sergeant as they came closer and closer to the five figures waiting for them in on the rocky shore.

"We'll hear a different story from this bunch of wogs this week, sergeant."

"Yes, sir. A week in the open air should have quieted them down."

The boat slowly neared the land.

189

"Cheerio, Major," Jeannot waved. "Top of the morning, and all that sort of rot."

The red-haired Welshman couldn't believe his eyes.

"St. Andrew's teeth! They look like they just came off parade."

"Good morning. Could you come in a little close so we don't get our feet too wet?"

"Great God! Where have you been all week? I think you must have gained five pounds each. You've cheated! I'll have you court-martialled for this! This is impossible. What have you been doing?"

"Just living off the land, Major. An old French Army secret. Here you are, Marie. *Allez—OOP*!"

Chapter 41

The British military intelligence mission to the capital of Switzerland had been in constant touch with the Oelrich factories since the late thirties, but they had never sent a man to the factory in Basel. They were content to let Hans-Jörg come to them to sell his proximity fuses and negotiate his contracts for the Manchester plant that licenced Oelrich designs to the British.

Now, however, pressured by higher-ups in Britain, an English representative made an appointment to speak with the head of the firm. Hans-Jörg received him in the board-room overlooking the Rhine. He even had the windows washed for the occasion.

"Captain Harley-Ffythe! Welcome. It's an honor to have you here."

"Oh, don't call me Captain. How are you, old boy? What an impressive place you have here."

"You just let me take you on a tour of the premises after we've had our little chat. Have a seat, sir."

"Oh, thank you very much."

"You're looking very fit. Skiing much?"

"Yes. I get away for some cross-country skiing every now and again."

They discussed the ski resorts near Berne.

"I went to school in the Bernese Oberland," Hans-Jörg smiled. "At Rosey—with that Pablavi fellow. Charming chap."

"Really. Did you know Prince Aly? Married Lady Guiness. Bit of a bounder, I'm afraid."

They discussed mutual acquaintances for a bit before getting down to business.

"Hans, old chap, I want to get serious for a moment. You know, you've always played the game, but really— the time has come when you must stop making those guns for old Adolph."

"My dear Captain Harley-Ffythe, you know that the moment I do, you'll get no more proximity fuses. Your steel comes directly from the Ruhr in German bottoms."

"Well now, we can purchase those fuses from the Yankees, you know."

"You wouldn't do that! We're loyal to old customers, and anyway I can supply you at a much lower cost per hundred than they can. I've prepared some comparison prices." Hans shuffled through some papers. "Even taking the American pre-war costs for comparable items, they simply cannot compete in either price or quality. After all, we have led the world in precision manufacturing for generations."

"All the same, old chap, you must cease making those guns. You could use your last shipment of Ruhr steel to produce enough fuses for the rest of the war."

"The Germans would invade in a moment if I did so. You remember last year. They had an armored division at the border, ready and waiting."

"They don't have any extra divisions to spare now, old chap."

"And the Swiss would blow up the factories."

"Shouldn't care to have the Swiss neutrality changed. I might be interned!"

"That's what I'm saying, old chap. I'd like to oblige you, but it's really quite impossible."

"Actually, I do have another trump to play," Harley-Ffythe took a photograph from his note-case. "I have good news for you. Your brother is alive and well in Scotland."

"No!"

"Here's a picture which we posed very carefully with Colonel Smythe."

Hans-Jörg examined the photograph. His expression seemed to indicate doubt.

"You'll notice last Sunday's *Times* there," the Englishman said. "You can actually read the date if you use a magnifying glass."

"Well, that's wonderful news," Hans-Jörg smiled grimly. "Of course, such photographs can be faked."

"We would never do a thing like that. However, accidents do happen in wartime. Your brother is very depressed. I should hesitate to think of his committing suicide."

"He's much too sensible to do that."

Captain Harley-Ffythe brushed at his salt-and-pepper Guardsman's moustache.

"You know, old chap, this war is not going to last forever. We will be the victors, and I can guarantee you, no representative of your firm will be able to enter any of the allied countries if you continue to supply the enemy this way."

"Ah—memories are short. In a few years all this will be forgotten. I'm terribly sorry I can't oblige you. Oh—it's getting toward tea time. I've taken the liberty of whistling up a proper English tea for you. Do you know, I found a place where I could have some scones made. With marvellous cream!"

"Scones? In Switzerland?"

"I thought you'd like that. Let me ring."

Old Hans Oelrich was sitting at home, alone in his gloomy study, its vast spaces lit only by a fire and by candles dripping from sconces on the stone walls. He jerked his head around at the sound of a knock on the door.

"Herein!" he shouted testily.

"Hello, father." Hans-Jörg came in hesitantly, careworn and harried by the responsibilities he faced every day alone.

"What do you want?"

"I have good news, father." He took the English photograph he had received from Harley-Ffythe from his pocket and put it in front of his father. "Peter is alive. In England. Here's a picture of him taken just last week."

"Nonsense. What are you telling me lies for? He's dead and gone. I have the telegraph from the Reichs Chancellery."

"No, father. Look—that's him. No doubt about it."

"Don't lie to an old man. He hasn't even written. I told him to write. If he were alive he would have written, or come home."

Hans-Jörg stared into the fire. His father was getting worse and worse. The old man had never been testy with him before the war. With Peter perhaps, but not with him.

"Father, you should get out more. Why don't you come over to the plant? We need you. God knows, I could use your help. The British are putting pressure on me again. They want us to cease production of the Flak 41. They're making all sorts of threats."

"Oh my God, they're coming for me!" The old man wrung his hands.

"No, they aren't, father. I won't let them hurt the factory. It means as much to me as it does to you. I'm not like Peter, kiting off to play at being a hero."

"Oh my God, they're coming for me!"

"No they aren't, father. Don't worry yourself." Hans-Jörg tried to get the old man's mind off his problems. "Oh, by the way, Neider said there actually was an error in the monthly report. I'm glad you found it."

The old man picked up his steel pen and went back to perusing a column of figures by the light of the flickering candles.

"Where's Peter?" he asked. "Peter should see these figures. He understands these things."

Hans-Jörg ran his hands through his hair and backed away toward the big double door. He felt more alone than ever.

Chapter 42

A medium-sized, athletic-looking young officer with what the Americans called a "butch haircut," wearing a new uniform marked with a U.S. and the silver bars of a first lieutenant, came out of the Windmill theater. On his arm was a dark-haired woman in the uniform of the French Army.

"Mais, j'ai pas compris un mot, Peter."

"Moi non plus," her escort laughed. "I can't understand Cockney at all, but those two fat men with the mandolins!"

"And the electric blue suits!"

They laughed and strolled arm in arm out of the Soho area towards Bond Street. It was Peter's first leave in London, his first opportunity to get away from the constant supervision in the isolated area in Scotland where he and Marie and Lieutenant Jeannot and others were going through rigorous training courses, isolated from almost all civilians and confined in a distant part of the British Isles that could be entered and left only after stringent inspection of identity papers.

It was Peter's first opportunity to wear his new American dress uniform, and to spend some of the cash the American Army supplied so abundantly to its officers. He was spending it with Marie in London.

As they strolled down Bond Street in the fifth year of England's war, evidence of the bombing was everywhere, but the taxis were still running, the underground roared, and the time-honored clubs on Bond Street still sported their retired Colonels in club chairs looking out through the great bay windows and pulling on their moustaches in deathless contemplation.

"Oh, look!" Peter smiled, and bustled Marie into an unobtrusive establishment that bore a royal coat of arms emblazoned on its inconspicuous street sign.

"Yes?" A balding old clerk shot his cuffs and looked down his nose at them. "We don't make for Americans, you know. No new clients a-tall, I'm afraid."

"Oh that's all right. I'm an old customer. I couldn't resist coming in. You used to have an old fellow named Farrington who travelled on the continent. Is he still with you?"

"*Mister* Farrington happens to be here. Would you like to see him?"

Peter fingered the silk foulards on a counter. "That might be nice."

"Whom shall I say is calling, sir?"

"Mr. Oelrich."

The clerk disappeared with a disdainful glance.

"We used to order all our clothes here," Peter explained to Marie. "Ever since I was a boy. Wonderful tweeds. My brother used to order suits by the dozen. This is like old times."

"Mr. Peter!" An impeccable old man emerged from the back room. "Mr. Peter! What a surprise!"

"Hello, Farrington. It's nice to see you again."

"How you've grown! Why—" he said, turning to Marie, "I remember Mr. Peter when he was only this high!" The old gentleman made a gesture.

"*Sous-Lieutenant Blancharde*, Mr. Farrington," Peter introduced them.

"How do you do. I remember Mr. Peter when he was just a schoolboy. And Mr. Hans-Jörg, now there's a proper gentleman. And how is Mr. Hans-Jörg, Mr. Peter? Well, I trust?"

"I trust."

"It's such a pleasure to see an old client. We're getting nothing but Johnny-come-latelies these days. Dreadful! Even Americans. Oh—excuse me—I mean..."

"That's all right, Farrington."

"No-one understands a proper fit these days." The old

tailor looked at Peter's new uniform and touched the flare of the jacket.

"You could do better than that, Mr. Peter. I believe I could find a bolt of twill for you. They don't make the pinks anymore, you know, but I have some put aside for special customers."

"Oh, no. I never get a chance to wear these—"

"You can't go around like that. How about a nice blue suit? Your measurements must be considerably changed. Let me see!"

Peter laughed, embarrassed, and let the man measure him.

"I take it you're accepting American currency?" he smiled.

"Oh, whatever you say, sir. Your credit is always good here. And of course, I'm looking forward to serving Mr. Hans-Jörg again when things get back to normalcy."

"My grandfather used to have his cutaways made here," Peter smiled at Marie.

"Oh, your great-grandfather too, Mr. Peter. We have served a select clientele for many generations."

"Well, be that as it may, you go ahead and pick out some shirts and ties for me, Farrington. Although I don't know when I will get a chance to wear them..."

"Oh, that's quite all right, Mr. Peter. They'll be ready whenever you say."

Peter escaped into the weak February sunshine, still laughing.

"Actually, I just went in there to say hello."

"You never cease to astound me, *Herr Leutnant*."

They went up another street and Peter peered at the numbers on the buildings until he spotted a building with a flag which had a red cross superimposed on a white ground, the opposite to the Swiss flag.

"Marie, I wonder if you'd wait a moment for me. I'll be right out."

"Of course, *cherie*," she smiled, making a mental note of their whereabouts.

"I won't be a moment."

Peter went into the building and stopped at the front desk.

"Yes, lieutenant. Can I help you?"

"Hello. I wonder if you would could send a postal card for me . . . to an old friend in Switzerland." Peter took out the post card he had written at his hotel.

"I suppose it's possible. We do maintain liaison through Lisbon. May I see it?"

Peter handed over the card.

Dear Vreneli,

I've tried again and again to get to you, but the war conspires to keep us apart. Soon it will be two years away from you and away from home. Yet, I think of you every day. I hope you will be waiting for me.

Love,
Peter

"Certainly. Lieutenant. It seems harmless enough."

"Thank you very much." Peter smiled and rejoined Marie on the sidewalk.

Chapter 43

They went to the Old Vic that night. "Hamlet" was playing. Peter knew it from Heine's *Sein oder nicht sein* translation, while Marie could remember *"être, ou ne pas être, dormir, rêver, peut-être..."*

As they emerged from the theatre into the darkened, bomb-shattered streets, the spell of the pentameter was still upon them, and Peter brooded on the tragedy of the doomed Nordic Prince and his fate.

They had one of the river suites at the Savoy, and when they came into the lobby, through the double, blackout-curtained entryway, they were surprised to hear the strains of music coming from the cafe.

They stood for a moment at the top of the steps leading into the gaily-festooned room with its myriad of dancing strangers, and they were still under Shakespeare's spell.

"I suppose the Germans are dancing tonight at the Ritz in Paris."

"And at Borcher's in Berlin."

"And somewhere, perhaps, Jean is looking up at the stars."

They went, hand in hand, to the lift that took them up to their suite.

Peter had a shower, and then put his trench coat on over his shoulders as he looked out the open window at the shadows of London below him. He heard Marie flick off the light as she came from the bath, and the room was in darkness, lit only by a bomber's moon. The docks, the ships on the Thames, the houses of Parliament stood out only as black shadows on the gray.

He felt her arm around his waist, her head on his shoulder. Months of war in the desert, and more months of training for war on parachute jumps and on obstacle courses in the open air of Scotland had turned Peter into a different man—different by far from the contemplative

199

and reserved student he had been. His body was young and hard, at the peak of its physical maturity, and he turned to Marie with a smile, lifted her up and carried her to the canopied bed.

In a broom closet on the floor below two technicians and a red-faced Colonel smiled as they listened through earphones to the steady bounce of a squeaky bed, an ear-shattering climax, then silence and a few low murmurs. Colonel Smythe rubbed his hands together and leered.

"Now," he said, "*now* we'll hear something."

Upstairs Peter turned on his back, holding Marie's hand, and stared at the ceiling.

"It's no good, Marie," he said. "We're making love, but we're thinking of two different people. Sometimes I almost feel you speaking to Jean, and often I close my eyes and think of Vreneli. It's no good."

"You're right, darling," Marie sighed.

Downstairs Colonel Smythe jumped up in irritation. "You're getting all this?" he asked one of the stenographers. "Why didn't someone tell me they'd be speaking French? You can't trust these bloody foreigners. I've wasted the whole evening." He picked up his coat, hat and gloves. "I want a transcript on my desk in the morning. And in English, too!" He opened the door of the broom closet and stalked out majestically, slamming it behind him.

Chapter 44

The O.S.S. resident operative was seated with the American Ambassador to Switzerland in their Embassy in Berne. In his hand he held a postal card. It had been tested for every type of secret ink and scrutinized for microdots.

"I wonder if you could go over to see this girl," he said. "Her fiance is in the U.S. Army, but it's a very delicate situation. I have an appointment tomorrow with this Oelrich's brother in Basel. This situation with the girl is rather different. You have an official position here, Sam. You could handle this, while I can't."

"All right. I suppose I could drive over there. But what about this other matter? It's a lot of money, and you'd be risking a lot of lives. You could get us all thrown out of this country, or tossed into jail. I don't want to sit out the war in a Swiss jail."

"Officially, you need take no notice until it's a *fait accompli.* Of course, I hope we can achieve our ends without shedding blood. But you can't make an omelet . . ."

Sam Woods was decidedly unhappy. "We'd better not crush too many eggs. After all, we're not at war with Switzerland."

"We might as well be. If the Germans have a good supply of those Flak 41's when we land in France, there'll be no tank movement possible."

"Well—I can take no official cognizance of your duties here. That's all I can say, your brother notwithstanding."

"That is all we ask. Just have that check ready. And if you wouldn't mind seeing this girl—it can't do any harm to do a favor to someone who may be influential after the war."

"Certainly."

The O.S.S. man took a second class ticket on the train to Basel. Hunched in a corner of the compartment in tweeds and puffing on an odiferous pipe that stained his graying mustache a tobacco brown, he might have been mistaken for a modest businessman of any nationality. His grayness blended into the background with the anonymity of the perfect spy.

He maintained his contacts with the S.S. in Switzerland, and he regularly met his agents in a little café in Zurich where they played chess and sipped cups of ersatz wartime coffee. But this assignment was a different matter. It irritated him that a German cannon factory could operate openly and without camouflage in the middle of the war and remain impervious to Allied air power. He was aware that they also made proximity fuses for the British and licenced their guns to be produced in English factories, but he was also aware that any armaments they made could also be supplied by American factories now that the U-boat menace had abated, and he had no patience with the British attitude of respect for the neutrality of Swiss soil.

As he took the tram over the Rhine bridge to the Basel suburb known as Oelrich, he reviewed in his memory the British Intelligence summaries he had read. The British had been in constant touch with Oelrich, but to no avail. The O.S.S. man felt that the time had come for someone to stop this factory from producing more guns for the enemy. And he was the man to do it.

Hans-Jörg Oelrich received him with a mystified cordiality.

"How do you do, Mr. York. Come in." He ushered him to a seat beside his father's desk, and sat back in his swivel chair.

"Your note said you were here on behalf of the Bethlehem Steel Company. We licensed some designs to them, but that was years ago."

"Actually I'm here on quite another matter. My

202

principals insist that you stop producing the Flak 41's for Germany. We have been reading the reports of Capt. Harley-Ffythe, and we are tired of being put off."

"Oh, you're a friend of Percival's?"

"Not exactly. Our interests sometimes diverge in spite of our wartime alliance. I am told that you have ignored every effort, even including threats to have your own brother shot while trying to escape captivity—and even the threat of postwar proscription."

"You can't be serious, old chap." It was very nearly Hans-Jörg's first dealings with an American, and he combined a continental disdain for upstarts with a fear of the unknown, uncouth power these blunt and blundering fools might have. The rapidity with which this gray nonentity had come to the point without any pretense of mannered fencing put him off.

"Let me make you a promise, Mr. Oelrich. If you don't stop production, we will bomb this plant into rubble."

"You couldn't. Think of all the innocent Swiss civilians you would kill."

"Accidents happen every day in wartime. We can always make reparations, but we cannot replace American lives lost storming your guns. Not at any price. And we don't intend to."

"Reparations? That's an interesting approach."

"And so is your approach, Mr. Oelrich."

"The dollar is quite a good currency."

"Mr. York" stoked his pipe and had a fleeting thought of a mercenary German soldier named Yorck who had fought his ancestors.

"The dollar is a currency backed by gold. On the other hand—we are not in the habit of bombing neutral civilians."

"It has happened—in France, in Holland..."

"Of course, there are always certain shifts when the workers are not there. Fires must be banked, and so forth..."

"Mister . . . York, isn't it? Perhaps we have a basis for discussion. Yes. I think I begin to see where we could come to a meeting of the minds. You Americans have the reputation of being good businessmen. Now if we could—"

Chapter 45

Hans-Jörg Oelrich looked around his office for the last time. It had been his father's office and his grandfather's before that, and one of his earliest memories was of coming there as a child.

"Ugly old brickpile," he muttered as he took several German medals out of his safe, threw their boxes on the floor, and dropped the shining baubles into his overcoat pocket.

He looked out of the window for the last time. The factory fires were banked for their annual cleaning, and all the workers were on furlough. He had even managed to have a Swiss national defense drill moved up a few days so that the Rhine Bridge was closed off and the only people on the entire premises were himself and his father. Of course, old Hans wasn't aware of much these days, but he would be safe in his isolated mansion. Hans-Jörg felt that his father would be proud of him if he could have understood what he had arranged.

"To be finally rid of this whole mess!" He smiled as he went down to get into his Mercedes for the short ride home. "And to have even the demolition paid for. And then to start all over, with all new equipment, all new factories—underground, if I wish, like Peenemunde." Germany, England—they were all being bombed into rubble. There would be more than ample demand for a new factory with experienced workers to supply arms to fight the Bolsheviks once this mess was over. What was it Zaharoff said? He tried to recall the old Russian who was one of the first worldwide merchants of cannon.

"Worldwide!" he smiled as he drove out the deserted gates for the last time. A worldwide concern! Swiss workers, American dollars, and German know-how.

He heard a menacing drone coming from the leaden sky, and he glanced at his watch. It wasn't even dark yet.

He turned his car lights off and stopped to peer out of the window. A flight of flying fortresses were coming right towards him on a heading from the northwest. He looked at his watch again in disbelief.

"The damned fools are early! Can't they do anything right?"

And then his world exploded with the fury of thousand-pound bombs blasting acres of factories into waves of flying steel and brick. The shock waves blasted the heavy Mercedes into the air.

"The damned fools, they might have killed me!" Hans threw his car into gear and raced for home. As the Mercedes skidded on the deserted tramway tracks Hans-Jörg looked ahead to see his house lit up like a Christmas tree. Every light seemed to be burning in the dusk. And running down the road from their tiny island, stumbling on the shoulders of the road, with his white hair flying in wild disorder, came his father.

"Papa, papa! Stop! You can't go over there." Vast explosions echoed behind him.

"They're destroying my factory! They're blowing everything up! Stop them! We've got to stop them!"

Hans got out and tried to force the old man into the car.

"No, father, go back. It's all right."

"They're blowing up my factories. The Germans are coming! We've got to stop them. They can't do this!"

Hans-Jörg slapped him twice, hard.

"Shut up, you old fool. I'm taking you home." He pushed his father into the car, and the old man suddenly stopped protesting, his blue eyes staring in front of him, uncomprehending, as Armegeddon blasted his factories into oblivion.

Shock waves still rocked the heavy car with explosive fury as Hans-Jörg raced to his house, got his father into the great hall, and searched for the fuses that would shut off all the lights.

The momentary darkness came just before the two bombs blasted first the roadway and then the entire west wing of the house, but Hans-Jörg got a final glimpse of his father in the middle of the great marble hall, lit by the explosion, his white hair straggling in mad disarray as huge blocks of granite began to fall around him.

And then he saw no more.

Chapter 46

The Allied Interservice Assessment Board, depleted by a number of members who were sojourning on the continent, was assembled for its weekly meeting. Among the items on the agenda was the analysis of the records and prisoner interrogations of the Seventh Field Engineer Battalion, which had been attached to General Rommel's staff in Normandy, the analysis of the German Naval files captured at Tambach, and a discussion of the methods for dealing with the new portable V-2 launching pads in Germany. Almost in passing, the O.S.S. representative mentioned an intercepted top secret German army circular.

"The O.K.W. is looking for English-speaking volunteers to serve under Skorzeny."

"What for?"

"That's what I'd like to know."

"Who are they going to kidnap now? Talk about gangster methods!"

"Perhaps we should re-inforce the King's Lifeguards, and not let the P.M. go kiting off to France."

"I'd like to see you stop him."

"They're calling for volunteers to apply to Skorzeny's training camp. Perhaps *we* should send someone. We can cut it as an O.K.W. order out of Berlin."

"I shouldn't care to send a man on a mission like that."

"We have no one who could play the part of a Nazi officer."

"We *have* a German officer. Up in Scotland."

"That Oelrich fellow? He's been out of the war for eighteen months now. They'd catch him in a minute."

"They'll be getting troops from all over Europe. They won't know each other."

"Frankly, if they catch him—he's expendable."

"So is his report."

"If that's the way you feel about it, I take it I am authorized to send him."

They went on to other matters.

It was Colonel Briggs of the O.S.S. who was put in charge of Peter's fate. He sent for all available records including several reports from Switzerland, Peter's Anglo-American training records, and his narrative of his service with the German Army. Then he sent for Peter himself. When Peter entered the room for the interview, he came to attention and saluted.

"Hello, Oelrich. Have a seat."

"Thank you, Colonel Briggs."

"You may have wondered why I sent for you."

"Yes?"

"To put it bluntly, we think it's about time you earn your salt." The Colonel looked Peter up and down.

"A man can live pretty well up in Scotland on a Lieutenant's pay," he said.

"Even better on a Captain's pay."

"Be that as it may—before we get into particulars, perhaps you could tell me a little about your service in Africa."

Peter narrated what there was to be told.

"Very well. That's enough. Your English has improved quite a bit."

"Thank you."

"A slight Scotch accent. You might pass for British, or Scottish. You could say you had a Scottish teacher in Switzerland."

"Why should I say that?"

Instead of answering, the Colonel picked up Peter's American army records.

"Your assessment scores at Bletchley were excellent. You're a good leader, resourceful, painstaking, careful. Only in one respect is there a deficiency. Can you guess what that is?"

"Colonel, if I have learned one thing in my military . . ."

"It's *motivation*," the Colonel shouted. "Are you for us or against us? Do you want to fight or not?"

Peter watched the red fade from the Colonel's face. Apparently an answer was now expected of him.

"Colonel Briggs, I am not pro-German. I was forced into the Wehrmacht. Nor was it my idea to become a spy. On the other hand, taking training courses is better than being a prisoner of war."

The Colonel was not terribly satisfied with that answer.

"Field Marshal Keitel has sent out a secret memorandum to the Wehrmacht asking for English-speaking volunteers to serve under Colonel Skorzeny. You know who Skorzeny is?"

"He's the man who rescued Mussolini."

"*Kidnapped* Mussolini."

"And you want me to volunteer for Skorzeny's group?"

"Yes. All we want is for you to parachute into Germany, proceed to Friedenthal, find out what they're planning, and radio us. Then you may get out in any way you can."

"They'd catch me in a minute. I've been out of Europe for two years."

"We can take care of that. There'll be officers from all over Europe there. We can get orders cut out of Berlin detailing you from the officers' replacement center in Frankfurt."

"And where am I supposed to have been for the last two years? Any identity you give me—I might see somebody from his unit."

"I have the best identity in the world for you. *Oberleutnant Peter Oelrich* of the Seventh Field Engineers Battalion. We captured the whole bunch in Normandy, including personnel records. You're listed as missing, believed dead. But we can put you into the records of that repple depple . . ."

"What?"

"Replacement depot. It will work. And I want you to do it."

There was a silence. Peter was very doubtful. The Colonel decided to take another tack. From his file of O.S.S. reports he extracted a postal card. It was in Peter's handwriting. He turned it over and over on his desk.

"We have contacted Vreneli Schmid for you," he said.

"Wonderful! Is she all right?"

"She's fine. She's teaching violin at the conservatory in Zurich now. You know—up near the University."

"Yes, I know." He could imagine Vreneli walking up the curved driveway to the Conservatory, violin case under her arm, her hands jammed into her pockets.

"Zurich itself is busier than ever. A lot of horse-drawn traffic, but there's still plenty of gasoline. They bring it in through Liechtenstein." The Colonel tapped the postcard on his desk and then went on.

"Of course, this mission *is* dangerous. It's strictly a volunteer mission. We'll understand if you don't care to take the risk. After all, you can get killed crossing the street, these days."

Peter looked down at the hat in his lap with its shiny silver bar glinting in the light.

"Perhaps you're right, sir. It's time for me to earn my salary. I'll take the job." Peter looked out the window at a walled-in garden. "However," he said, "I'd like to ask for one special favor. I'd like to write a letter to Miss Schmid. You could even deliver it to her after I leave. Would you do that?"

Colonel Briggs looked at the postcard in his hand. It seemed little enough to ask—perhaps a condemned man's last wish.

"All right, Oelrich, I'll recommend it. I can't promise that my superior officers will approve, but I'll recommend it."

That night Peter sat down in his barren bachelor's quarters and took pen in hand. The letter was hard, to write.

8. IX. 1944

Dearest Vreneli,

I am hoping this letter will get through to you. This war seems to go on and on. Each day without you is like a year in purgatory. When I think back of our days together, it's like a paradise lost.

They've asked me to go on a long trip. It's not dangerous, but I don't know when I'll be back. When I do return, I'll come to you, no matter where you are. I'll find you, and I'll marry you. This is a terrible way to propose, isn't it?

But I want to know that you'll be waiting for me. It will help me to get through. I love you, and there is nothing in this world I want more than to be with you. There is nothing more in this world I could ask for.

I've seen other places now. Perhaps I'm no longer the nice young man you know. But if you'll have me, I want to spend the rest of my life with you. I've never known a happiness, a contentment like that I had with you.

Remember that I loved you, and I love you now, and I will always love you. Never stop thinking of

Peter

Chapter 47

While Peter's orders to Friedenthal, near Berlin, were being inserted into the O.K.W. teleprinter traffic, and copies forged in England, Peter spent the better part of two weeks preparing for his assignment. He practiced radio telegraphy with the latest in miniaturized senders, a new model built to look like a German portable radio. It even received on the AM band. He memorized a simple code and broadcast schedules. He got his choice in officer's equipment and clothing from the prison camp in Scotland where the pitiful remnants of the 7th E.B. were imprisoned.

Painstakingly, he studied the battalion war diary and personnel records. They were appalling. Major Dreieck was dead. Lieutenant Wolfschmidt was long since dead. Sergeant Horner, and most of the others he had known. The battalion had survived the long retreat with Rommel in Africa, and had been reconstituted in Frankfurt before being posted to coastal defense under Rommel in Normandy. They had spent six months designing and installing tank traps and underwater obstacles on the Normandy coast. But when the invasion finally came, they had been decimated by air attack, and then surrounded and captured by Patton's tanks when they retreated. Peter went down the lists of soldiers he had known, and memorized their fates. He memorized the names of replacements, and studied their personnel files. With the help of the O.S.S. he concocted a story about his escape across France during the retreat, and a tale of reporting to the Officers Replacement Center in Frankfurt.

"Would you like to go up to Ringway and take a parachute refresher course?" Colonel Briggs asked.

"If it's all right with you, Colonel, I'd prefer not to practice any more of those jumps from four hundred feet.

There's no sense in practicing something you have to do perfectly every time. Too many broken arms and legs from that height. Anyway, I get very nervous with the British. They have a certain fanatical dislike for anyone who speaks German."

"I'm afraid you'll have to be nervous then. Our only night fighters and jumpmasters trained for this are all British."

"God save the King!"

In London, a Colonel Smythe was consulting with his commanding officer in an office overlooking the Horse Guards Parade. The General was crisp and correct in the red tabs that marked his General Staff appointment.

"And you're convinced that this—this Oelrich is a double agent?"

"My dear Roger, I can smell a Nazi from a hundred feet. This fellow is up to no good."

"Old boy, we can't risk offending our noble allies from across the water. It was foolish of you to let them take him into their army."

"We didn't dream they would be foolish enough to use him on a mission."

"They're such amateurs! So trusting. So naive. And I can't tell you how irritated the Chief is with this bombing of Basel." The general stroked his white mustache. "You can do what you please," he said, "but we musn't offend the Americans."

"Accidents happen on those spy-flights. I'm sure I could arrange one for him."

"Officially, of course, I can't give you any written orders. But there are casualties every day. Actually, it might give Canaris a good object lesson to have one of his spies drop in without a parachute."

"Consider it done, sir."

"I don't want to know anything about it, Cecil."

"Of course not, Roger."

Word was received from Germany that duplicate travel orders could be forged, and that Peter was accepted for Skorzeny's training camp at Friedenthal. The moon was waning, and no better time for the jump could be expected.

Peter was dressed to the teeth with his parachute, portable radio, sidearms, bedroll, two "looted" bottles of French cognac, some drafting tools, Iron Cross, and spare uniform. He was perspiring in the cool autumn evening as he waited to board the black shadowy airplane that was to take him to Germany.

He checked his billfold again for his military identification cards, Deutschmarks, souvenir occupation francs, a picture of Rommel decorating Major Dreieck, paybook and small change. Then he checked his parachute again.

"All set, Oelrich?" Colonel Briggs looked concerned. He had driven down with a British colonel to see him off. "Anything we can do for you?"

"My—friend Vreneli. But I don't know what you could tell her."

"We'll tell her you're alive and well, and looking forward to the end of the war."

"That's God's truth."

They went to the plane and were met by the jumpmaster, a sergeant-major.

"You've got your orders, sergeant?"

The British colonel smiled and patted the man's arm.

"Right you are, Sir."

"*Bon voyage*, Oar-lick," the colonel said.

"Don't take any chances in reporting, Oelrich. You've got the schedule. There's no hurry, but we do want to know what they're doing there."

They shook hands again and closed the door. The inside of the plane was black as death.

Peter was the only passenger. The plane headed out

over a runway lit by two distant guidelights. In a few minutes they had climbed above the cloud cover and headed east over France.

Once they had reached their flying height, the sergeant lit a cigarette. His wind-burned face and the trim on his uniform gleamed red in the Mephistophelian gloom.

Peter looked up at the static line, and down at the well, the hole in the floor through which he would soon make his exit. Then he checked his watch, closed his eyes, and tried to think in German again after all the many weary months.

A sudden rush of wind made Peter open his eyes. The sergeant-major was opening the hole, and smiling up at him wickedly. Peter checked the time and the air speed repeater, and stood up to stretch and get his body moving.

"Right-oh, Kraut. Keep your pecker up!"

Performing the drill automatically, Peter handed his ripcord to the sergeant for attachment to the static line, sat down, and dangled his legs in the hole. He stared down at the black void that was Germany as the sergeant came behind him to push if his equipment got stuck. The plane slowed perceptibly.

"All right, *Leutnant*, GO!"

Peter automatically checked his ripcord and it pulled free from the static line. He twisted and grabbed, and pulled the laughing, screaming sergeant with him down the hole.

The slipstream hit with a sledgehammer blow. Peter kicked free and clawed for his ripcord. No sooner did the parachute pop open than he banged into tree branches that broke his fall.

All was silence. Only the drone of a climbing airplane disturbed the night. Full of pain, Peter checked himself, and then his equipment, and gathered his small chute together before he climbed down.

By the time he found the sergeant's body, motionless in the middle of a shallow pond, there was no time left for digging. Peter dropped the chute and spread it out so that it would appear that the sergeant had had a malfunction. It was four kilometers to the train station at Rockitnitz, and dawn was coming.

Chapter 48

Peter walked rapidly over the frozen ground beside the road to Rockitnitz. Daylight was just beginning to break. He heard a cock crowing in the distance. A Simca staff car roared past him, but otherwise he saw no signs of life.

At the Rockitnitz railroad station more than a dozen persons were huddled sleepily on wooden benches near the pot-bellied stove that warmed the waiting room. Peter thought he recognized one of the civilians, an old man with a straggly white mustache who sat huddled in a corner reading the *Völkische Beobachter*. Yet there was nothing for it but to stalk on by, put down his valise and ask the ticket seller for a first class ticket to Berlin-Friedenthal.

"Ja wohl, Herr Oberleutnant. Moment, bitte."

While the railway clerk leafed through schedules and timetables to find the fare to Friedenthal, Peter felt the hair rising on the back of his neck. He remembered now who the old man was. He was a salesman who had called on his father in the late thirties. Peter had seen him several times in waiting rooms or conference rooms at the Oelrich factory.

"Yes sir, Lieutenant. Here you are."

While Peter fumbled with his notecase, the clerk glanced at his Iron Cross and his uniform. He then examined with interest the money Peter gave him.

"Occupation marks."

"Yes. I'm just recently in from France."

"Well, I suppose they're good."

Peter picked up his valise and backed clumsily toward the door leading to the train platform, trying to keep his back toward the corner where the old salesman sat.

The platform was deserted except for an old reserve corporal on guard duty. Peter put down his valise, looked at his watch, and put his hands in his pockets to keep warm.

"Papiere bitte, Herr Oberleutnant."

The overage corporal had piggish eyes peering from a lined, puffy face. Peter dug into his tunic pockets for his forged travel orders and his Wehrpass, and then dug into another pocket for one of the bottles of French brandy. The corporal cast his eyes over the papers.

"Chilly this morning," Peter said, taking a swig.

The corporal grunted, eyeing the bottle.

"Care for some?"

"Sure." The corporal wiped off the top of the bottle with his palm and drank down a long pull. "Mmm—real French stuff."

"Liberated by me, personally."

He handed back the papers. "Afrika Korps," he muttered.

"Yes."

"I lost a cousin there."

Peter stuffed the papers into his pocket, keeping his back toward the windows of the waiting room.

"Train on time?"

"It should be. There was a break in the line yesterday, but they've got a Yugoslavian gang out fixing it."

Others were coming out on the platform now. The corporal saluted and moved on, checking papers on a random basis. Peter sidled to the edge of the platform and kept his back turned to the crowd. He felt decidedly uncomfortable at the medley of German dialects that assaulted his ears. He kept hearing new slang words that were hard to figure out.

The train chugged into the station on schedule, and Peter found his way through crowded corridors to a first class compartment. The plush seats were old and worn, but still decorated with the Reichsbahn antimacassars. Peter put his bag carefully up on the rack, made himself

219

comfortable by a window, and pulled his hat down over his eyes to feign sleep.

Once the train got started he slept for several hours. Businessmen and farmers came and went during the day, for the train seemed to stop at every little station. His tickets were taken, and once an S.S. enlisted man checked his papers. Peter began to relax and lower his guard.

The conductor was calling the Berlin stops when he re-checked Peter's ticket.

"Berlin-Friedenthal next stop, *Herr Oberleutnant*."

Peter hooked up his tunic, got down the valise, and made for the exit. It was still open country they were going through, pleasant wooded hills and pastures. Friedenthal—Peaceful Valley—was only a small suburban railway stop.

A young Luftwaffe lieutenant got off at Friedenthal too. Otherwise the platform was deserted until an S.S. corporal came out of the waiting room.

"Friedenthal?" Peter asked.

"Yes. Lieutenant, you too?"

"Orders for Friedenthal."

"All right. Let's go. I have a Volkswagen waiting."

They loaded their bags into the car and climbed in. It was a short ride through a tiny village and out to what once must have been an old farm estate. The guards waved them through the gates without stopping them.

"Adjutant's office, right over there." The corporal stopped by a converted stable, and they got out. The fresh-faced Luftwaffe officer held the door for Peter.

Signs painted in old-fashioned script identified the various offices leading off a central corridor as being for ordnance, engineering and liaison, and some were identified with numbers only. At the end of the corridor was the adjutant's office. Peter knocked and they entered.

"Yes, gentlemen? Are you volunteers?"

"Yes."

"I'll take your papers into Captain Radl. Have a seat."

They sat down on a sofa, and Peter picked up a copy of the *Berliner Illustrierte*. It featured a picture story on Rommel's state funeral. Peter found it depressing.

"Are you one of the English-speaking volunteers?" the Luftwaffe officer asked.

"Mmm..."

"I hope they're not too tough. I've forgotten everything I ever knew about English."

"Uhuh."

"Captain Radl will see you now, *Herr Oberleutnant.*"

Peter walked into the inner office and found an old-young captain leafing through his travel orders and Wehrpass.

"Oelrich? Sit down. Welcome to Friedenthal."

"Thank you, Captain."

"So—you're an engineering officer? How good is your English?"

"It's pretty fair, I think. I had three years in school, and took a few summer trips with my father to England and Scotland," he lied.

"Could you pass for American or English?"

"Scottish maybe—for a little while. Not American."

"Well—we'll see. You come sit with me at dinner tonight and I'll introduce you to the chief of staff. At any rate, we can always use another engineering officer." He noted Peter's Iron Cross with approval. "We always have a lot of projects going. Do you know anything about Ami equipment?"

"We used a lot of enemy material in Africa. I once examined a Sherman."

"A Sherman? Could you read a field manual on the Sherman tank?"

"Certainly. Anything technical."

"Well, maybe we'll get somewhere. You wouldn't believe the quality of the officers we've been getting:

Sergeant," he yelled, "give Lieutenant Oelrich a room assignment. Dinner's at seven-thirty, Oelrich. I'll see you then."

"Yes sir. Thank you, sir."

Peter retrieved his bag and followed the sergeant's directions to a new-looking Bachelor Officers' Quarters that fronted on a small airfield. Peter found his room, hung up his extra uniform, plugged in his portable radio and turned on some music. After taking a quick shower he put his feet back into his heavy jackboots, put on his fresh tunic, and went out to find the officer's mess.

Radl was at a table with three other officers including a beefy giant of a man wearing the Knight's Cross, who could only be Skorzeny.

"Yes. Oelrich, isn't it? Otto, a new man from France. Engineering officer. Knows English."

"Hello," Skorzeny half stood and shook his hand, and then went back to his conversation with an S.S. officer who had only nodded.

"And this is our chief of staff, Baron von Foelkersam."

"How do you do. Have a seat."

"Oelrich says he knows some English. I thought you'd like to meet him before we assign him."

"Fine." Von Foelkersam turned his head away to continue his conversation with the other officers about the Russian campaign, leaving Peter to eat his soup and enjoy the black bread he had gone without in England, not realizing how much he missed it.

Radl broke up a piece of bread and swished it around in his soup plate.

"Old Russian hands. Sepp is just in from the Russian front. The boss served there in '42; and Adrian was with the Brandenburg Regiment. His grandfather was a Russian admiral."

Peter looked around the room. The furnishings were by no means luxurious, but the officers looked young and

222

alert. They wore every conceivable uniform in the German services.

Major Von Foelkersam broke off his conversation and began asking Peter questions in English. His command of the language was fluent and British.

"Have you had any contact with the Americans?"

"Very little," Peter recited the story he had concocted of the retreat of the 7th E.B. across France. He hadn't expected to be telling it in English.

"How about written English?"

"I'm good on technical works."

"How are you at writing reports?"

"So-so."

"Radl will help you. He's our red tape expert. Listen—we've got idiots coming in here from all over the Reich who claim they can speak English. I'll put you in charge of sorting them out. You find another written test for them—I've got an old Professor to help you with that—and interview each of them in English, and then grade their English and assign them. Radl—can you give Oelrich a sergeant for the paper work?"

"Yes. I've got a new one you can have. Used to be a company clerk."

"All right. I'll take you over after dinner. There's a lot of reading I want you to do, too."

He went back to his questions about the latest developments on the Russian front, leaving Peter still mystified about the purpose of all the English language expertise being assembled.

As they walked to the chief of staff's office after dinner, Peter found out more about him. Adrian Ritter von Foelkersam had served on the Russian front in the crack Brandenburg division. "But they started throwing us away on ordinary front-line duty. Some of the best brains in Germany building road blocks. So when I heard about Skorzeny's commandos, I transferred over."

When they got to Foelkersam's office they put the night duty officer to work. "Get this man a desk—no, two desks and an office, and send him the whole English-speaking load." Foelkersam gave him and Peter a stack of orders and rosters on the English-speaking volunteers.

"Classify the whole lot. Send the best to translator's school. Good men you can assign as specialists—tanks, infantry, what have you. Send them to our training batallions, or to the schools. Make your reports to Radl."

"Now here—" the chief of staff handed him another stack of reports, some in English, some in German. "We're operating a sabotage school, a weapons school, and so forth. You go through these reports and familiarize yourself with the British methods. I'll have you take a look at our schools next week to see if you can suggest any improvements based on your reading."

Peter gathered up a stack of papers and piled them on the desk the duty officer had assigned him, and took the others back to his quarters for study.

They turned out to be reports based on prisoner interrogations, and in some cases training manuals for Ringway, Pemberley and schools up in Scotland—the very courses Peter had attended. There were complete training manuals on small arms, radio telegraphy and coding. Peter skimmed through them and felt content that at least this part of his work would be easy.

Chapter 49

Von Foelkersam was already in his office when Peter reported to work the next day, met his sergeant and the old man who gave the English tests. "Do you have a place to give the tests?"

"A room downstairs."

"Let me see one of the tests."

Peter studied it. It ran rather quickly from the elements of grammar to paragraphs from Shaw and Maugham upon which there were reading comprehension questions.

"Let's add a page of military terminology . . . in British and American. Sergeant—you make a list with words like 'truck,' 'tank,' 'rifle,' 'machine gun,' and so forth, and get them translated. Professor, you make up a set of duplicate words with their translation: like 'spanner' and 'wrench,' 'petrol' and 'gasoline,' 'bonnet' and 'hood,' and so forth."

"Yes, sir."

There was a man waiting at Peter's desk. Peter made a sign that he would be there in a moment.

"How about Americans? Do we have anyone who knows idiomatic American?"

"We did have a naval rating, but he's off on a small arms course."

"See if you can get him back. Check with Captain Radl."

"Yes, sir."

Peter sat down at his desk and introduced himself to the Wehrmacht sergeant who was waiting. *"Wehrpass, bitte."*

The sergeant handed over his paybook.

"Hermann Goering Division—you were in Sicily?" Peter asked.

"Yes."

"You fought against Monty?"

"Against Patton's tank division."

225

"And you know English?"

"Two years in high school."

Peter began asking his questions in English. "How are the Americans, good soldiers?"

"Yes, Lieutenant."

"Did you examine any Sherman tanks?"

"Yes, Lieutenant."

"Have they added to the armor plating in the front of it?"

"Yes, Lieutenant."

"Were you in a line company, or what?"

"Would you repeat that over?"

"Did you fight in a line company?"

"Yes, Lieutenant."

Peter began to get suspicious. "How would you like to jump in the river?" he asked.

"Yes, Lieutenant."

A few more questions established that the sergeant's English was rudimentary at best. Peter noted it on his record and sent the man to take a written test, but he suspected that the sergeant would be more valuable in a regular infantry assault company than in any other capacity.

As the days wore on into weeks, Peter found that his interviews discovered few volunteers who spoke English well at all, but that they uncovered a great deal of information about troop movements, new equipment, and tactics. Peter made notes on these bits of information, coded them and sent them off to London using the miniature sending equipment concealed in his portable radio. He sent it off at his regularly assigned hours, but had to wait several days before a confirmation of reception came through a code phrase used on a certain Radio London broadcast.

The commando courses being operated at Friedenthal didn't seem very serious when compared with the ones

Peter had taken in England. The students were willing enough, but the instructors were half-hearted. When, from his limited knowledge of codes and coding, Peter recommended that certain methods be discontinued, saying he had read about them in prisoner interrogations, the non-com in charge of the school had only one comment. "Oh—it's not important. We'll never use them anyway. You can always get access to an Enigma machine, and that's unbreakable." Peter didn't find it worthwhile to argue, although he reported it to von Foelkersam.

At the small arms school he was able to show the instructors new methods for clearing jams on the Sten gun, to show them how to keep a Thompson submachine gun in working order, and how to load the circular drum efficiently. The young officer in charge soon came to call upon Peter as an expert on foreign ordnance and tactics. When Peter showed them the American method of shooting from the hip with handguns, however, they dismissed them as "gangster methods."

Coming back from lunch one day, Peter spied a new Sherman tank which had been captured in France, and stopped to inspect it to see what changes had been made. After climbing in and out and banging on the armor plate, he found he had been joined by Skorzeny, who was banging the armor plate too.

"Good afternoon, Colonel."

"Oh, hello. You're Oelrich, aren't you?"

"Yes, sir."

"Foelkersam says you're quite an expert on ordnance. Know anything about these things? They're having trouble getting effective hits on them."

"I think this is case-hardened steel. I've never seen it before." Peter stopped, for he wasn't sure how much was known about case-hardened steel in Germany.

"Where did you learn about that?"

"A technical paper, I think."

"It would make good roadway supports for bridging."

"Tensile strength is excellent, Colonel."

They went on to discuss the angle at which a Flak 41 would have to hit the tank to penetrate, and from that to further talk of bridging.

"We used some steel-reinforced concrete on a bridge I did in Vienna," Skorzeny said.

"Did you see the new Bailey bridge the Americans have?"

"No. I've never been on the Western front."

"It's very practical. A good design." Peter went on to compare it with the FT104 and 105, and Skorzeny expressed considerable interest about the methods used for standardization of parts. It was getting late, however.

"Colonel, I wonder if you could excuse me. I have a man waiting for me in my office."

"Certainly. Perhaps we'll see you at dinner tonight."

"I'll look forward to it."

It wasn't until several days later that Peter saw Skorzeny again. It was after dinner one evening, and he saw von Foelkersam playing a chess game with the Colonel in a corner of the officer's mess. He went over to kibitz the game.

Foelkersam glanced at his watch, and made a few bad moves.

"Oh well. Do you play, Oelrich?"

"Yes, sir."

"You take over. I've got to get to the railhead. We're supposed to be getting in some Ami jeeps, and they won't last five minutes if I don't take charge of them personally. Do you mind, Otto?"

"Go ahead. Better you than me."

Pete sat down and immediately castled. Skorzeny began puzzling out a new strategy.

"How's our British brigade coming?" he asked.

"All right. I just wish someone would tell me what the purpose of this whole thing is."

"Oh—somebody's brainstorm. We're supposed to

supply a whole brigade to infiltrate the British and American lines during an attack—capture bridges and road junctions. In enemy uniforms."

"That sounds like a good way to get shot if captured. Especially if we ask them to speak English or American."

"Are they that bad?"

"Wouldn't last for two sentences, most of them."

"The latest is, we're supposed to be Americans—all of us."

"We don't have more than a couple dozen who can even begin to speak American, or even look American."

"Did you start that school affair?"

"Yes. We've got an ex-sailor who's trying teach the boys to walk and look like Amis, but it doesn't work very well. They keep clicking their heels together every time an officer walks by."

Peter lost his first chess game. They started another, and began talking about a new method for continuous welding of railroad tracks. From that they went on to discuss bridging innovations the Wehmacht had been trying.

It was a pleasant evening. Peter found that Skorzeny had had his own engineering office in Vienna before the *Anschluss*, and looked forward to returning there, and to seeing his wife and child more often. They drank the better part of a bottle of excellent French wine, before calling it a night. As they were leaving, Skorzeny slapped Peter on the back and called him by his first name.

"Thank you for the games, Colonel."

"Call me Otto."

"Yes sir. Good night, Otto."

"Good night, Peter."

As he walked back to his quarters, already composing his report in his mind, Peter realized that never before had a German field-grade officer asked him to call him by his first name. Even Dreieck, close as they had been, had never completely relaxed from military formality.

Chapter 50

"What do you think of that new officer, Adrian?"
Skorzeny was playing chess with his executive officer.

"He seems competent enough. A good engineering
officer, and he gets things done. His English is not all that
wonderful."

Skorzeny pondered a Sicilian defense.

"Tell me, Adrian, did you ever kill anyone?"

"Of course. What do you mean? I'm a soldier. You
were in Russia—you must have—you have a Knight's
Cross..."

"Yes, but I've never pulled a trigger. I've ordered others
to, but I never have."

"How strange."

A silence fell as von Foelkersam tried to plan an attack.
When he had finally moved, he started talking again.

"You're not a professional soldier. At the War College
they had lectures on that. They said that as many of as
25% of the troops on the line never actually fire at the
enemy, and officers even less. Our weapons aren't even
designed for killing the enemy. Pistols, swords, swagger
sticks, marshal's batons—they're for coercing the enlisted
men, not for attacking the enemy." He warmed to his
subject. "There are a lot of officers who consider it
beneath their dignity to shoot weapons. That's work for
the working men—the enlisted men. And there are a good
many men who just don't like killing."

"How do *you* feel about it?"

"It never bothered me. I don't lose any sleep."

It was Skorzeny's turn to move. He considered
carefully.

'What about this Oelrich fellow?" Foelkersam asked.

"I'm going to put him on staff rather than line. He
doesn't seem like a battle leader to me."

"Nobody thought you were either."

"Actually, I'm not. I've done more by not shooting than by shooting. People would rather talk, or obey orders, than shoot. I saved Schusnigg's life that way, years ago. I probably saved Mussolini's life by telling my men not to fire."

"And you think Oelrich is the same way?"

"That's the way he struck me."

"Then put him down as a staff engineering officer. That way you can keep your eye on him."

"I think I'll do that. Thank you for your advice."

Chapter 51

In London, Peter's report of the training of three battalions of English-speaking troops was disregarded. Smythe gave it as his opinion that Peter had become a double agent, and was feeding them false information mingled with true trivia. Colonel Briggs also found the idea of a large group disguised in an enemy uniforms to be beyond the realm of likelihood and didn't argue too vociferously for the distribution of reports.

"Bury it in the weekly intelligence digest," he told his subordinate officer. "That way we're covered. No one reads those damned things anyway."

Peter was spending more and more time with the various school detachments and helping engineering officers to get captured American and British equipment into working shape. For every American jeep they obtained and put into working order, two others had to be cannibalized. For some reason the distributor rotor was almost always missing on jeeps, and Peter made a casting so that they could manufacture their own.

American and British uniforms were being stored in a warehouse near the railhead at Friedenthal. Peter was sorting them out and translating a lot of American sizes into German clothes sizes one day when a messenger arrived from headquarters.

"You are to report to Colonel Skorzeny immediately."

Peter got into a jeep and drove to Skorzeny's office as quickly as he could. He wondered what the colonel had in mind.

Peter ran into the office and froze at attention.

"Oelrich! Get a couple uniforms and your kit and report back here in five minutes. We're flying to Hungary immediately." Skorzeny was dressed in civilian clothes and had on a gray wig with matching shaggy gray mustache.

"Yes, sir."

Peter sprinted for his quarters and quickly packed a uniform and a set of fatigues and steel helmet, and his shaving equipment. At the last moment he grabbed his portable radio.

When he got back to headquarters he found the Colonel still packing papers into a brief case. Skorzeny looked up. "Never mind the radio. You'll have a field radio. I changed my mind. You order up a two-ton truck and the troops Radl gives you and start driving. Register at the Hotel Breslau in Budapest. Wait there for further orders. If anyone asks, say you're from—the Adolf Hitler division on your way to the Eastern front—but it's top secret. *Radl*, cut orders to that effect and send them after him by courier."

"Yes, sir."

"Now get moving. You'll be my liaison. We're going to kidnap Admiral Horthy."

Peter got on the telephone to the motor pool to have a truck brought immediately, and then to his own office to summon his sergeant. When the sergeant arrived, Peter issued quick orders.

"You'll have to get the Professor to take over any last-minute volunteers who arrive, and you make sure Radl gets his report for classification and assignment. Oh—and lock this radio up in my desk. I don't want anybody fiddling with it while I'm gone."

It was a long and difficult drive in a bouncing truck full of armed commandos. Peter drove or acted as a co-pilot, reading the road maps, getting as much sleep as he could, and being thankful that there was no air strafing to be expected. A motorcycle courier overtook them in Bavaria with the forged orders.

When he arrived in Budapest, he looked at the hotel, and decided that it was too obvious to move in a group of armed German commandos. He drove to the railway yards where he commandeered a group of sidetracked sleeping cars. After bedding down his troops, he took a taxi back to the Hotel Breslau, registered under his own name, bought a tourist map of the city, and went up to his room. A telephone call came for him as soon as he got in the door.

"Yes?"

"A Dr. Wolf on the line, Lieutenant."

"Put him on."

"Hello, Peter? This is Wolf." Peter recognized Skorzeny's voice.

"Ja wohl, Herr Doktor."

"I'm staying with some friends. Come on by and say hello."

"All right. What's the address?"

He wrote down the address, grabbed his city map, and took a taxi to the intersection nearest there. It was an ordinary four-story house. Peter knocked and was admitted by a civilian who looked like an S.S. man in mufti. He was shown into a downstairs parlor dominated by an 1870 cavalry saber mounted over the fireplace, and by Otto Skorzeny.

"Hello, Oelrich. It's about time. You've got the boys with you?"

"Yes, sir. Tucked in bed down at the railway terminal."

"Fine. We have a job tomorrow morning. Out in the suburbs. Horthy's son is meeting with a bunch of Yugoslavs. They're going to surrender the whole damned Hungarian Army to the enemy. *Steiner!* Where's that street map?"

"I've got one here, sir . . . if it's on this map."

They laid the map out on a table and found the location of the meeting, and then laid out their troop dispositions.

"You'd better get over there yourself and reconnoiter. I've already looked at it, and I have to stay here near the radio."

"Yes, sir."

"Do you have any civilian clothes with you?"

"No. I don't have any."

"*Steiner*—get this man some civilian clothes. Give him a list of sizes, Peter. While we're waiting, you'd better get over and alert your troops. You can take my car. You've got a radio? Get on to Radl. I'll give you a list of supplies and troops I want sent by air. We're keeping this radio open for incoming messages."

Peter took the Mercedes diesel car that Skorzeny pointed out and drove to the railyards. It was a matter of minutes to tell the well-trained commando sergeants what time to have their troops ready and waiting, and to show them the dispositions on the street map.

It took longer to code his transmission for London and to tune the radio in on the frequency which he used for reports, and still longer to put through Skorzeny's appeal to Friedenthal for additional troops and supplies.

When he got back to Skorzeny's hideaway, he changed into the civilian clothes which had been hurriedly assembled for him, and reported to the Colonel.

"Take a look this square here," Skorzeny said, pointing it out on the map. "You'll see how to position the troops. We'll have some civilian cars parked there, and they can hide inside so it won't be too obvious. Your truck goes here, with about ten men. Keep out of sight until I give the word. Now—get over there and look it over, and be back at dawn with your troops. I wish I could go with you—but—" Skorzeny, with his height and scarred face, was instantly recognizable all over Europe. Even in civilian clothes, he could hardly go out in public without drawing attention and possible recognition.

"Peter, I can't tell you how important this is. If we lose Hungary, we lose our entire production of bauxite. And without bauxite, we can't produce jet planes. Now—get going."

Now he understood. If they successfully kidnapped the son of the Hungarian head of state, they could stop him from withdrawing Hungary's armies from the war. And the words about jet planes—it was the first Peter had heard about the possibility of jet-propelled manned airplanes.

Peter scouted the area his troops would cover the next morning, and then returned to the railyard to get a few hours of sleep. He wouldn't be able to send off another message to London until the next evening, and he wasn't sure that his transmissions were getting through anyway. It also entered his mind that if the English were somehow able to communicate with Admiral Horthy through the Russians or the Jugoslav surrender delegation, and were able to warn that the Germans were trying to kidnap his son, the extra protection sent would make it certain that Peter would be among the first to die.

Chapter 52

Five o'clock came, and they moved out to their positions. Peter armed himself with a pistol and hid his face behind a newspaper on a bench in the square overlooking the planned meeting place. After a while he heard a car drive up and watched as a tall gray-haired tourist got out to gawk at the fountain in the middle of the cobblestoned plaza, and the old buildings that surrounded it.

"Good morning, Peter."

"Good morning, Dr. Wolf."

Eight o'clock came, and then nine, and Peter's stomach began to rumble. A bakery opened. Peter strolled in and bought bags of breakfast rolls, and then distributed them around to his troops in their hiding places around the square. Skorzeny was still sitting on the park bench when Peter got back from his rounds and sat down again to peer out through the hole poked in the center of his newspaper. "Dr. Wolf" puffed nervously on a curved Austrian pipe that threatened to set his moustache on fire.

"All set?"

"Yes, sir. I've got them doing exercises to keep their blood circulating."

Four big black limousines pulled up to a house across the square. One of them was flying the flag with the two-headed eagle of the regent of Hungary. Peter raised his whistle to his lips.

Armed guards tumbled from the front and rear cars and formed a cordon.

"Wait," said Skorzeny. "No. Don't do a thing. It's the Admiral himself. We can't have an incident. Go call off your troops. Walk slowly."

Peter dropped his pistol belt, casually threw the newspaper over it, and walked slowly across the square, his hands in his pockets. Going by the truck around the corner, he muttered, "Forget it. Make a U-turn and get the hell out of here!" He walked a circuitous route to call off all of his trigger-happy troopers, giving them change to take streetcars if necessary, and instructing them not to get picked up by the police. "Tell them you're under top secret orders. It's still early. Go straight back."

Peter went back to pick up his pistol, and then sat in Skorzeny's car. The Colonel was very unhappy when he returned.

"It would have been beautiful! King, rook and pawns, for a pawn sacrifice! But—we have to follow orders." He started the car. "We'd better get back to my safe-house."

No sooner did they get back to Skorzeny's hideaway than an officer in civilian clothes hurried in.

"They're meeting again on Sunday. You'll have another chance."

"Who's meeting?"

"Nicholas Horthy, and Marshal Tito's representatives."

"Where?" They got out the city map.

Now there was time to lay out a more foolproof plan. When "Dr. Wolf" reconnoitered he found that the meeting was to be in an office building, and that there were offices for rent right upstairs. In his disguise as a travelling chemist, he rented the upstairs office and laid out with Peter a plan to take the Regent's son and his "co-conspirators" from the inside before any troops could be called in. This time there were to be two truckloads of troops waiting right around the corner, and still more concealed in delivery vans within running distance of the building.

Sunday morning dawned quiet and clear on the Danube. This time the troops were buttoned up tight in their trucks, with containers of hot soup and black bread to munch on. Peter was in civilian clothes in the fourth floor office they had rented, watching from the windows. He kept his armed men back from the windows, but he kept a constant watch on the street below from behind the drapes. He saw "Dr. Wolf" making a casual circuit of the area every half hour.

The quarry arrived, again in limousines. Peter waited until he could hear them enter the offices on the floor below, and then signalled his men.

He took the elevator down and knocked at their door. As soon as it opened he heard his non-coms behind him, running down the stairs, machine guns at port arms. As they bulled their way into the room, a young, dark-complexioned man started screaming, "You can't do this! Get the hell out of here. What do you think you're doing? Do you know who I am?" The more practical men with him reached for weapons. Peter silenced one of them with a blow to the throat, while the others were slugged with gun butts. Young Horthy ran to the window.

"Guards!" he shouted. Peter ripped down the moldy velvet curtain, threw it over the young man and tied it with the silk-tasseled tie-back rope.

"Sergeant, throw this over your shoulder!" he said.

The huge non-com picked up the struggling, kicking sack containing Horthy, threw it over his shoulder and headed for the stairs. Outside, gunfire was echoing from the ancient stone buildings. Peter backed out of the room, locked the door from the outside, and ran down the stairs. The sergeant and his two men were hesitating in the doorway. Outside, bullets were ricocheting off the cobblestones. Peter pushed his men back inside and peered out into the square. Across the way he saw Skorzeny, still in civilian clothes, leading an S.S. group running out of the side street. The gunfire seemed to be coming from the building next door.

"Sergeant," Peter said to one of the men sitting on the moving figure trussed up in velvet, "Give me a hand grenade."

The sergeant pulled a potato masher from his belt harness and handed it to Peter by the wooden handle. Peter pulled the pin, peered out, and flipped the grenade onto the balcony of the neighboring building. It blew, and down came the balcony—balustrade, cement, marble and all, to block the doorway.

"Now!" Peter yelled, and they ran out into the square and threw the still kicking bundle that was young Horthy into the back of Skorzeny's car. The colonel ran up with the commander of the S.S. company.

"To the airport. Commandeer anything you see. Get him to Berlin!"

The captain got in the car and roared away, while Skorzeny and Peter headed for the nearest van, signalling their men to pick up their wounded and retreat. As they drove away, three companies of Hungarians came double-timing into the square in perfect formation, four abreast, with rifles at port arms.

Concealment was now futile. They drove to the Hotel Breslau, German Army headquarters, and Skorzeny sent for his uniform while Peter went up to change. The next move was up to Admiral Horthy.

It wasn't long in coming; As they met in the Kommandatura headquarters with generals of every stripe, Admiral Horthy broadcast on the radio that all Hungarian troops were to lay down their arms and surrender forthwith to the Russians opposing them. The Hungarian chief of staff in the Carpathians had already deserted and crossed the lines.

From Berlin, General Jodl sent a message for the highest ranking German officer in Budapest to fly immediately to the Hungarian headquarters in the Carpathians. Surprisingly enough, the line commanders had refused to surrender without proper written orders, and it was not difficult to keep them in check, to prevent them from surrendering.

At the Kommandatura, the General Staff officers were flushed and worried. Potential bloodshed was coming much too close to their comfortable desk chairs.

"What are we going to do?" they asked. "We have less than a divisions here, and the Hungarians have three division in this area, not to speak of the guards on Capital Hill."

"Horthy's still the key to the problem," Skorzeny said. "He's blockaded up there in the castle. Every entrance is mined and sited for anti-tank guns. We would have to destroy the entire citadel to get him!"

"I've got my siege mortars. I'll blast them off the hill in no time." Insane zeal shone from the piggish eyes of General Bach-Zelewski, the butcher of Warsaw. "A 45-inch mortar, the biggest shell since 'Big Bertha'. We blasted the whole ghetto to rubble in Warsaw."

"Tempus fugit," Skorzeny said, turning to the ranking officer. "Can you give me a tank column and five hundred men in trucks, immediately?"

"Yes. I guess I could divert that bunch headed for the front."

"Have them line up in parade order right now. I've reconnoitered that castle. I will lead the troops in."

While the general ordered up the Tigers, Skorzeny got a wire to the German Embassy, now blockaded on Capitol Hill overlooking the city. "Keep them talking," he ordered. "Talk about our ancient alliance, about Emperor Franz-Joseph, about anything—but keep them talking."

"Come on, Peter," he said. "Let's go."

They got into an open staff car and took off at speed, leading the column of tanks through the city and up the hill.

"Keep those hatches open," Skorzeny shouted back to the tank commanders over the roar of the engines, "and salute everything that moves. Just like passing in revie ."

As they moved up the hill toward the first roadblock, Skorzeny stood up and held onto the roll bar, straightening his uniform and Knight's cross as if on

241

parade before the Führer. Peter shrivelled down in his seat, waiting for the land mines that would blow them into the sky.

They roared up to the Vienna Gate, and Skorzeny gave a flashy salute as shadowy figures emerged from guardhouses. They clanked through without slowing. Next came the long, climbing avenue, sited for anti-tank guns, that led to Castle Barracks with its machine guns in sand-bagged emplacements. Again Skorzeny's salute and smile got them through. The guards knew that the column had entered through the Vienna Gate without gunfire. They assumed that orders had been changed.

Again they breezed through and came out onto Castle Square before the huge pile of the Regent's palace. Three heavy tanks faced them, their cannons in motion. The Hungarian officers, seeing the approaching storm, kept the cannon barrels moving until they pointed straight up in the air.

A huge brick wall blocked the entrance to the castle. Skorzeny motioned his driver to turn aside, and jumped out to direct traffic. The first tank smashed straight through the wall, and the others were sent around to the flanks. Skorzeny shouted, "Come on!" And Peter followed him on the run. A Hungarian colonel emerged from a guardhouse, pistol at the ready. Peter kicked it out of his hand and picked it up. "Sorry, sir," he said, and ran after Skorzeny up the stairs. "Come on," he shouted to the colonel, gesturing him to follow, beckoning him with the hand that held the colonel's pistol.

Skorzeny was shouting at another colonel who had appeared. "Come with me. I've got to see the Commandant immediately."

At a window a machine gun was opening fire on the German troops in the courtyard below. Skorzeny picked it up and tipped it out the window to crash to the cobblestones below.

A Hungarian general appeared. Skorzeny crashed his

heels together, coming to attention and saluting.

"Sir," he said, "the castle is in German hands. I beg of you to surrender and send out officers to stop further bloodshed." He was laying on his Austro-Hungarian Empire accent in layers as thick as whipped cream on Vienna coffee.

"What has happened?" the general mewled, as a gaggle of Hungarian officers entered the room, still pulling at their braid-bedecked uniforms.

"Courtyard and main entrance secured, sir." One of the Friedenthal non-coms was saluting and waiting for orders.

"Sir," Skorzeny addressed the general. "Please ask your troops to stack arms." Gunfire was echoing from the gardens in back of the castle.

"All right," the general said, crestfallen.

"Thank you, sir," Skorzeny smiled and turned to the younger Hungarian officers before they could speak.

"Gentlemen—Captain: you'll be my liaison officer. Please have your men stack arms and then report back here. Major, will you go down and tell my tank officers that everything is under control? Thank you."

The amazed and astounded staff officers, not knowing what else to do, salivated like Pavlov's dogs and trotted off to obey orders.

"Colonel," Skorzeny saluted the head of the palace guard and addressed him respectfully. "Would you please make sure your troops stack arms? Of course, officers must retain their sidearms. Oelrich, you damned fool, give the colonel his pistol. I apologise for my assistant, sir."

Peter bowed and presented the Luger, butt first, to the dumbfounded colonel of the guard, then went down to the radio truck to report to Budapest headquarters that the castle was secured.

When he got back upstairs he found Skorzeny on the dais in the throne room addressing the assembled

Hungarian officers, now resplendent in full uniform.

"Gentlemen—Germany and Austria and Hungary have never quarrelled. We have always fought shoulder to shoulder against the common enemy. Today the godless horde of Bolsheviks stands at our gates as did the Turks six hundred years ago. We must . . ."

Peter noticed an astounded flunky in white tie and tails, the gold insignia of the keeper of the wine cellars hanging on a gold chain around his neck.

"How about a little drink?" Peter asked, throwing the strap of his Schmeisser around his neck so he wouldn't have to hold the gun in his arms. "Cognac for two hundred. *Verstanden?*"

"Servus." The *maitre d'hotel* looked like a startled rabbit as he scuttled off to the kitchen.

Peter followed Skorzeny into a less imposing reception room after his speech, and sank onto a satin couch. "This is not for me," he complained.

Skorzeny gave a booming laugh that echoed in the high-ceilinged room.

"Oelrich, why don't you go home and make cuckoo clocks?"

"I wish I could."

Peter followed orders to send a message direct to Hilter's Wolf Lair announcing the capture of Castle Hill, and was the bearer of the return message of congratulations. Skorzeny was ordered to take possession of the Castle until further notice and to locate Admiral Horthy at all costs. The Admiral had disappeared.

Yet within a few hours he was located, and tendered his abdication. The last Admiral of the Hungarian Navy, the last Regent representing the Royal and Imperial power of the Hapsburgs, the last independent ruler of Hungary was gone, to be replaced by Otto Skorzeny, the Constable of Castle Hill.

As Peter came from the radio truck and mounted the

marble staircase yet again, he was pushed out of the way by twenty immaculate waiters, each with a silver tray, a bottle of 1850 cognac, and ten glasses.

When he got to Skorzeny, who by now had found a small side room and had taken off his heavy boots and tunic, he was pushed aside by the *maitre d'hôte*, his golden medallion like a sunburst hanging on its chain in the middle of his boiled shirt beneath his white tie.

"Cognac for two hundred, *Herr Oberst-Leutnant*!"

Chapter 53

The Constable of Castle Hill gave a banquet that night in the imperial banquet hall; but the glories of war, like the privileges of high title, are fleeting. Later that evening he had Peter load up a truck with the finest wines to be found in the vast cellars of the castle. The next morning Peter headed up the truck convoy back to Friedenthal.

It was a long, tiring drive. As they came close to the Swiss border, Peter was tempted. Home was only a few miles away, but he knew Switzerland would never admit him in uniform, and would deport him as a deserter if he did cross the border. And he knew that the S.S. would shoot him for desertion if they got a chance. It was a temptation, but not much of one. Peter turned his little convoy north, toward war and destruction.

Upon arrival, he gave instructions for the safe storage of the wines and the unpacking of the equipment. He turned in his vehicles, and then reported to Radl at headquarters.

"Hello, Captain. We're back. All present and accounted for except for the fellows who stayed there with the colonel."

"I know."

"When is he getting back?"

"A few days, I suppose. Peter—what can you tell me about that radio of yours?"

"Nothing. Why?"

"It was a spy radio. It had a transmitter in it. Your sergeant was using it and he opened up the case. Where did you get it?"

Peter was mortally afraid. He hesitated before answering. "In France," he said. "I liberated it from a bistro in Joinville."

"You are in a lot of trouble," Radl replied. "Some smart-ass reported it to S.S. headquarters. They sent out an order for you to be picked up and sent to Spandau under guard."

"Oh, for God's sake!"

"They said there's been an 'arrest on sight' order out on you for years, and also that you were reported missing in action. The records are all screwed up."

"Yes."

"Look, Peter—the Waffen S.S. and Himmler's bunch are two different things. I'm going to put you under guard until the boss gets back. We'll let him handle it."

"Whatever you say."

"You go ahead and get some sleep, and I'll put a guard outside your quarters. I'll tell them to act as your personal guard under your command—just in case Himmler's boys come around."

"Yes, sir."

Peter threw up his hands in mock dismay, and walked back to his quarters, now without music. That night he tossed and turned, trying to figure a way out of his predicament. There seemed to be no escape. If he could commandeer a plane and fly to Switzerland, he might get himself interned just as the American pilots were. On the other hand, they might turn him over to the nearest border guard, something they couldn't do with the Amis. And too, if reports were true that the Oelrich factory was bombed to rubble, it would be unlikely that his father and brother would still have enough influence to keep him out of a Swiss or German jail.

It took Skorzeny to solve the problem. He settled it as soon as he returned to Friedenthal. "Peter," he said, "this is the most idiotic bureaucratic mess I've ever seen. You're a man with an Iron Cross, one of my best soldiers, and those idiots want to throw you in jail. I won't allow it! I can't fix it right away—not until I find the right opportunity to speak to the Führer about it—and God knows when that will be. With him, you don't speak until spoken to.

"But, by God, I'm going to backdate orders to von Foelkersam for you to report to the *Sperrgebiet* near Nuremberg—the restricted area where we're training our 'Americans'. You go down there until we're ready. There's no-one allowed in or out of the area. It has a complete security black out. I'll guarantee that Himmler's boys won't get in without shooting, and they're not known for attacking armed soldiers, the idiots.

"You go down there, and I'll straighten things out as soon as I can. All right?"

"Yes, sir," Peter answered. There wasn't much else he could do.

Chapter 54

The restricted area near Nuremberg was one which Peter had never visited. All the English-speaking volunteers he had classified and sent on for further training were now concentrated there, over three thousand of them, under the command of von Foelkersam. They constituted Skorzeny's 150th Brigade. Captured American material was coming in at the railhead every day.

Baron von Foelkersam was harried and nervous when Peter reported to him.

"Well now. I hear you had a good time in Budapest while we were slogging in the mud here."

"Too much gunfire for my taste."

"Oh, come now. I was told there were only a half dozen casualties. Better than Gran Sasso! You should have been *there*. We were out of those gliders and into that hotel before Mussolini could get his glasses on."

"How are my Anglo-Saxons coming along?"

"Just terrible. When I saw your reports to Radl, I didn't believe it. But I do now. We can't even get a hundred good men who speak American out of the whole Reich. It's incredible."

"The whole operation should be junked."

"We can't do it. It was one of the Führer's brainstorms. Maybe it will work. Who knows? Look . . . you'd better get to work. The orders came through—we're supposed to go in as Americans. You make a final choice of the best linguists and form special companies. We'll give them the best equipment. Take the office at the end of the corridor here, and start interviewing them. Do you need a new assistant?"

"Yes. The last one disappeared."

"So I'm told. Well, go over to B barracks and pick one up."

During his time in England, Peter had never been in an

American military camp. The nearest he came was the supply depot where he had picked up his uniforms the day he was sworn in as an American citizen. On his walk across the barracks square, Peter was surrounded by American uniforms. Some of them still had prisoner of war triangles sewn on, others had fading bloodstains. No two uniforms seemed to match.

One line of "G.I.'s" was listening to a "master sergeant" who was lecturing them in English. As Peter walked by they crashed their heels together and came to rigid attention. The "non-com" glanced at Peter, then turned back to them screaming, "No, no! Never click your heels together. Americans don't do that. And I've told you a million times—ignore the officers. If they don't talk to you, don't even see them."

He turned around and saluted Peter in a casual, American sort of way.

"Hello. You're Muller aren't you?"

"Seaman First Class Henry Muller, Lieutenant."

"Oh, yes." Peter remembered now. This was the merchant sailor who had grown up in New Jersey and had been drafted in 1939. "How are your Americans coming along?" He glanced at the motley lineup, hardly a squad. They were still standing rigily at attention, their chins tucked in, backs ramrod straight, stomachs pulled in.

"They're awful, Lieutenant. We're going to get shot the minute we cross the line."

"Well, who knows? Maybe it will work yet. Trust Uncle Otto. By the way, that man on the end is wearing officer's pants with an enlisted man's jacket."

"Yeah? I'll fix it up, boss."

"Okay, sergeant."

Peter walked into barracks B, and someone shouted "Achtung." All the men jumped up. "Never mind—go back to work," Peter said.

Peter went to find the quartermaster's depot. If he was supposed to look American, he wanted to get a comfortable uniform. Peter chose a woolen shirt that bore sergeant's stripes, a sweater, and several pairs of drab woolen trousers. There were no boots in his size, so he had to keep his German Army jackboots.

"How about some brown oxfords?" he asked. "I believe that's what they often wear."

"We can get you some from the Brown Shirts uniform."

"Do that. How about neckties?"

"We don't have any. They don't wear them on frontline duty."

"Really? In that case, I'll do without."

Peter went back to his office. His new sergeant was waiting there, together with a soldier in an American field jacket who had two black eyes and several ugly cuts on his face.

"What happened to you?" Peter asked, in English.

"I vas sent to mix in the American P.O.W. camp. Somehow, dey found me out."

"For God's sake! Did you learn anything?"

"Sure did, Mac. I can't pass for American."

"Well, you're better than some I've seen. Sergeant, send this man over to Muller's squad."

Over the next several weeks Peter re-sorted the volunteers again. Of the hundreds he called in for re-evaluation, only fifty were able to sound or look convincingly American for more than a few minutes. Peter tried to screen them. They were formed into a special platoon, and Peter tried to obtain for them the best and most authentic of the captured American equipment.

Radl came personally from Friedenthal with a trainload of American materiel. Peter met him at the railhead.

"Hello, Peter. Got a dozen jeeps and some armored cars for you. And two Shermans."

"Two? I thought we were supposed to get a dozen!"

"Retreating is no way to capture equipment. We'll have to convert some Tigers and Panthers."

"There's no way we can make a Tiger look like a Sherman."

"You'll figure out something. We've got every confidence in you. By the way, Otto sends his regards. He's up at the Chancellory every day now. The Führer wants him to attend all the staff meetings."

Peter was looking at the armored cars as they were unloaded. "Wait a minute, Captain." He went over and checked the dashboard on one of the cars.

"Radl—this is a British vehicle. They're all British."

"They are?"

"How are we going to explain British vehicles in an American sector? You know what they say about the Americans. They shoot first and ask questions later."

"Well, maybe you can make them look American somehow."

"Radl, this whole operation is a mess!"

"Nevertheless, it's *our* mess. How about lunch?"

They got into one of the jeeps and drove off to the officer's mess. "Not very luxurious, I'm afraid," Peter said, "but we've got good wine."

"Yes. That Horthy had good taste."

Von Foelkersam joined them at lunch. "How are you Radl? What's the latest at Friedenthal?"

"Otto says we've been promised three thousand jet fighters for the offensive."

"Whatever that means. I sometimes think Fat Hermann goes off into opium dreams."

"You know, Rommel once said that he saw Goering in an uniform with six stars!"

"Unbelievable!"

They sank into their *Kässler Rippchen* and washed it down with a 1907 Mouton Rothschild.

"Where did you get all the jeeps, Radl?"

"Requisitioned them. I think every officer on the Western front had one for his own personal use, but when I called them in, they disappeared. So I sent out foraging parties. You wouldn't believe where they had them hidden. One was covered by a manure pile!"

"Do they run?"

"Every one of them."

"What about tanks? They expect us to hold road junctions and bridges without armor."

Von Foelkersam stroked his chin. "Peter," he said," Perhaps you'd better take charge and convert some Tigers. We can't count on any more coming through."

"It's an absurd assignment, Adrian, but I'll try."

Peter joined the ordnance officers that day, and every day for a week thereafter, to lay out plans for the fabrication of sheet metal panels to change the appearance of Tiger tanks to look more like Shermans. They welded them directly to the armor plate. Even after they painted them olive drab and added the white star, they wouldn't fool anyone who'd ever seen a Sherman at a range of less than a mile.

All of the British armored cars broke down when they were tried. They had obviously been abandoned. The four American armored cars were in good running order, but no more were forthcoming.

Skorzeny had put in for American guns for two anti-tank companies and an anti-aircraft company. The guns arrived, and Peter helped the gunners translate the instructions for dry loading and range adjustment, but when the shells finally arrived, a whole trainload, they exploded the next day, flattening a whole section of the training camp.

"Don't worry," von Foelkersam said half-heartedly, "When the Amis start to retreat we'll be able to get all we want."

The winter was getting colder, and the issue of American overcoats was welcome. Then came the day when they were recalled. All of the front line troops were wearing field jackets, and authenticity was demanded of Skorzeny's 150th.

With over three thousand men confined to the brigade area, cut off from all contact with civilian life and from the rest of the army, and training secretly with American uniforms and foreign equipment, gossip was rampant. Rumors, bad enough in any army unit, became wild beyond belief.

Peter heard stories that they were being trained to cut across France to relieve the surrounded garrison in Lorient. He was told by the best of authorities from the non-com's mess that they were to head for Paris and capture Eisenhower. Yet neither Radl or von Foelkersam seemed to be any better informed. Skorzeny was confiding in no-one.

Peter's future seemed bleak, like that of the German army itself. He could be of very little more use to the allies, and it appeared that there would be little chance, if any, to cross the lines to the allied side without getting shot. In Africa, easy as it was to get captured, many prisoners were taken. In Europe, few survived to tell the tale. He felt he would have to take his chances with the forward group who were to go disguised in American uniforms, and try to find a way to get through the trigger-happy front line troops to the rear areas without getting caught. Even then, his own men might shoot him.

After Peter had installed German field radios in the American armored cars, he decided to make one more radio report to London. He coded his final message on the back of cigarette papers so that he could swallow them quickly if he got caught. His messages were scheduled to be received in the evening. It was several days before he found an evening when the ordnance shed was deserted and he could get unhindered access to a field radio. His message was short, succinct, and sad:

254

150th Armored S.S. Brigade training with American uniforms and equipment including 4 Shermans, 12 jeeps, 20 trucks, 6 Panzer VI disguised as Shermans, artillery and A.A. companies armed with Flak 41. Operation Greif said to be for relief on Lorient or kidnapping of Eisenhower. Large number of piloted jet-propelled aircraft believed set for attack. Last message. Now under suspicion.

Old acquaintance.

After he burned the message on the cigarette papers and walked over the frozen ground back to his lonely room, Peter looked up at the stars and wondered how long he had to live. He was a man without a country, living by his wits, and his wits had brought him to a camp built on frozen mud, surrounded by doomed soldiers in ramshackle equipment going on a fruitless mission that could not be saved by jet planes or buzz bombs or any other magic. Peter remembered the endless line of British tanks after Alamein. No matter how many died, they still kept coming.

Chapter 55

Peter felt that the end was near when Skorzeny teletyped from Friedenthal to schedule a brigade inspection and review. It was a bright December morning when Skorzeny drove down from Berlin in a borrowed Mercedes SK. "Beautiful car," he said. "We used to race them in Austria. Actually that's why I joined the party."

He was exhilarated by his drive, and resplendent in his uniform, medals shining in the bright December sunlight. "Parade at eleven?" he asked.

"Yes, sir," Peter answered.

"Then I've got a little time. Peter, you come along. First, the quartermaster's. Let's look at some uniforms."

They drove in the jeep Peter had appropriated for his own use. The warehouse was still filled with American Army clothing. Skorzeny inspected the setup with some pride at its neatness, but then he got almost querulous as he drew the supply sergeant aside.

"I don't suppose you have anything my size?"

The sergeant looked up at him. "No, sir. No jackets, no boots. Maybe pants and shirt—and a sweater. You could stretch the sweater."

"All right. Pack them up for me, and have them put in my Mercedes."

The mess hall was spotless, and the kitchen smelled of baking bread.

"Hello, boys," Skorzeny said. "What's in the pot? *Gib' doch ein Schluck.*"

The colonel was a German war-god with his smile, his scar, his size, his magnificent tailored uniform, and his friendly Austrian accent.

"Mmm—that's tasty. I wish I could stay for lunch. Peter, send the sergeant here a couple bottles of our Hungarian wine." He turned to the mess sergeant and shook his hand. "They're for you personally."

The sergeant was beaming. "Hey, Colonel. When are we going to Paris? When do we get our field kitchens?"

"Too bad, sergeant. No field kitchens. I'm trading butter for guns—field kitchens for fire power. That's why I want you to feed them well while they're here."

"You mean we don't get to go?"

"Next trip. I'll bring you some cognac. I'll see you then. Goodbye."

They strode rapidly to the nearest barracks. The charge of quarters reported, all excited at a personal inspection by the man who had rescued Mussolini.

"1st A.A. battery C.O.Q. Private Knebel *Herr Oberst-leutnant*. Heil Hitler."

"Hello, Knebel. Glad to get out of the parade?"

Skorzeny ran a white-gloved finger across the tops of the wooden wardrobe chests, inspected the shower heads, and down on his hands and knees to check the bottoms of the toilet bowls for cleanliness.

"Twenty minutes, Colonel."

"All right, Peter. Let's go. Thank you, Knebel. You keep a good barracks here."

Peter dropped him at the hastily erected reviewing stand and then drove off rapidly to change into his makeshift American uniform. He just made it before the whistle blew, and led off the parade with ten jeeploads of "G.I.s" in helmets and green field jackets.

"Okay, you guys," he said, switching to English with the broadest transatlantic accent he could muster, "Look American. Stick your hands in your pockets. Don't sit so damn straight."

"Für Oberst Skorzeny?"

"Goddam right. You—Flegelhofer—chew some gum and park it on the jeep when we pass the reviewing stand. Steinwerfer—light a cigarette and keep it half hidden."

Peter put the jeep into its lowest gear and led off, driving the ten jeeps to the front of the column of tanks and armored cars. As they passed the reviewing stand in their lowest gear, he grinned and threw a sloppy salute to von Foelkersam and Skorzeny.

"Hi you, Mac," Skorzeny smiled.

Peter's "Americans" smiled nervously.

"Hey you guys," Peter yelled. "Answer him—all together: 'Hi-ya, Colonel.'"

"Hi-ya, Colonel."

Skorzeny laughed.

Peter parked his jeep and motioned the rest to unload as planned.

"Line up here. Hands in your pockets. Wave to the troops. Remember—look sloppy!"

Leaving his motley crew, he joined the ranking officers on the reviewing stand. Skorzeny was still in a good mood as the two Shermans clanked by, their commanders waving and grinning as ordered. Then came the disguised Tiger tanks, and the trucks full of soldiers in variegated American uniforms, and the batteries with their instantly recognizable 88's. Skorzeny began to look grim.

"Is that the best we can do?"

"The High Command say we can get all the Ami stuff we want as soon as we break through."

"Good Christ, Foelkersam! These troops look about as American as Steinhäger schnapps." Skorzeny fixed a smile on his face and saluted as the units passed.

"Adrian, I want each and every soldier to have a complete Waffen SS uniform with him. I don't care what the legal eagles say, I wouldn't send them through the lines dressed like that—except maybe the first bunch."

"My group, Otto?"

"Your group, hell, Peter! You're not going through the lines."

"Then what have I been training for?"

"If I can't go, you can't go. And anyway, if Himmler's boys picked you up in American uniform, they'd shoot you on the spot."

"Oh, come on, Colonel."

"You're going to be my field adjutant, just like Budapest. Don't argue." He saluted the last unit.

That night at the officer's mess, they had a formal dinner. Radl had flown down from Friedenthal, and Peter and Adrian von Foelkersam were in attendance. The best wines were broken out, and for dessert they had a fruitcake *flambé* with cognac.

"Merry Christmas, boys," Skorzeny said, although it was only the tenth of December. "This will be your first holiday dinner, and maybe your last. We'll celebrate Saint Nicholas' day in Paris, or not at all."

"Happy Christmas, and a victorious New Year."

"Sieg heil!"

Peter sipped some Armagnac and thought of the last three Christmases—the lonely one with his father, the unreal Christmas with Rommel and Dreieck at Fort Zinderneuf or whatever it was called, and the still more fantastic Christmas in wartime England, with plum pudding and carols in French—strange uniforms and strange languages—and never, never with Vreneli.

"Zu den Gefallenen," he toasted, raising his glass.

"Someday it will be over, Peter." Skorzeny said softly. "It can't last forever. The Amis and the English will realize that they've got to knock the Russians out of Europe. Jesus! They're almost in Prussia, and they've got Poland!"

"I'm ready to quit anytime you are, Otto."

"Don't talk that way. Look, Peter, somebody will have to rebuild this mess some day. The railroads are destroyed, the bridges, the public buildings. Someone's going to have to rebuild it all."

"Here's to the survivors."

A sergeant was brought in with his accordion, and they all sang.

"Ich hatt' ein Kameraden,
Ein bess'rer find'st du nicht..."

259

"Schatz, mein Schatz,
Reise nicht so weit von mir...

"Stille Nacht, heilige Nacht,
All' ist Ruh'..."

Chapter 56

It was the middle of the night. It was the sixteenth of December. It was a quiet area in the snowy hills of Belgium. The Sixth Waffen S.S. Panzer Army was lined up for the attack. Its power led back for miles on the frozen roads—thousands strong with the latest and best weapons Germany could produce. At the spearhead, just behind the shock troopers, were ten jeeploads of German soldiers in American uniforms, ready to sprint through any gap. One mile behind was the 150th Waffen SS brigade, in motley American uniforms, waiting for a breakthrough.

It was snowy, and a white fog engulfed the mountain passes. At exactly 3:17, huge searchlights turned a blinding white light on the low-lying clouds, on the banks of fog, and white-clad figures walked forward, guns in hand, as the deafening music of trucks and tanks and artillery explosions came from powerful loudspeakers sited in the trees. With a banshee scream never before heard, silver fighter planes streaked low out of Germany at speeds never before seen, silver air machines with no propellors, flying faster than line pilots had ever flown. German soldiers raised their rifles in the air and shouted. Hitler's secret weapons of revenge were screaming through the sky, giving them hope.

On the American side, green troops ran to the rear, musicians and cooks were issued rifles they didn't know how to shoot, and grenades that could blow up in their hands. Staff officers and entertainers, junketeers and at least one hungover novelist staggered with blood-shot eyes from their downy comforters, or refused with arrogant immutability to believe that their coddled lives, their well-protected luxurious existences, could be threatened.

At Barraque-Michel, Colonel Smythe, still celebrating

after a nine-course dinner, was machine-gunned in the belly by S.S. General Heiligenkreuz as paratroopers rained from the sky. *Obertsturmbannführer* Jochen Peiper led his black-clad SS men from the open hatch of a Tiger tank as Baron Hasso von Manteuffel watched. General George Patton screamed in his piping voice that "we can still lose this war," as well as something about bringing back the dogtags by the truckload if he regarded it as necessary. Field Marshal Bernard Law Montgomery planned to tidy up by withdrawing from his fortified goose egg.

A mile behind the German front, the 150th was still waiting to jump off. Otto Skorzeny, with Peter at his heels, slogged uphill past a line of stalled tanks and trucks, slogged through mud torn up by tank treads to the top of a hill. A huge V-2 rocket launcher on its specially built transport truck was jack-knifed across the road. Seven hundred men were waiting in trucks for something to be done. Three miles of vehicles lay stalled behind.

"What the hell is a V-2 doing in the front line?" Skorzeny yelled.

"We're supposed to set up in Bastogne and fire at Paris, Colonel."

"Get the hell out of those trucks and tip this thing into the ditch!"

Skorzeny drew his Walther and fired into the air. The troops came tumbling out of their warm trucks.

Still further ahead, by a ruined railway overpass, eight more tanks were stalled. Bridging equipment was piled up by the roadside.

"What are you waiting for?" Skorzeny asked.

"Center section of the bridge isn't up here yet. The truck must have got stuck in the mud."

Peter and Skorzeny walked back to their troops. They could do nothing but wait until a breakthrough had been made.

Several miles west of them, Seaman Henry Muller with

a jeepload of "American" troops found a crossroad with signs pointing to Krinkelt and Rocherath. They quickly wrapped explosive cord around it and blasted it off its base, and moved on.

At a larger intersection they almost collided with a column of the American 14th Cavalry. Terrified at the firepower they faced, Muller shouted, "Scram, fellas! They've broken through all around us!" The Germans were so obviously afraid that the 14th Cavalry turned at speed and went back the way they had come.

Twenty miles behind the moving American front, Lieutenant Jochen Brauer, whose team had just blown four gaps in the command telephone lines between the headquarters of Hodges and Bradley, drove up to a fidgety crew manning a big gasoline truck.

"Petrol, please," he smiled. Six M-1 rifles came up and covered the Germans, safety catches clicking off ominously.

At Baraque-Michel an excited American major who had just interrogated six German paratroopers telephoned to Shaef headquarters in Paris.

"The prisoners say that Otto Skorzeny has a whole brigade of troops in American uniform who are heading for Paris to capture Eisenhower! They all speak perfect English. The name of the operation is 'Grief'—that means 'kidnap!'"

Still far behind the German lines, Skorzeny was having lunch with Oelrich, Radl, and most of the officers of his disguised brigade. With their worn green field jackets and khaki sweaters, they were a different crew from those who had celebrated Christmas near Nuremberg the previous week.

"As soon as Dietrich breaks through the American lines, you head for the bridges over the Meuse. I can't repeat often enough—your job is not to fight, it's to secure those bridges and prevent the Amis from blowing them up."

"But when, Otto? We're already hours behind schedule."

"I'll locate General Dietrich, and find out," Skorzeny said, standing up, huge and strange in his tight foreign sweater. "Peter, you come with me. Adrian, you go around and make sure we're in contact with all of our units so that we can pull out fast when the time comes."

They bounced across frozen fields to locate Sixth Panzer's farmhouse headquarters. General Dietrich was cursing over a field telephone. He seemed drunk. "Take that goddam village," he was screaming. "Get your tanks up front!"

"The Americans just brought up the Second division, General. You can't send them against that."

"That division is ten miles behind the lines."

"Not any more. They're throwing A.P. at my men. And we can hardly chip foxholes in this ground."

"By God, you find a way to take that village, or I'll get a new commander!" He hung up the telephone with a crash.

"General," Skorzeny said, "I've got a whole brigade ready to go. Do you want me to take that place?"

"No. We're saving you for the breakthrough. Sit tight."

Peter and Skorzeny kept out of the way as Division commanders came and went, marking their positions on map overlays, crying for reinforcements, demanding supplies that were bottled up in traffic six miles behind the front.

"Peter," Skorzeny took him aside. "This is not going to work. The element of surprise is gone. You get back to the boys and break out the paint brushes. Tell them to change into German uniforms, and see if you can organize some hot food for them."

Peter found his jeep and drove back over frozen fields to the crossroads where the 150th was cowering in the cold. He located the truckful of paint cans and passed out brushes. Within an hour the tan and olive drab of their vehicles was painted over in gray and white, and the white stars of the American insignia were replaced with stencils of the black cross that identified German equipment.

"Pack up all the American uniforms and put them in the paint truck," Peter said, "and wait for further orders."

Von Foelkersam drove up in an armored car. "Peter, I've got some dinner organized at that farmhouse just below the hill. We killed two cows and we found a basement full of potatoes. Bring the men down, a company at a time."

"Yes, sir."

The troops were beginning to emerge from their truck cabs and armored cars in the long leather jackets and steel helmets of the Waffen S.S., expressing relief at not having to go into battle dressed as Americans. The lectures of legal officers notwithstanding, they felt sure they would have been shot as spies if captured.

Peter had some dinner and packed a steak and baked potatoes into a heated metal ammunition box to take to Skorzeny, together with his S.S. uniform.

The arguments of Sepp Dietrich with his divisional commanders were still raging. Skorzeny went out to the barn to eat his dinner sitting in the jeep, the plate and ammunition box resting on heated bricks in the back. Peter pulled a bottle of burgundy from his jacket pocket. They shared it, drinking from the bottle.

The Sixth Panzer Army was bedding down for the night, its first objectives still in enemy hands. Skorzeny returned to the command post and studied the maps.

"General, you need more power. I've got a brigade ready to go. Send us in. We'll break you through." Dietrich, flushed and smelling of liquor, agreed.

"Pull your artillery up behind this ridge," he said, pointing to a curve on the map. "Open up at dawn, as soon as you can aim the pieces. Your tanks can go in from the south. We've got to get through and start running. Peiper's already halfway to Clervaux."

Skorzeny and Peter split up, Skorzeny taking orders to

the tankers, Peter relaying orders to the artillery. The guns were in position by midnight, Peter helping to place them just below a ridge that overlooked the village. Ammunition was at hand, ready to load.

At winter's late dawn the bombardment started with ranging shots and increased to a deafening roar as two batteries of 88's opened up on a village soon reduced to rubble.

From his hill, using the battery commander's tripod-mounted range finder, Peter could see Tigers and Shermans stenciled with the black cross rolling up from the south. The artillery fire lifted and the tanks had rolled up to the outskirts of the village when the first of them exploded.

A single 57 milimeter gun had been sited to fire from the village, and it blew off the tank turret. The two following tanks ran off the road and slowly plowed forward through the fields until they were hit by bazookas. Peter saw infantry running forward as he got into his jeep to report to Skorzeny.

The colonel was directing fire towards a church steeple when Peter found him. "Oelrich," he said, "find that Ami 57 and see if you can fix it. We hit it with an 88."

Peter found the street and walked up to the gun past the flattened remains of a jeep that had been run over by sixty tons of Tiger tank. The American cannon was blown off its mounting. The breech block had been bent beyond repair. Four American soldiers lay, blasted and dead, beside the gun.

Armored cars from 6th Panzer arrived to mop up the town. The 150th went forward again, with fewer tanks and less ammunition, although Major von Foelkersam had been sent to the rear to speed up resupply.

To the east of the village a road curved through the snowy fields and rolling hills. As the heavy tanks, led by Skorzeny in an armored car, rolled through the fog toward a ridge of hills, artillery smashed down at them from prepared positions. Skorzeny's men retreated, picking up the wounded.

The radio in Skorzeny's command car, now bouncing on the rutted roads, antennas whipping wildly, crackled with new orders.

"Hello, Skorzeny?"

"Yes, sir."

"Get your ass down to Clervaux. Relieve Peiper. Clean up the mess and wait for further orders. You hear me?"

"Yes, sir."

Peter got out the maps and found Clervaux. It was a little manufacturing town on the road from Germany to the Meuse. Somehow, something there had stopped Peiper and his SS tank force, at least temporarily.

"We'll make a tanker out of you yet, Peter," Skorzeny smiled, flushed with the heat of battle. "Now—let's see where we're going."

They sent out two patrol cars in front. The convoy was still under distant artillery fire from the mountain ridge, but they knew they would soon be out of range.

Chapter 57

The road to Clervaux was wide and smooth, and clear of the enemy except for some small amount of sniping. The weather was lifting, raising the spirits of the troops. For once they were making some time, and were not under heavy attack.

It was late afternoon as they rolled down the highway, holding their speed down to that of the slowest tank. Peter didn't think anything of it when Skorzeny tapped his arm to point out a light plane buzzing overhead, poking its nose briefly through a break in the overcast. Skorzeny stood up to scout the area with field glasses, and bent to study the map.

His instinctive forebodings, one of the marks of the experienced field commander, were proved out some fifteen minutes later as they raced for the cover of a distant wooded hill. A flight of enemy fighter planes began to strafe the column with cannon and machine guns. While tanks and armored cars ran for the woods, troop carriers bounced off the road in every direction, overturning and scattering their men as soldiers jumped out, running from the terrible machine gun fire that ripped through their black jackets, such good targets against the white snow. Trucks blew up into blazing pyres, and a Tiger tank exploded with a roar, blocking the highway and forcing others to detour with agonizing slowness through the fields as the anti-aircraft batteries tried to unlimber fast enough to get a few shots at the low-flying aircraft.

Even in the woods, the barren trees gave little cover to the dispersed armor. Another tank was hit, and the ammunition on its rear deck exploded in every direction.

As the flight of fighters ran out of ammunition and turned away, unscathed, into the gray cover of the clouds, the brigade had been brought to a complete halt, and the afternoon light was dying as wounded men bled their lives away and froze in the fields of Luxembourg.

"Oelrich—go back and make sure the wounded are picked up. We'll assemble in the woods."

Peter took an armored car and drove back through the rutted fields around blazing trucks, directing the men to the woods ahead. Fires were extinguished, and burned-out vehicles pushed off the road. The wounded were loaded in troop carriers that made their slow way forward, bouncing and jerking to the accompaniment of groans and screams as blood seeped down from the truckbeds and made a ragged trail in the snow.

Dark had descended as Peter came back with the last of the wounded and the best of the vehicles. Troopers were standing near their vehicles eating rations from cans and packages. Small fires had been built to warm up some of the food, and soldiers stood around them warming their hands and cursing the luck that had brought the brief but deadly demonstration of air power.

Skorzeny was chewing on black bread, standing over a map laid out on the hood of a command truck, and trying to read it by the light of a flashlight. Other officers stood with him, trying to locate their position on the map.

"Nine dead, Colonel, and twenty-three wounded. They'll probably go before the night is over. We lost three trucks, two tanks and a troop carrier," Peter reported.

Shots rang out. All of them scrambled for cover beneath the trucks.

"Franc-tireurs!"

"Man hat geschossen!"

"Christ—the Maquis," Skorzeny said. "We'd better organize a perimeter defense and set up guards. *Put out those fires!*" he shouted. "You make good silhouettes."

He handed their map coordinates to Peter and told him to report to Dietrich. While Skorzeny scuttled away in the

269

dark to organize patrols and a defense line, Peter started the engine on a command truck and cranked up a field radio.

"Greif to Brownshirt, Greif to Brownshirt. Come in. Come in." After several tries while he fine-tuned the radio, Peter got an answer.

"Come in, Greif. Come in. Identify yourself."

"This is Lieutenant Oelrich from Greif. We are regrouping. Our coordinates are—"

"Who the hell is this?" a new voice came over the frequency. "This is Major General Bayerlein. Who the devil are you?"

Peter re-adjusted the radio. Somehow he had locked into the frequency of the German southern force, and identified himself to a General who was an Afrika Korps veteran. He could only hope that Bayerlein hadn't understood his name, or didn't believe what he had heard.

Single shots were coming in from all around their perimeter, and grenades exploded in the night as Peter tried yet again to get through to Dietrich.

"Goddam FFI," Skorzeny cursed as he climbed in the truck. "Who would have thought they'd be this far north?"

He took over the radio and spoke to General Dietrich.

"*Ist dass ja der Sepperl?*... We're taking sniper fire, and we can't send back our wounded... Yes, I know, but they did it. We had casualties and lost some equipment... Yes. We'll be there. *Ja wohl, Herr General. Heil Hitler.*"

Skorzeny signed off and looked around the darkened truck. "Turn off the engine," he shouted to the driver. "They'll be firing at the sound."

Peter heard more explosions, and then the death rattle of Schmeisser fire as a patrol tried to flush out the snipers. He chewed on his bread and gulped wine from a bottle.

"Now we're paying," Skorzeny said, shivering in the

cold. "We're paying for all the mistakes of Himmler's bully boys. The civilians all hate us."

"It's enemy action, Otto."

"Of course. They supply the guns, but the FFI couldn't exist without help from the civilians—all of them, not just a few collaborators. There'll be the devil to pay if we lose this."

They put on their heavy overcoats over their leather jackets and tried to sleep.

The sniper fire continued to grow as shots were loosed off at every moving shadow. Bullets pinged off armor plate, ricocheting blobs of jagged hot steel. Another truck blew up and more shots rang out as troopers silhouetted against the blaze tried to put out the fire.

"Jesus and Mary!" Skorzeny cursed, getting out of the truck. "I sent out a patrol. Can't these idiots even flush out a few civilians?"

Cursing, he went out again to widen the perimeter protection and fire his troops to clean out the snipers. When he came back he was still cursing. "Three more dead. They murdered one of the sentries. Cut his throat. They're sub-humans. This isn't war."

"Well, you can't blame them. They didn't invite us here."

"If they'd act like human beings, they'd be all right. As it is, we should shoot them all and replace them with good Aryans."

"Come on, Otto. You don't believe all that master race stuff, do you?"

"You'll have to admit, by and large, we *are* a wonderful race."

"And a little bit crazy too. Any nation that could get into a two-front war and then do it again in twenty years, that's insanity."

Skorzeny tucked his overcoat around his legs and tried to stop shivering.

"It could be that some fanaticism and extremism has to go with greatness. We can't all be plodding engineers."

"How about Hitler? Is that fanaticism, or insanity?"

Skorzeny was silent for a moment. "You haven't met him, Peter. He's a great man."

They tried to sleep, but the firing kept increasing until it sounded as if every farmer within miles had been attracted by the sound of gunfire, and lay in wait, hunting rifle in hand, to spot a German target. An ammunition truck exploded in a flare of flaming gasoline, and the shells blew off in every direction. Peter peered out of the armored command truck to see the troops cowering under their vehicles, hoping that a stray shell wouldn't hit the gas tank.

"Christ, let's get out of here," Skorzeny said. "We'll take casualties all night at this rate. Peter, you lead off, and I'll clean up the mess. Take the tanks and leave the armored cars with me."

In the glare of the burning trucks, they ran from vehicle to vehicle, telling the troops to load up.

In an armored car, headlights blazing to avoid running over bodies, Peter led the tanks out of their burning circle and onto the highway, taking sniper fire all the way and for a half mile on the road; while Skorzeny led the armored cars in a cavalry raid around the camp, dodging trees and machine-gunning any figures that moved, finally sending up star shells to light the hills when all of the troops were loaded up and fleeing.

When they stopped to take a count, some miles away, they found that they had lost more men to the FFI than they had lost in the air attack.

Chapter 58

Dawn saw them on a mountain road overlooking the town of Clervaux. The road snaked and doubled out of the hills and across a river to a little manufacturing town dominated by a monastery and a castle. Burned out Panther tanks still smoked by the roadside as evidence of yesterday's fighting, and firing could be heard from the town. Skorzeny stood by the road surveying the town through binoculars as his haggard troop clanked past him down the road. Little movement was visible in the town. At the railway station, a Swastika flag flew from a tower.

"Keep bottled up, and go in slowly," Skorzeny shouted to his tank commanders as his armored car raced forward to regain its position at the front of the column. "Peter, repeat that on the command channel and then try to raise Colonel Peiper in town."

The 150th, after taking fire for almost 12 hours, needed no reminder to keep down. Peter repeated Skorzeny's orders, and then tried to contact the commander of the tank force in Clervaux.

They clanked up to the railway station and a Tiger commander waiting there pointed out the house where Peiper had taken shelter for the night. Skorzeny returned the salute of the sentries and went inside, Peter at his heels.

"Colonel Skorzeny reporting as ordered," he saluted the little Lieutenant Colonel who greeted him.

"Well, the famous Skorzeny. Got any gas?"

"A couple truckloads."

"I'll take it. How about ammunition?"

The giant Skorzeny looked down on the diminutive lieutenant colonel. He wondered why there were so many small men in this command—Model, Manteuffel, and now this pipsqueak.

"You won't take anything without orders from Dietrich."

"Then get on the radio. He'll back me. I'm the best tank commander available." The little colonel grinned with restless energy as he settled his peaked cap on his head. The skull and crossbones of the death's head insignia gleamed white on his hat.

"Why don't you fellows get some sleep?" he said. "You look tired. Have a rough day?"

"We do as we're ordered, Colonel."

"And so do I. Right now I'm heading for Bastogne and the Meuse. You can play garrison for a while. There's still some shooting on the other side of town. You'll have to clean up at least a corridor to send supplies forward safely."

He went out and began assembling his task force in order to move on. Skorzeny sent his commanders in armored cars to scout the town before Peiper pulled completely out.

"Peter, set up a command post here, report in, and then get some sleep. I'll be back in a while."

Peter took over the office being vacated by Colonel Peiper, set up radios and a courier service, found a town map, and had some hot food for the first time in 36 hours. As Skorzeny set up command posts and observation posts in the town for the different companies, radio operators reported in and Peter marked their locations on his town map. Finally he turned the headquarters over to a junior officer and went upstairs to flop down on a stripped bed next to a snoring sergeant. He passed out immediately.

While Peiper's tank battalions went South for more fighting, Skorzeny's decimated brigade took over the occupied and re-occupied town of Clervaux to the accompaniment of ceaseless gunfire. The once-cowed civil population, having had a taste of freedom, were shooting at the Boche whenever and wherever possible.

Guns, ammunition, and explosives came from some-where. Snipers appeared from nowhere.

The German attack had bogged down at Bastogne. For want of gas, for want of ammunition, for want of the crushing power of fear, the German army was making its last desperate effort around a barricaded town that covered the approaches to the Meuse, the approaches to Paris.

General Dietrich, constantly prodded from Berlin, finally ordered all available men up to attack Bastogne. The attack included Skorzeny's brigade. They set up a headquarters at a little crossroads village near Bastogne, and prepared for a coordinated attack at dawn.

Chapter 59

The incredible cold of the night was something the survivors of the 150th would never forget. Peter and others learned from the veterans of the Russian campaign. They kept their hands under their armpits to keep the fingers mobile. They left weapons and ammunition always out of doors so that the metal wouldn't sweat and then freeze. They rubbed frozen ears and noses gently to restore circulation.

The attack was set for an hour before dawn on a wide front before Bastogne. The troops huddled together in barns or vehicles or around fires like Napoleon's army before Waterloo. Food and drink were thawed over exhaust pipes, and corpsmen kept plasma under the hoods of trucks and morphine syringes beneath their armpits. All waited for the terrorizing bombardment of the cannon to reduce the enemy, and then deployed in the dark and the fog to attack behind a rolling barrage over the snowy slopes up towards the stone buildings of Bastogne.

While von Foelkersam was in the rear directing battery fire, Skorzeny went from group to group on his brigade front energizing the men and instructing the officers on how to space them out and how to use the terrain for natural advantage. Peter followed.

The first high-velocity magnesium flares went up an hour before dawn, lighting up the targets, and the troops stood up, ghostly in white shrouds, to walk up the long deadly hills toward Bastogne. The huge spotlights made blinding artificial moonlight by lighting up the clouds, and the white spectres of the 150th disappeared into the blinding fog to walk their last mile.

A withering artillery fire came down on them as the hills, already zeroed in by the Amis, exploded with flying steel.

Anti-personnel shells burst in the air before hitting anything, spreading their shrapnel over a huge area. Troopers ran forward heavily, their oversized boots and heavy woolen shirts soon soaked with sweat in spite of the cold.

Skorzeny went from area to area in a tracked command truck. On one hillside the artillery was so deadly that the men were bogged down, trying foolishly to dig in the frozen earth, to chip out some protection from the deadly A.P. bursts.

"Bring up some reserves, Peter," Skorzeny shouted, and jumped out of the half-track to get the terrified men on their feet and moving again. Peter cranked up the radio and ordered up a truckload of reserves, giving the co-ordinates from the map he consulted with the light of a field flashlight. Skorzeny ran from man to man, hitting them with a dull American bayonet he had picked up, prodding with the point of it, hitting them with the flat of the blade, or banging on their steel helmets, deafening and galvanizing them with the noise as it drew the attention of others.

"Come on, do you want to die here? Move! Keep walking! It's safer up the hill than here."

The first foxhole line of the enemy was being overrun. Peter saw one of their captured Sherman tanks moving up and down the line of frozen foxholes, machine-gunning the Americans hole by hole. And then the tank was flamed up and blasted out by bazooka fire.

The 150th used its advantage well, walking forward, invisible in the brightly lit fog and snow, to wipe out forward artillery observers. The enemy artillery became less accurate.

The Troopers took advantage of every fold and hollow in the hills to hide from the small-arms fire that rained down on them from invisible positions. The rattle of the German automatic weapons would be followed by the heavier, slower fire from the American machine guns and

277

BAR's, with their greater range and accuracy. The fog echoed the sounds of explosions until the battle seemed to be all around them, terrifying in its nearness.

Skorzeny came galloping back to the half-track, his eyes red with the fire of battle.

"Turn around! Get over to the Ligneuville road." He hit the driver on his shoulders, then seized the radio.

"Radl, this is Greif. Bring up the big ones and the reserves to Point A3." He had memorized the map co-ordinates. "We're getting outflanked. Hurry!"

The halftrack bounced and clanged down a hillside to the paved road that led from Ligneuville to Bastogne. An American bazooka team lay frozen into grotesque positions by the road, their blood black in the snow, their faces turning ruby red in the dawn.

A turn brought them face to face with another road block of railroad ties, and a rocket flew at them to explode on the frozen shoulder of the road, flaring red and gold in the black and white. The halftrack stopped and backed around the curve even faster than it had come.

Cold dawn was coming up white behind the clouds as the last of the Tiger tanks clanked forward. It was covered with troopers hanging onto the cannon barrel, holding to the armor plate, flattening themselves to the heat of the engine coming through the armor plate.

"Off!" Skorzeny shouted. "Into the ditches!" He jumped up on the tank and shouted into the ear of the tank commander, pointing around the curve of the road.

The Tiger moved forward as Skorzeny jumped off and into the ditch with the infantrymen. As soon as it turned the corner it blasted with the 88 at the barrier of railroad ties, and tried to bull through it.

The ground exploded all around them. Bodies flew through the air. An artillery salvo, timed to explode simultaneously, blanketed the curve: roadblock, tank and half-track. The Americans had called down a planned time-on-target salvo on their own position.

Peter was thrown from the half-track into a snowbank. He got up and began to run back the way they had come. Then he stopped and instinctively turned away from the road. More 105 shells were screaming through the air to blast the curve. A rising sun was burning away the fog, and an incredibly cold wind, invisible and icy, blew away the remnants. Peter could suddenly see for miles across the rolling hills. Spread out in straggling lines, the 150th came into view—some walking forward, and some squatting in the snow, firing forward at nothing, others already frozen like statues.

The Americans saw too. They must have had an endless supply of ammunition. A tremendous barrage of shells began falling. Peter saw truckfuls of reserves blown into the sky, bodies with arms flapping in the air like rag dolls thrown to the ceiling. A copse of trees sheltering a company of Skorzeny grenadiers disappeared in one blast—the trees and all seeming to rise in the air and falling back as bloodied kindling.

The line of soldiers kept walking forward as A.P. shells decimated their files again and again. The 150th was being destroyed before his eyes.

Skorzeny came running by. "Stop and dig in! Take cover," he shouted. "Peter, what the hell are you doing? Standing around? Get back to Ligneuville!"

Dazed and numb with cold, Peter walked south, away from the devastating artillery fire. He saw a farmhouse that had been converted into a field hospital. Already the wounded were being brought in. They lay moaning in corners, on the floor, in chairs, on the dining table. Peter sank down by a wall, indifferent to the babble of the dying men around him. He put his hands under his armpits, hunched his head into his shoulders, and tried to become invisible.

Chapter 60

It was a long walk back to Ligneuville. Peter found himself staggering down the road past shattered remnants of the brigade, some of them without guns, their faces frozen and turning wine-red, pus running from open sores where their ears used to be, frozen feet shuffling through the rutted frozen snow.

He stumbled into the hotel at Ligneuville to find the communications center manned by one sergeant, fallen asleep across his switchboard. Upstairs, Skorzeny was chewing on moldy bread. The smell of brewing chicory ersatz coffee came from a pot on top of the porcelain stove.

"Where the hell have you been?" the colonel asked.

"Damned if I know. I woke up in a field hospital."

"Wounded?"

"No. No frostbite even. I guess it was the first place I saw."

"You're about as much help as a broken leg. Come on, drink some coffee and let's get to work. You get out and find out what's left. Report in here by field telephone or send runners. Find out what material there is and organize squads."

"Yes, sir."

The command line telephone rang. Peter put down his coffee and answered it automatically.

"Yes. Luttwitz? How many men? Hold the wire." He turned to Skorzeny. "Captain Luttwitz. He's got four trucks and a half track He's picking up the men who are left in front of Bastogne."

"Let me talk to him." Skorzeny took the radio telephone. "Hello, Luttwitz. Take a look around and pick up anybody who can walk. Organize squads and send them back under a non-com or an officer. Have them report here. Look carefully, They may be hiding somewhere and freezing."

He hung up. "Well, that's a start."

Peter finished his mug of ersatz coffee and stood up. "I'd better go look around."

"Don't get lost this time," Skorzeny said, making a note of the number of troops and vehicles reported by Luttwitz.

Peter went out and tramped to the edge of the village, digging out soldiers from wherever they had flopped. As he found officers and sergeants, dazed and almost in shock, he directed them to search out troops and report to the hotel.

After an hour of trudging about in the snow he returned to headquarters. The former brigade headquarters on the ground floor had come to life. The field radio was in operation, and soldiers were reporting and being sent out to scrounge food.

Upstairs, Skorzeny was yelling into the telephone.

"*Ja, Sepperl.* I have about sixty men so far. There may be another thirty or forty wandering in. The rest are all dead...Artillery. Completely wiped out. Every tank, every gun. They've even got 105's cited to fire in a 360 degree arc...Yes, sir. I'll report in." He put down the telephone connecting him to General Dietrich.

"Assemble the men in the town hall, Peter. Let's see what we've got."

The survivors of the 150th were zombies, their eyes red holes in their faces. Powder burns blackened their hands. Frozen fingers and noses glowed red.

"All right, you bastards," Skorzeny addressed them. "This is all we have left. I just talked to Dietrich. We're being pulled out as soon as Peiper arrives with the 'Death's Head'. We're going back to Clervaux. Garrison duty while Peiper does our job up here. So try to look like soldiers, even if you aren't."

It was a bitter blow to Skorzeny to turn over his

command area to the cocky little Colonel Peiper after having suffered a defeat.

"So. The great Skorzeny flies again?" Peiper smirked. "Just like Gran Sasso—only it wasn't the Italians you were raiding this time, eh?"

Skorzeny gave him a map showing his troop quarters and headquarters.

"It won't be a bunch of Russian peasants you're facing this time either, Peiper."

"We'll see. Those Americans are fat and stupid. In the meanwhile, take care of Clervaux. Come now, I just turned that village over to you the other day. What happened?"

"You'll find out. I herewith turn Ligneuville over to you. And Bastogne, if you can get it. *Auf Wiedersehn, Herr Oberststurmbannführer.*"

"*Gleichfalls, Herr Oberst-leutnant.*"

Skorzeny and von Foelkersam made a tour of the field hospitals while Peter organized the troops for their drive to Clervaux. Captain Luttwitz led the way in a blacked-out truck, while Peter, Skorzeny and von Foelkersam brought up the rear. It was a sad parade that entered Clervaux to resume command of the village. Peter went upstairs to the former brigade headquarters to put in lines to reestablish radio contact with Army Headquarters and OKW in Berlin while Skorzeny took the report of the garrison they had left behind.

"Increased firing from the castle, sir," the lieutenant in the downstairs headquarters reported. "They've got a 57 milimeter cannon up there and I didn't have enough troops to storm the castle."

"Why didn't you blast them out?" Skorzeny asked petulantly.

"The walls are eight feet thick, Colonel!"

"What artillery do we have left?"

"Only what you brought back, sir. You didn't leave me anything but a bunch of typists and one Volkswagen."

"Christ! Does that cannon interdict the supply route to Bastogne?"

"Yes. They're running a gauntlet out there. The service troops are giving me hell. They've lost I don't know how many trucks."

Skorzeny didn't even make it up the stairs to his former headquarters. He went out immediately to inspect the tactical position on Castle Hill.

The Bastogne survivors fanned out to the houses where they had been previously quartered and pleaded for food like tattered beggars. If they didn't get it, they killed.

Chapter 61

When Major von Foelkersam came in from his reconaissance with Skorzeny, his arm was bleeding.

"Adrain—what happened?" Peter asked, looking around for bandages.

"Sniper fire. It's nothing." Peter bound the wound with gauze. "Hurry up. I've got to drive back to Bastogne and borrow some artillery from Peiper. That castle has to be blasted out."

"Do you want a driver? Sergeant—find a driver for the Major."

"Not a cannon to our name! This is the end, Peter. They'll break up the 150th for sure and split us up into replacement depots. No more brigade, no more Friedenthal. We're finished."

"Don't think about it now, Adrian. And look—stop at a field hospital and get that wound dressed."

"No time. No more time." He walked out and slumped into a Volkswagen to sleep on his way to Bastogne. Peter went upstairs and ducked as a sniper bullet smashed through the window and ricocheted off the stove. Keeping out of sight, Peter pulled the blackout curtains.

The telephone rang. Peter was expecting a call from Captain Luttwitz.

"Hello, Luttwitz?"

"Is this the headquarters of the 150th?"

"Yes."

"General Schellenberg here. May I speak to Colonel Skorzeny?"

"He's out on reconaissance, sir. Can I take a message?"

"All right, Luttwitz. The Colonel asked me to make inquires about this so-called Lieutenant Oelrich. We have reason to believe he was recently in England. Your man may be an impostor or a spy. He should be put under arrest immediately. I'm referring the case of Reichsführer Himmler. Is that clear?"

"Yes, sir."

"And my best personal regards to the Colonel."

"Yes, General."

"Goodbye."

Peter hung up the field telephone, breaking out into a cold sweat.

When Luttwitz and Skorzeny returned they brought with them a huge salami and some wine. The officer's mess was silent as they waited for von Foelkersam's return.

Sniper fire rang out through the night, even though Skorzeny's orders now kept sentries off the street. The FFI ruled the night streets in Clervaux, and their cannonfire blasted the supply road by day.

Von Foelkersam returned, weakened by his wound and pale after the jolting ride to Bastogne and back.

"No cannon. Peiper said he couldn't spare one. He gave me a *panzerfaust*, and a dozen rounds."

"Oh, God. We'll never blast out that gun. Those castle walls are eight feet of solid stone, and if we blast one turret, they'll just drag it to another place. Do we have any flares? Star shells?"

"Nothing."

"We'll have to wait until morning." Skorzeny ran his hand through his hair distractedly.

"Luttwitz, you go out and organize the troops for a full-scale assault on the castle. Start with the *panzerfaust* at dawn, but if you can't silence it, we'll have to go in. I'll hear the firing. I'll be there to lead."

They finished the wine.

"This is the end of the road, Otto," von Foelkersam said. *Finis Germaniae*."

"The Führer has promised..."

"Do you believe what you hear on the radio?"

"We've got to win, Adrian. Otherwise it's the fall of the

West. Can you imagine what the Russians would do to Germany? You were in Russia."

"*Finis Germaniae.*"

Chapter 62

Dawn had not yet seeped through the bullet-riddled blackout curtains when the shelling started. This time the cannon was not firing at the highroad. An artillery spotter hidden away somewhere was walking the blasts in toward Skorzeny's headquarters. Distant *panzerfaust* explosions came from near the castle as Luttwitz fired at the muzzle blasts, but the incoming shells were nearer and nearer as Peter and Skorzeny pulled on their boots. As the explosions came closer, fear started adrenalin pumping through their veins.

"They're after *us*! Let's get out of here, Otto!"

A shell blasted the command post on the floor below them and severed the lines of their field telephones.

"Come on, Otto. We can't do any good here."

They grabbed their overcoats and ran down the shattered stairs, keeping close to the wall. Cordite smoke and groans came from the blasted-out command post on the ground floor.

They ran up the village street. Shells were still falling. A deafening blast threw Peter against the wall of a house. When his vision cleared he saw Skorzeny on hands and knees. Blood was flowing from a cut over his eye. Peter got him to his feet and half carried him to the nearest house. The door was locked. Peter took Skorzeny's Walther and blasted the latch off the door. Inside there was a dark hallway and a double door leading to a parlor. Standing there wearing the beret of the Free French, a field telephone in one hand and a 45 caliber pistol in the other, was Robert de Bourgival. He raised his pistol slowly.

Peter pulled Skorzeny back and out the door again. He staggered with him further up the street, expecting a bullet in the back at any moment. Around the corner were the abandoned vehicles of the troopers now dying in the command post. Peter loaded Skorzeny into a Volkswagen and moved out to the east, away from the artillery. A machine gun nest was dug in at the edge of town, protected by sandbags and barbed wire.

"Is there a field hospital around here?" Peter shouted over the roar of the artillery.

"That way—" the gunners pointed east down a small road.

The hospital was a combination farmhouse and slaughterhouse. Peter helped Skorzeny inside and sat him down at the door of the *abbatoir* to wait his turn.

"Peter—go find Adrian," the Colonel gasped, holding his head. "Tell him to take command. I'll be back with you as soon as I can."

"All right, boss."

He found the chief of surgery and told him who was waiting, then went back to the Volswagen parked by the door. By cutting across a frozen potato field he was able to circle around to re-enter by a different road the village he had just left. The artillery had stopped. An ominous silence filled the streets. He saw no more soldiers though his speeding vehicle was fired on from the windows of several houses. Two command trucks were still on the corner of the street where Skorzeny had been wounded. Peter stopped the car and took off his overcoat so that it could be readily seen that he wasn't armed. With the hair rising on the nape of his neck he walked down the middle of the street to the house where he had seen de Bourgival. The rattle of distant small arms fire and the sound of his own boots crunching on broken glass in the street were the only sounds he could hear. Wetting his dry lips, he began to whistle "Auld Lang Syne."

The door was open. Still whistling, though his lips were drawn back in a grimace, he knocked on the shattered door and entered slowly, his hands half raised and well away from his body.

De Bourgival was still in the parlor, now accompanied

288

by two boys in civilian clothes who turned their Sten guns on Peter as he walked slowly through the doorway.

"*Bonjour*, Robert. I came to surrender."

"*Adieu*, Peter. Welcome back to the First French Highlanders!"

Chapter 63

The Allied Inter-Service Assessment Board was sitting again in London, its chairs filled with deputy commanders and deputy's deputies since most of the older officers were inspecting facilities at the Ritz in Paris.

"Gentlemen," Colonel Briggs was saying, "General Donovan has asked me to advise you that our Lieutenant Oelrich will no longer be available for debriefing or interrogation."

"Bloody spy! He should be shot," said a Major in a new uniform. "My predecessor was decidedly of the opinion that he was always serving the Germans. I know for a fact his brother was, until you Americans violated all ethical and moral standards by bombing poor defenseless Basel."

"Major Harley-Ffythe, you have had three months to interrogate Oelrich, and you've been treating him like a war criminal. Now enough is enough. In fact, we have given him a D.S.C., and I would recommend that you give him a medal too. His factories in Manchester alone ..."

"I'm recommending that we confiscate them as German war reparations."

"A Swiss corporation?"

"I shall leave it up to superior authorities," Harley-Ffythe sniffed.

"Eh—Colonel Briggs—I have a most peculiar request from one of our prominent FFI officers. He has recommended this Oelrich for a Chevalier's Cross of the Legion of Honor for services to the First French Highlanders. I've never heard of such a group."

"Nor have I."

"Gentlemen," the chairman brought them to order, "Shall we get down to something substantive? We have a report that a Major General Skorzeny is fighting the Russians in East Prussia. Does anyone have any information ..."

First Lieutenant Peter Oelrich was seated by the balcony window of his suite at the Savoy having lamb chops, new potatoes and a glass of 1938 Rhine wine. Below him the city bustled with business, the Thames teeming with traffic, taxis beeping like distant black beetles, barrage balloons still holding up the island although the Luftwaffe was only a memory in these last days of the war.

When Robert de Bourgival had passed him up the channels to the French Headquarters in Paris, Peter had been happy to get out of the war. He had begun to have the feeling that every hour he spent with the German Army might be his last hour on earth.

But then came complications. At Shaef, the British officers had kept him virtually imprisoned even after Colonel Briggs had complained. He had had two months of debriefing by the British, the Americans, the Shaef staff.

"Was Operation *Greif* intended to kidnap Eisenhower or not?"

"I don't know. That's what I reported by radio. That was the camp gossip."

"Did you believe it?"

"I don't know. Skorzeny played his cards close to his chest. Now, I think, he had no intention of letting the 150th go in dressed as Americans. Only the scouts ever did."

"You have no idea how much trouble it caused us."

"It was only ten jeeploads. Forty men."

"Why would they call it *Greif* if it wasn't for kidnapping Eisenhower?"

"*Greif* is a mythological bird. It's just coincidence that it means 'grab'."

"Could Skorzeny have been promoted to Major General?"

"Maybe. With Hitler, anything is possible."

"How bad was his wound?"

"Not bad. I left him at an aid station. That's the last I saw of him. The whole town was being taken over by the FFI."

Even after he had been brought back to London, Peter had undergone endless hours of interrogation at the "safe house" hospital outside of London. The OSS seemed to want a minute-by-minute report on his doings in Germany, Hungary, Belgium and Luxembourg. Only in March had they let him move out and take a suite at the Savoy, but he still had to report to a British naval archives office and spend long hours in writing appraisals and analyses of captured German documents.

Peter went to the window and stared out at the gray Thames, the gray buildings, the leaden sky. He had tried to contact Vreneli, to contact Basel, but wartime restrictions were still on. He was as cut off as if he were on the other side of the world. And the war still went on. On and on.

A knock came on the door. Peter glanced at his luncheon table.

"Herein—entrez," he stammered, "Come in."

General Donovan was there with a gray pipe-smoking civilian.

"Peter, this is—our man in Zürich."

Peter offered his hand.

"I'm afraid we have some bad news for you, Mr. Oelrich," said the man known as Mr. York. "As you know, your factory in Basel was 'accidentally' bombed by the American Air Force. It was totally destroyed. We have just been able to confirm positively that there were only two casualties: your father and your brother. I'm sorry to say they're both dead."

Peter turned away and stared through the window at the dull sky, seeing memories of his handsome brother playing tennis, his father at the head of the dinner table, at his desk, commanding, vibrant.

"It's totally incomprehensible," the man went on. "Your brother knew perfectly well when the raid was scheduled. He wasn't even supposed to be on the island. Or if he was, all he would have had to do was to go down into a basement. It was a freak occurence. One or two bombs on your father's house. They must have stuck for a split second in the bomb bay, and overshot."

"Peter," General Donovan put his hand on Peter's arm. "You don't have to say anything. I've made arrangements for you to go on terminal leave, and you can take the next plane for Paris and Zurich if you wish. I can even get you a diplomatic passport."

"That's very kind of you, Bill."

"The least I could do, Peter."

"Mr. York" cleared his throat. "There is one more thing, Peter." The General nodded at "Mr. York" who went to the door and beckoned someone from the hall.

"Vreneli!"

"Peter!" She ran to him, and burst into tears.

"*Schatzi. Schatz*, don't cry. Everything's all right now." He kissed her and pulled her close.

"Oh, Peter," Vreneli smiled through her tears. "You're changed. I didn't know whether to come or not. They wanted to surprise you..."

"I'm terribly glad you came. You're all I've been dreaming of for three years. I'll never change when it comes to you!"

"Well, children," Donovan coughed. "We'll leave you alone. I'm sure you have a lot to talk about."

Several days later the American ambassador to the Court of St. James was rather confused to be officiating at the wedding of an American who stood before him in a Savile Row suit decorated with the rosette of the French Legion of Honor, marrying a Swiss girl who apparently spoke no English.

"I still don't understand, General," he said to the best

man after the ceremony, "if she's Swiss, why does she need an American passport to get into Switzerland?"

"Well, never mind, Mr. Ambassador," said Donovan. "It's one of those wartime weddings."

"I only hope they don't repent in haste."

Peter had kissed the bride, who looked radiant in the white wedding gown she had somehow managed to bring along from Switzerland.

"Where would you like to spend your honeymoon, Vreneli?"

"St. Moritz?"

"How about Manchester?"

"Aarau?"

"We'll see, Mrs. Oelrich."

"Oh, Peter!"

Chapter 64

He had turned up the collar on his American Army officer's trench coat, and wore no hat, unlike the stolid Swiss in their homburgs and fedoras. He wore gray flannel slacks and had removed the military insignia from his coat. He felt very civilian.

Vreneli put her arm through his and snuggled her cheek to his shoulder. It was May, and still cold in Basel. They had spent a week with Vreneli's parents, but Peter was anxious to get started on his new life. They had taken the train to Basel, checked their bags at the station and then boarded the tram marked 'Oelrich'. Peter did not know what he would find at the end of the line.

"It's going to be depressing, you know," Vreneli said. "I've seen it."

"I know. But I suppose I'll have to look at it sooner or later."

"There's nothing left. It's bombed flat."

"I'll still have to pay taxes on it."

"End of the line."

"They don't go over the bridge anymore," Vreneli explained.

"Merci veilmals," Peter thanked the motorman.

"Blöde Usländer," the man muttered under his breath.

They walked across the bridge arm in arm; the cold wind blowing off the river whipped at their legs. May of 1945 was a cold, cold month, and all over Germany ex-army officers huddled together in the disguised remnants of their military uniforms, sharing the cold of defeat with their victorious brothers in France and Belgium and an England without coal.

From the center of the bridge the scene of desolation was like a medieval landscape from Breughel, or "The Gleaners." Little roadways had been cleared through the rubble, and it appeared that frugal Swiss burghers were gathering usable bricks into neat piles, and loading twisted bits of steel into wheelbarrows to be taken away.

"Nothing. Nothing left."

They walked through the damp and decaying brick dust of what had been one of the biggest factories in Switzerland, a place where Peter had spent so many quiet hours at drafting tables. Peter looked back at the small but sturdy bridge to Basel, and envisioned the great eight-lane bridge he had once designed to hook up with the Autobahns of Bavaria. "We could still do it," he muttered, "—or someone could."

"What, dear?"

"Nothing."

They walked on. The ragged gray gleaners of brick looked up at them without recognition, a joyless glance. Peter hoped they would not recognize his coat as being the same as those worn by the officers who had bombed this place into desolation.

Grass was starting to grow by the end of the deserted tram line. Peter looked at the heavy, jagged, burned-out rubble that had been his father's house. Atop a six-foot pile of 19th century granite building blocks lay an old Homburg stained with rain. Peter picked it up, looked inside to see the initials H.O., and cast it aside.

"My inheritance," he said.

As they turned sadly to walk away, a little man in a worn loden coat emerged from a hole in the ground. Surprised to have visitors, he looked at them with suspicion, and then his face lit up with visible pleasure.

"*Herr Peter! And Fraülein Vreneli!* Welcome home. *Welcome home!*"

"Hello, Neidig! What a surprise! And a pleasure." Peter embraced the old bookkeeper and shook his hands, smiling broadly.

"How do you like my bride? We got married in London. *Gott verdeckel*, it's nice to see a familiar face. I thought you were probably dead. What are you doing down in that hole in the ground?"

"You're married? Wonderful. Congratulations! You have a lovely little bride. The moment I saw her, I liked her."

"A long time ago," Peter smiled sadly, remembering the cold, formal dinner when Vreneli had met his father and Neider.

"How about Klara? Is she still alive?"

"Oh, yes. Retired now. I see her often. It's only a few years, Herr Peter—a little more than three years. We don't die off so fast." Neidig slowed down. "Except his Honor and your brother. They were the only—casualties—in the bombing."

Peter looked over at the battered Homburg he had cast aside.

"But what are we standing here for?" Mr. Neidig said, "Come on down to the office."

"What office?"

"Wait until you see!"

He ushered them down a rough staircase chiselled into the stone. At the bottom of the second flight they came into a huge cavern cut into the bedrock. Peter recognized it as the old family wine cellar.

"Of course, many of the wine bottles broke, but we cleaned it up, and we salvaged a generator to make electricity."

Stretching in orderly lines were scores of machine tools—drills and punch presses being installed. Familiar-looking foremen were bolting the machines to the floor and connecting them to D.C. lines.

"I took the liberty of ordering some machine tools, Herr Peter. I hope you don't mind. I'm sure bridge components will be very much in demand in Germany, not to mention France and Belgium and Austria and Poland, as soon as we can get steel up from the Ruhr. I'm told their steel factories are still capable of production."

297

"*Nanu*, where are you getting the money for all this?"

"Oh, I got a temporary court order, but now, of course, as sole heir, you can have almost immediate access to your company funds. Come into my office, and I'll show you the books."

Still chattering, Herr Neidig escorted them into a little glassed-in cubicle and took neat and orderly ledgers from a locked filing cabinet.

"I've sent most of the workers off on vacation, half of them each time. They had a lot of vacation time coming. I hope you will approve. The foremen I've kept on full salary. You wouldn't want to lose them, Herr Peter. I'm afraid there's going to be a lot of competition for trained labor."

Peter looked at Vreneli. She was as astounded as he, but she concealed her excitement behind the prim smile of a proper Swiss *Frau Direktor Oelrich*.

"I was thinking of going back to the F.I.T."

"Oh, I hope not, Herr Peter. You'll be much too busy. This was just a start, to hold us together until you came back. You'll be able to hire your old Professors if you want to. But we need someone here to make the decisions. And we'll need a European sales force. And we have to build a factory."

Neidig laid out the ledgers for Peter's inspection. There, neatly reduced to figures handwritten with a steel pen, were millions in German gold, Swiss Francs, blocked English pounds, and American dollars from the reparations check for destroying the factory.

"The American check was here before the dust settled. They're very good to do business with."

"Yes. I'm an American citizen now since I served in their Army. And Vreneli is too."

"But Peter is going to be a citizen of Aarau," Vreneli smiled. "The cantonal council said they would put it through as soon as we could submit the papers."

298

"Well, well. The first Swiss Oelrich."

"But not the last, I hope."

"I hope."

Chapter 65

In a small ski resort in lower Austria, a giant of a man, stoking a curved pipe that, like his moustache, was part of his disguise, spit out the vile tobacco taste and tramped heavily in his ski boots down the single snowy street to the post office.

After waiting and waiting for trial, after answering thousands of questions by every military authority in Germany, Otto Skorzeny had tired of the endless delay, the endless red tape, the endless questions.

He found that he had become the mystic nemesis of the mysterious west: the scar-faced kidnapper, the S.S. giant, Hitler's protegé. About him they wrote endless stories made up out of whole cloth, yet they couldn't find any charges upon which to try him in a military court.

Tired of waiting, anxious to rejoin his wife and children, Skorzeny had very simply got into a car and escaped. Once out, recognizable over all of Europe, he could yet never be caught. Perhaps no-one was looking for him since they could neither convict him of war crimes, nor did they want to "de-nazify" him.

Adopting a variety of disguises, Skorzeny rejoined his family and travelled through France, Spain and Austria, often recognized and photographed, his presence reported even in countries he had never visited. Yet, as a fugitive without a legal passport or work papers, he could not take up his profession again.

Skorzeny, again disguised as the chemist from Dresden, opened the silver cover on his pipe bowl and lit it again before entering the post office.

"Any mail for Dr. Wolf?"

The clerk took a sheaf of letters from the box marked "W" and leafed through them. "'Wagner, Wozek, Woden—Wolf.' Here you are, Herr Doktor."

"Thank you very much."

"Servus."

He took the letter outside and slit it open carefully. It was from Switzerland. He had never been there.

6. März, 1947

Office of the President
Oelrich Industrien A.G.
Oelrichstrasse 1
Basel, Switzerland

My dear old Comrade-in-arms:

I'm sorry to have to address you in that way instead of in terms of the great respect in which I have always held your name. Herr Dr. Hjalmar Schacht has kindly advised me how to contact you. I should like you to consider taking a position with our firm to initiate and operate a design and sales office in Spain. I can obtain a Nansen passport for you, and I am sure all your old skills will come back, plus the fact that your international connections will be very useful to you and to our firm. We have done well in Germany, but now Spain too must be rebuilt, and yes, with German and Swiss know-how.

I may also say that on my recent business trip to North Africa, I was in Cairo, a city I had long wanted to visit. There I met some fine young officers who think highly of you and your tactics and would like to meet you.

With great pleasure I remember the many cheerful talks we had at Friedenthal during those dark days that are now past. I trust you have been able to rejoin your wife and family. I too am happily married now and the proud father of a growing boy whom we have called Hans.

So if you can make yourself available for this position, through which I am sure you can build a fine new life for yourself and your family, please advise me and I will send the appropriate papers and funds via the American or Swiss authorities.

301

Hoping that I shall have an early opportunity to greet you again in person, I am

Most sincerely yours,
Oelrich Industrien A.G.
Peter Oelrich, Dipl. Ing., Pres.

HEROES DIE YOUNG
Rick Sandford

BT51361 $1.75

War

When Jeff Parton got to France he knew nothing about combat, and he figured he was lucky to have battle-hardened Gil Ryder for a buddy. Ryder would teach Parton what he needed to know to stay alive—and sooner or later this education would pay off!

Setting: France, 1944

MISSION INCREDIBLE
Lawrence Cortesi

BT51346 $1.50

War

The five-man crew of the downed B-25 survived the crash, but they were separated. Each one had to fight his way out of the New Guinea jungle alone. And when they got home each one had a different story to tell. Somewhere in those stories was the truth about a Japanese ambush!

Setting: New Guinea, World War II

ESPIONAGE
William S. Doxey

BT51363 $1.95

Spy

The leaks were impossible. The only way the Russians could have gotten the information they had was if they could read minds. James Madderly, parapsychologist, was given an order: Find out if it was true, and, if it was, stop it from happening again!

Setting: London, Finland, Leningrad, contemporary

MAYHEM ON
THE CONEY BEAT
Michael Geller

BT51353 $1.75

Crime

Angel Perez took round one—he had Bud Dugan busted down from detective to patrolman. But Dugan wasn't throwing in the towel yet, and when his ex-partner was found dead—apparently of an overdose of heroin—Dugan was back on the case, with a big reason to nail the heroin kingpin Perez.